~ Acclaim for Ally Shields ~

"I can't wait for the rest of the series from this exciting new
author because I will definitely be reading them all."
— The Romance Studio (5 Star Review)

~ Look for these titles from Ally Shields ~

Coming Soon:

The Guardian Witch Series
Fire Within (Book Two)
Burning Both Ends (Book Three)

Awakening the Fire

Guardian Witch Book One

Ally Shields

Etopia Press
1643 Warwick Ave., #124
Warwick, RI 02889
http://www.etopia-press.net

AWAKENING THE FIRE

Copyright © 2012 by Ally Shields

Edited by Narelle Bailey
Cover by Annie Melton

Print ISBN: 978-1-939194-26-8
Digital ISBN: 978-1-937976-82-8

First Etopia Press electronic publication: September 2012

First Etopia Press print publication: November 2012

~ Dedication ~

To family and friends who have been so supportive, with special thanks to the following:

Kathleen Marsh, fellow writer and invaluable critique partner; Phil Douglas, my most faithful beta reader; my son David, who helped brainstorm glitches in the plot; and to my editor, Narelle Bailey, for pulling it all together.

Chapter One

The crickets stilled. Ari paused to scan the shadows in the sudden silence, looking for the source of the magic vibrating in the air. Maybe she was imagining things. A chill scurried across her skin, and she rubbed her arms, setting off a jingle from her protective charms. No. No mistake.

Tense seconds passed as she waited. When the crickets started singing again, she knew that whatever had triggered her alarms had moved on. She took one last look around before shaking her head and setting out along the path. It was close to midnight, the end of her regular patrol of the city. The Goshen Park gates were chained, the trails quiet, the playgrounds deserted. So why did she feel so unsettled?

The faint buzz of her witch senses had started earlier, like ants marching across her neck. Her uneasiness had gained strength at nightfall, grown persistent when she entered the park. Ari scanned the thick undergrowth as she approached a heavily wooded area. A quarter moon filtered through the autumn foliage. An owl hooted. Tiny rodents scampered in the ground debris. Ordinary things.

A crunch of leaves broke the expected pattern, and her head snapped around, fingertips tingling this time. Two eyes glowed in the dark, and she froze as the gargoyle in the underbrush snarled at her. As she watched, the ancient, three-foot creature snatched a furry lump from the ground. Laboriously flapping his heavy wings, he took to the air, clutching a rabbit carcass in his talons. Ari let out a soft sigh, eased her stiff shoulders, and resumed her steady stride. Nothing but a successful evening hunt.

Nearing the center of Goshen Park, she picked up the pace again. She could almost feel the silken sheets of her bed. She passed the west fountain and noted the lights and water were off. Visiting hours for humans ended hours ago. Warning signs forbidding night access dotted gates and posts. Standing on the east edge of Riverdale's Olde Town, the park provided a barrier between the modern, mostly human world, and the original city where the Otherworlders lived.

At night the park belonged to the predators of Olde Town.

Annoyed by her overactive sensitivity, Ari kicked a rock from the path and listened to it rattle across the pine needles. Had she misread the signs? Maybe this edgy feeling was about the witchcraft class in the morning. Explaining her job as a Guardian, what it was like to be a supernatural cop, was hard enough, but the young girls, usually visitors from the modern side of Riverdale, always asked about spells and potions. She could handle the curiosity, but the inevitable requests became tricky. Could she please, *please*, turn some girl's ex-boyfriend into a cockroach? Maybe she could. Probably she could. The thought was interesting, even tempting, but Ari wasn't about to admit it. Humans were already paranoid enough. Being new at the job didn't make her stupid.

Ari jumped at the sudden scream that rang out on the still night air. She whipped around as she reached out with tendrils of her magic. The musky scent was unmistakable. *Lukos anthropos.* Werewolf. Propelled by adrenaline, she raced toward the sound. Another scream brought her to a moonlit clearing.

Ari skidded to a halt. A werewolf the size of a Great Dane, two hundred pounds of rippling muscle, crouched before a human teenage couple. The wolf's russet tail lashed back and forth. The kids clung to the trunk of a giant oak. As the dark-haired teenager attempted to shield his girlfriend, the spunky blonde reached around him to swing a stick at the wolf.

A stick? Well, better than nothing, but not by much.

Ari extended her fingertips. A pale blue flame leaped from her fingers to the wolf's left flank. He yipped in pain, the stink of singed fur filling the air. The creature swung his massive body around and charged.

Ari fired a second stun as the werewolf jumped into the air. The flame shot harmlessly past. With a split second to spare, she snatched the silver dagger from her waist sheath and swung it upward. The blade slid into the wolf's side as the creature hit her, rolling them both to the ground. Warm blood oozed across her hand. Her nostrils filled with a rancid dog smell.

Undeterred by the knife wound, the wolf reared his head, striking with his long fangs as Ari jerked her head aside. His jaws snapped so close to her cheek that she felt the waft of his hot breath.

Ari braced one arm and shoved, delivering a jab to the throat with the other. She pivoted, breaking free. As she sprang to her feet, she struck out with a sharp kick to his head. The wolf fell back.

She grimaced. No more nice witch.

She unleashed her magic again, the bright blue flame of a full stun smashing into the werewolf's side. He flew through the air, smacked into two trees, and dropped. His legs twitched once.

Her eyes narrowed as she waited to see if the fight was over. When he didn't move, Ari turned to the kids. "You OK?"

The boy squinted at his friend in the dim light. "Yeah, I think so. Becca, you OK?" When the girl nodded, he looked back at Ari. "Was that what I think it was?"

Ari raised a brow. "Depends. If you think it's a werewolf, then, yeah. You don't want to mess with them."

"No kidding," he muttered, throwing another glance at the wolf. "Sure is a big sucker. Never seen one before. Not up close."

And you're lucky you survived the introduction, Ari thought. Why didn't these kids stay where they belonged?

Where they were safe? Olde Town was no place for the inexperienced or the faint of heart.

She sighed and shifted her attention to the girl he'd called Becca. Now the danger had passed, she sniffed and blinked back tears. Ari looked her over for injuries. Becca wore a mini skirt and tights, now ripped at the knees. "Are these from the wolf?" Ari pointed to the scratches.

"No, I fell. When it was chasing us." Becca fingered her torn leggings. "Guess I won't wear these again."

Ari nodded, relieved that Becca didn't have something worse to worry about. No danger of lycanthropy, an incurable shape-shifter virus with a 20 percent chance of transmission. While natural-born werewolves were proud of their heritage, those changed by infection frequently felt very differently. Some resorted to suicide. It was a tough adjustment. At least in this case the kids wouldn't have to face that possibility. They were white-faced and shaken from their experience but otherwise okay.

"Are you some kind of cop?" Becca asked.

"How'd you do that zapping thing?" the boy interrupted. "Awesome! Had to be magic."

"Witch magic," Ari said, dusting off her jeans and inspecting the bloodstain on her white top. Her favorite white top. "I'm Ari. A special kind of cop. I patrol the park, among other things." She gave them a knowing look. "You know you're not supposed to be here. It's off-limits at night."

"We weren't hurting anything." The boy turned his head away. "Just messing around." His neck turned red as he spoke.

Uh-huh. Ari cut off an automatic grin of understanding. She had been fifteen not so long ago. Eight years hadn't destroyed her memory.

"Well, I don't care what you were doing. You can't do it in Olde Town. Go back to Riverdale before he wakes up." She jerked her head toward the wolf.

That got their attention.

"Holy crap, I thought it was dead." The boy snatched his

ball cap from the ground and helped Becca brush the pine needles off her jacket. She jerked the jacket zipper closed and turned toward Ari, starting to say something. Before she got the words out, she focused on something behind Ari. "Look out!"

Ari whirled into a crouch, prepared to fight. But there was no immediate danger. The werewolf staggered to his feet, his body swaying with the aftereffects of the stuns. He raised his snout, sniffed the air, and swung his massive head toward Ari. The yellow eyes locked on hers for a long moment. Predatory, assessing…a warning, even? He shifted his focus to the kids. When the muscles in his haunches tightened, Ari moved to block a new attack.

Behind her, the teens raced toward the east gate and the bright lights of Riverdale. Their self-preservation instincts had kicked in. Finally. Sometimes, there are damned good reasons to flee from the bogeyman in the dark.

Ari glared at the wolf. "OK, big boy. Your move."

Her fingers tingled with anticipation. Full firepower. Whatever energy the earlier fight had used up, her levels had already recharged. It didn't look like the wolf could say the same.

He shook his fur, as if attempting to shed the remaining dizziness. Taking a step toward her, he stumbled sideways. With a last snarl in her direction, he turned toward the woods. Stretching his legs into a lope, he stumbled again and settled into an uneven hobble. The graceless exit left a trail of snapping branches as he crashed through the underbrush.

Ari took a quick look at the disappearing figures of the kids. Almost safe. The predators wouldn't follow them into the lights. In the morning, she'd report the wolf's behavior to her superiors at the Magic Council and to the local werewolf leaders. The attack would need to be explained, punishment given.

As she listened to the fading sound of the wolf's retreat, she frowned over his behavior. Attacks had become rare over the last fifty years, especially since the treaty renewals in the 1990s. Maybe he was just a rogue. But she wasn't sure this incident was so easy to explain. She remembered the way he'd looked at her, the challenge in his eyes.

Chapter Two

Ari retrieved her knife from the forest floor. The woods were quiet again. Still, she lingered, reluctant to leave. An ominous prickle persisted at the back of her neck, keeping her rooted to the clearing. She scanned the trees, opening her mind to the smells and energy in the wind.

A sharp round of applause shattered the silence.

A shadowy figure stepped from the shelter of the trees. The stranger stopped, silhouetted against the light of the moon. "Very nice, if a little overdone. I do not think he will return soon."

A rich, masculine voice, softly accented, rolled over her. Ari's pulse leaped. Her witch blood surged in response to the unmistakable vampiric energy, and she snapped into defensive mode.

The vampire stayed in the moonlight. An easy target for witch fire, Ari thought. Maybe he wasn't hostile. More likely, he didn't think she was any kind of threat. Either way, her advantage. She'd been underestimated before.

"You need not be concerned," he said. "I intend no mischief."

The distinctive cadence of Italy in his words trailed a feathery caress along her skin. The sound wrapped itself around her in lazy curls. A quiver swept up her arms, and she shivered. Ari quickly blocked the intrusion. She needed to keep her wits about her.

"No magical probing," she snapped. "Your tricks don't work on me. I'm stronger than that." Yet even as she spoke, she felt the pull, smooth as silk and slightly wicked. Her blood hummed in response, as if her magic recognized his.

And liked it.

He chuckled. Audacious. Bold. Sexy? Ugh, contrary to popular fiction, seduction wasn't something Ari associated with vampires. Federal civil rights laws, new treaties, and citizen status didn't make them any less dangerous. They were predators—useful in the military, but not exactly her idea of boyfriend material.

"I heard there was a new guardian, but not that she was a fire witch." The vampire moved closer, his feet skimming soundlessly over the layers of fallen leaves and pine needles. When he came to a halt, the moonlight illuminated his face, revealing dark eyes and strong, lean features. A lock of black hair had fallen across his forehead. He was dressed casually in black jeans and a crew neck T-shirt. "Our meeting is fortunate. Always good to know the local authorities." He cocked his head. "You are not what I expected."

Not again. Ari was sick of comparisons to her mentor. "Sorry to disappoint. Who are you? What do you want?"

"Did I say I was disappointed? On the contrary." His gaze swept the length of her. "You are much younger, prettier, than your predecessor. But then Yana served a hundred years or more. Disappointed? Not in the least. I find you and your talents…most interesting."

"Is that meant to be a compliment? Never mind. I don't care." Ari raised her chin and looked him straight in the eyes. "If you think I'm a pushover because I'm young, you can think again. I'm good at what I do. I've trained my entire life."

His eyes narrowed at her bold stare. She thought she'd made her point, until he laughed. Ari bit her lower lip. Had she been too quick on the uptake? Again. Or was she reacting to vampiric magic? She nudged up the strength of her magical defenses.

"Your entire life," he murmured. "As long as that. Impressive."

Ari snorted but didn't take the bait this time. She waited to see what he'd do next. Unfortunately, he had the same idea, and they stood staring at each other.

The vampire acted unbothered by the silence. He stood at ease, his body relaxed but waiting. The breeze ruffled the unruly, black hair that curled over his ears. He looked thirty or less in human years. Yet, despite his present efforts to hide it, she felt an underlying hint of power that said he was older. Much older. Awareness of him filled all the available space.

Whoever he was—she hadn't forgotten he didn't answer the question—his continued watchfulness made Ari uneasy. She moved her hand closer to her dagger. Although blood hunting was strictly forbidden, with a penalty of immediate execution, she didn't trust any vampire to play by the rules.

His lips curved under her scrutiny, a hint of amusement reaching his dark eyes. Humor? That surprised her. As their humanity fell away, vampires usually took on a distinctive look: cold, predatory, reptilian. Except for the newborns, and this guy didn't feel that newly minted.

In a rare flash of vanity, she wondered what he thought of her. The long, dark blonde hair wasn't very witchy. And her five-five frame was more boyish than curvy. But the long-lashed green eyes? All witch, and her best asset. Great-Gran's eyes. Her mother's eyes. Ari jerked herself back from this weird train of thought. What was the matter with her? This wasn't a hot-looking date.

Whatever was going on behind the vampire's hooded eyes, he kept it to himself. He made no overt aggressive moves, simply stood there. Wasn't that typical predator behavior? Lure the unwary into a sense of safety? Well, he could forget it. Wrong prey, bloodsucker.

She took the initiative. "I know what you are, but I'll ask again, who are you? What are you doing here?"

He moved then, gliding forward. She was startled when he

bowed with all the grace of an old world aristocrat. It didn't quite fit the jeans and T-shirt. "Andreas De Luca, at your service, madam witch. And you are...?"

"Arianna Calin. Guardian for Olde Town." She hesitated, then stuck out her hand. She really didn't want him touching her, but getting along with both the human and magic communities was part of the job.

He accepted the gesture, grasping her hand in long, cool fingers. Ari felt a spark of energy, but its relative neutrality told her how good he was at controlling his magic.

"Arianna." With his eyes never leaving her face, he repeated the word, his voice rolling it around. "Not exactly a Romani name."

"No, should it be?" Her gut clenched at his unexpected remark. How much did this vampire know about the Calin family of witches? About *her*?

As if she'd spoken aloud, he said, "Your great-grandmother was the witch Talaitha. The last great fire witch in this region." His smile said he knew he'd surprised her. "Talaitha is a Romani name."

How did he know that? What right did he have to use her name so freely? Ari was tempted to confront him, but it would have confirmed what might be a guess on his part. Talaitha was one of Ari's given names. An ancient name. Since the old names held power in her world, she was reluctant to share it. Especially with a vampire.

Andreas De Luca examined the hand he continued to hold. His fingers were inches away from Ari's silver bracelet. Although he didn't make direct contact with the trinket, he didn't act bothered by the sight or presence of the charms, most of which were considered dangerous or at least harmful to vampires. The miniature silver cross, the vial of holy water, the protection stones. Ari lifted a brow. Interesting reaction.

"These slim fingers have inherited Talaitha's gift for fire," he said, using her great-grandmother's name again, as if he knew it bothered her. "A rare and coveted talent." His smile broadened, bringing charm to his attractive face, and he lifted Ari's fingers to his lips in a brief kiss. Before she had a chance to react to this unexpected gallantry, he turned her hand over and nipped the palm with wickedly sharp teeth.

"Ouch!" She snatched it back, leaped away, and glared at him. Her witch senses flared with a rush of hot energy that ran to her fingertips. Ari clenched them into fists.

His rich laughter rang out. The real thing, no magic this time. Grinning, he threw up his hands as if to ward off retaliation. It defused the moment.

"It's not funny," she snapped, getting herself under control. Unclenching her fingers, she stared at the small drop of blood that welled from the broken skin. Her brain warred between anger and a strong desire to get the hell out of there.

"You are too tempting." A hint of teasing entered his voice. "Such smooth skin. And sweet-smelling blood." He ruined the milder tone by widening his grin to show a glimpse of fang.

Ari scowled. If he was trying to freak her out, it was working. A dangerous game for both sides. "Just stop it," she said, her voice all sharp edges. "State your business or get out of here. I've had enough, Mr. De Luca."

"Andreas will do." His voice was smooth, urbane. "I fear you have assumed some evil purpose on my part, when I truly meant no harm."

"Yeah, I can see that." Ari looked pointedly at the blood on her hand.

He sighed. "Yes, well..." Some emotion flitted through his eyes. Regret? Uncertainty? Puzzlement? His next statement made her wonder if she'd seen anything.

"Only a small bite, after all." When she bristled, he seemed to reconsider his words. "All right. Not my best moment." It was a matter-of-fact statement. Not a real apology, no remorse. A muscle twitched at the corner of his mouth, as if he was enjoying the situation. Before Ari could think of a good retort, he changed the subject. "As for what I wanted, nothing. I heard the screams and came to help."

"You came to help," she repeated. He nodded, and she went on, her voice thick with sarcasm. "Of course, I should have guessed. Fearing some innocent was in danger, you came charging to the rescue."

"Something like that," Andreas agreed. "You arrived before me, and my services were not required."

Yeah, right. Ari rolled her eyes. He'd had plenty of time to make up a better story than that. He was lying, and he didn't care if she knew it. Arrogant bloodsucker.

He frowned, took a sudden step toward her. "You appear to doubt my word, Ms. Calin. Why is that?"

So, the vampire's skin was not as thick as it seemed. Ari shifted her position a step to the left, increasing the distance between them. He mirrored her actions, closing the gap. She moved again, so did he. His eyes glittered in the moonlight. A sign of danger or mischief? Ari didn't feel particularly threatened. Perhaps she should. After all, she had baited him. To be honest, this macabre moonlight dance was more weird than frightening.

"Your story is pretty unlikely. In my experience, vamps don't give a damn about anyone else. So who were you tracking? The wolf or me? I hope it wasn't the humans."

Andreas raised a dark eyebrow. "In your experience? Have we not agreed that you have none?"

"Very funny. You know I didn't say that." Her face flushed. "And it's not smart to keep pushing me."

"But it is tempting," he murmured. Then he smiled again. "Perhaps an apology is in order. I have been too long in the close company of my own kind. If you can overlook my shortcomings, perhaps we could start over."

Wary of his conciliatory manner, Ari tilted her head in doubt.

His eyes widened. "I really am harmless."

Ari lost it. Laughed aloud. It was the most absurd thing he could have said. When Andreas started to protest, she waved a hand to stop him. "No, no. Please, spare me." She swallowed her laughter and eyed him, trying to read his mood. "All right, why not? A new beginning."

He cocked his head and leaned forward. "Shall we seal this understanding with a kiss?"

"I don't think so." She stepped out of reach, lifting her hands to hold him off. "We've had enough close contact for one night."

Too late, Ari realized her mistake. Never give ground to a predator. He appeared beside her in a blink, his quickness catching her off guard. She hadn't seen him move.

He didn't touch her, but his lips were close to her ear as he whispered, "What are you afraid of, young witch? Surely not of me." His magic was back, raising the hairs on Ari's arms.

She turned her head away, not stepping back this time, but creating a little space. "I'm not afraid." Her voice was steady. Good girl. This was just another test. It wasn't the first time an Otherworlder had demanded she earn his respect. She could handle anything this vampire dished out. And he hadn't tried to harm her. Not yet, anyway.

"Not afraid?" he repeated softly.

"No. Now back off. I know how to defend myself." Maybe she couldn't match his strength or speed or invade his mind. But Ari had the fire magic. Crimson fire that would turn him to charred bits. If he attacked, the oath of abstinence taken by every white witch didn't count. Self-defense was a given. Plus she had the silver dagger. No rules about using it. Her fingers touched the dagger's handle.

"Should we test your skills?" His voice was silky as velvet.

The scent of his exotic cologne floated around her face. A momentary distraction, until she remembered the fangs. Much too close to her throat.

"Is there some reason for this?" she asked, sounding more breathless than she liked. Her palm, now sweaty, closed on the hilt of the dagger.

"You are frightened. I can smell your fear." Andreas sounded surprised. He sighed, eased back, and studied her face, as if seeking the answer to some unasked question. "You do not need the dagger. I shall bid you good night and go before my poor manners betray me again. Perhaps, but no... Until our next meeting, little witch." He gave that brief, courtly bow again. "Another time," he said with a slow smile.

And then he was gone. As swift and untraceable as the wind.

Hot air exploded from Ari's throat. She hadn't realized she was holding her breath. Not afraid? Who was she kidding. Andreas De Luca was dangerous, in more ways than one. The leashed power around him was almost a tangible thing. Wild energy still pulsed in the space where he stood moments before. She moved away, unwilling to remain so close to the remnants of a primitive power she didn't comprehend.

Thinking back, Ari could have kicked herself for all the things she should have said and didn't. She'd been outmaneuvered. The quick mood changes, charm to menace and back again, had kept her off balance. Why had he affected her so much? She'd dealt with vampires before. What was different? The magic, or something indefinable?

Ari had to admit, he was definitely a hottie. Not a thought she wanted to dwell on. He was a vampire. Nothing hot about that.

Shoving him from her thoughts, Ari took a quick survey of the clearing. He'd been right about one thing. She might have overdone the witch fire. The woods had taken significant damage. Broken limbs, scorched trunks. The smell of singed wood and fur still clung to the night air. She grimaced, wondering what the park custodian would make of it in the unforgiving light of day.

Ari's frown deepened as she thought about the wolf, the vampire. A fleeting image of the future crossed her mind, drawing a shiver. She would see them both again. And that might not be a good thing.

Chapter Three

Emergency lights marred the night sky. Red, blue, yellow. Four days of quiet had passed since the wolf incident, but ten minutes ago Riverdale dispatch had notified Ari of a suspicious fatality in residential Olde Town, just five blocks from her apartment. The area was high on the bluffs, above the vampire entertainment clubs and the tourist district, and canopied by tall trees.

Human law enforcement officers and emergency vehicles already blocked the roadway. Two cops in blue uniforms guarded the front steps of the three-story, yellow-brick apartment building, built in the 1920s. Her ID got her an immediate pass.

She bypassed the elevator and climbed the stairs. She might have done so out of habit, a natural avoidance of enclosed spaces with no escape route, but she was also into predator thinking. They would choose a less public route to their prey. She was looking for signs of dark magic or any other Otherworld energy that would explain why she'd been called. Ari sniffed the air. The enclosed stairway was dim, not particularly clean, and reeked of stale cigarettes. She kept her hands clear of the grubby railing. Discarded gum and candy wrappers, an empty beer bottle, and smashed cigarette butts littered the steps. Normal clutter. By the time she passed the second floor exit, her witch senses triggered, sending a light pulse up and down her arms.

Still no visible clues of what was ahead.

Ari pushed through the stairwell door and stopped, adjusting to the cloud of gloom that hung over the hallway. A violent death then.

Lieutenant Ryan Foster looked up from his notepad. Blond hair, big blue eyes, hunky build, would-be lover. So far, she wouldn't. Unlike the patrol officers on the first floor, he wore jeans and a sweatshirt. Off-duty attire.

"Hey, Ryan," she said, regaining her composure.

Instead of his usual grin, he frowned and pointed to the floor. "Watch your step. That's my evidence."

Ryan was Ari's liaison to the human police force. They'd worked a couple of burglaries since June, and she'd met him several times while apprenticed to Yana, the former Guardian. They'd had drinks after a crime scene or two, and he'd made his interest in her obvious. His curt greeting today was out of character.

"I'm watching." She stepped over the bloody spots. "What happened here?"

"Look for yourself." Ryan jerked his head toward the open door on his right. His tone held a warning.

At first the scene looked normal enough. Pastel walls, worn wooden floors, cheap garage sale furniture. Typical apartment fare. As soon as Ari stepped across the threshold, the metallic smell of blood hit her hard. A red haze clouded her vision, and she could almost taste the sickening sweetness on her tongue. Bent over, her hands on her knees, she swallowed twice and fought the urge to back away. After a moment, she straightened and rounded the corner toward the kitchen. Table, chairs, mirrors, pictures — all had been churned by a giant eggbeater. Wherever she looked, objects were smashed and splintered, including the victim. The body of a young, human female, maybe sixteen or seventeen years old, lay in a crumpled heap.

Ari blanched from this latest shock. Why the hell was a human child living in Olde Town? Surrounded by predators? A runaway maybe, doomed from the moment she put down her rent deposit. Ari shook her head to clear her mind and tamped down her witch senses.

A large jagged section of what had once been a Formica dining table hid much of the victim's still form, and Ari stepped closer. The girl's legs lay twisted awkwardly under her body, jeans and tube-top ripped by claws or teeth and stained with darkening blood. Red hair splayed around her face; her head flopped against her left shoulder. Something had twisted her neck with savage force and tossed her carelessly on the floor. She might have been a broken toy, a ragdoll no longer wanted. Except for the blood.

The reason for dispatch's call was obvious. The scene shouted Otherworlder strength. Shape shifters, vampires, demons…the list of possibilities in the magic world was long.

"Neighbor heard a commotion and called it in." Ryan had followed her into the room. "By the time the first officers arrived about 9:40, the apartment was empty. Except for the body. We're canvassing the neighborhood, but so far no one's admitted seeing anything. Big surprise, huh? Plenty heard it, but no one came out to see what was going on. Nobody wants to get involved." Ryan grunted softly and glanced at his notebook. "Victim's name is Angela Raymond. Lived here alone. The next door neighbor," he jerked a thumb toward the apartment on the east, "says she has at least two boyfriends."

"Do we know who they are?"

"Sort of." He consulted his notes again. "Suspect one is a big, muscular vamp, name of Vince or Victor. Black hair, Caucasian. Looks to be in his thirties or forties. The other guy is human, also Caucasian, name unknown, age estimated at twenty, average build. Not much of a description on him. Maybe he'll come forward on his own. Considering the condition of the room, I'm liking the vampire for this one."

"Hmm." Ari slipped on a pair of gloves and remained noncommittal. Ryan's biases against certain magic races didn't need encouragement. He was assigned to the Inter-Community Division (ICD) of the police department only because his brother was married to an elf. That didn't mean Ryan liked vampires, demons, or werecreatures. Ari was thankful he tolerated witches.

They started working the scene. Although Ari tried to pick up any identifiable smells of Otherworld energy or the tingles associated with dark magic, her sensory system was overloaded by so much blood. As she helped Ryan sort through the mess, she spied a familiar pamphlet on the kitchen counter. Startled, she turned and peered at the girl, envisioning her in a blue *Viva La Difference* T-shirt.

"Ryan?"

The tone of Ari's voice got his attention. He looked at her sharply.

"Can I see the victim's face?"

"Sure. Photos already captured the scene." He leaned down and pulled the hair away with a gloved hand. "Medical examiner's been here. Thirty seconds and he was out the door."

Ari studied the girl's battered face and took a deep breath. Violent death was always hard to take, but she'd seen this victim alive. It made a difference.

"She was at my class Monday. And the human boyfriend too. At least the guy I saw fits the description." Ari pointed to the counter. "That's the flyer."

"Are you sure it's the same girl?" He walked toward her. "Any particular reason you remember them?"

"Oh, yeah. Boyfriend was a creep. Totally screwed up the group. It started out pretty normal. You know, I've told you about the classes. The guy wasn't there at the beginning. This girl," Ari nodded toward the body, "wanted to buy a love potion in the worst way. Just wouldn't give up. Believe me when I tell you, she was intense."

"Aren't all teenagers intense?"

"Not like this." Ari paused, the scene vivid in her mind. Angela had stood out in the crowd of mostly teen girls. Insistent, verging on desperate. Ari had felt sorry for her, especially after the boyfriend walked in. He butted into the class, loud-mouthed and angry. Angela had turned red with embarrassment.

"The jerk boyfriend came in with an attitude, ranted and raved about Otherworlders, and then stomped out. He seemed to hate witches in particular."

"So, he wasn't a fan." Ryan showed the first spark of humor for the day. "Doesn't make him a killer."

"Fine, laugh at me, but this guy was a real dipshit."

"Did he make threats? Against you or the girl?"

"No. Pretty much like I told you. Insults, wild accusations. Otherworlders are demonic. Illegal drugs are produced by dark magic. Accused me and *my kind* of conspiring to control the human race. Crazy stuff."

Ryan's forehead creased in a brief scowl. Even he didn't believe that kind of drivel. "Maybe he was on drugs. The autopsy will tell us if she was using." He picked up the pamphlet and dropped it in an evidence bag. "All right, from what you've said, this guy has a nasty temper and was on the verge of losing control. If he got mad enough, maybe he could kill." Ryan glanced toward the victim again. "But look at this scene, Ari. I'm not convinced a human could do this. It took a lot of force."

"And we've got claw or teeth marks. Yeah, I get it. But I'd like a chance to jerk his chain."

Ryan gave her a sly grin. "I'll try to arrange that. Give my sketch artist a detailed description before you leave." He scanned the room quickly. "We'll play this as usual, if that's OK. My department takes the lead with human suspects and physical evidence. You handle the magic stuff. Otherworlders won't talk to us anyway. I hope the ME gives us a better cause of death, but I'm not counting on it."

Ari agreed. Unless the medical examiner found evidence for the magic lab to analyze, his autopsy report wouldn't help at all. The cause of death was sure to be multiple trauma, but the assailant hadn't been human. The cause of death wouldn't narrow the pool of suspects. Too many Otherworlders possessed the necessary strength, and the natural weapons, to inflict the victim's injuries.

It was after 5:00 a.m. when they left the crime scene. They had a few potential leads. Ryan's officers located two witnesses who reported a silver sedan in the neighborhood; another described a black van. They would try to locate both. Bags of debris had been sent to the lab for analysis and a rush put on the reports. They'd found no evidence of forced entry or an apartment-wide search. Except for the kitchen/dining area, the rooms were undisturbed. That had tentatively ruled out random violence and burglary, leading them to one inevitable conclusion: the victim had known her killer.

Ari's first job was to find the vampire boyfriend. As she left Ryan outside the victim's apartment building, she glanced at the sky. Streaks of gray indicated dawn wasn't far away, too late to search for a vamp, and she'd be sharper after three or four hours of sleep anyway.

By the time she collapsed across her bed, the sun peeped through the window. She drifted off with a final weird thought: their prime suspect would be doing the same.

Chapter Four

It was just after 8:00 a.m. when Ari appeared at Claris Denning's storefront.

"Coffee," Ari croaked, setting the bell jingling as the door closed. Even over the rich smell of herbs and spices that habitually permeated the shop, she identified the tantalizing aroma of rich, black caffeine. Humans had definitely got one thing right. Coffee was essential, and Claris always had the pot on.

A young woman with long brown hair tied at the back of her neck looked up and smiled. "Hard night?" Without waiting for an answer, Claris nodded toward a beaded curtain at the back. "It's brewed." She set down an armful of dried herbs, sorted and tied in small bundles, and smoothed her long skirt. Claris tried hard to present the expected Mother Earth image at the shop, and her amiable personality fit, but Ari had seen her too often in cutoffs and a skimpy tank top to be deceived.

This morning Ari paid little attention to her friend's attire. She made mumbling noises, so intent on her mission to the coffee pot that she failed to respond to her friend's question. She disappeared behind the multi-colored beads as Claris watched with a tolerant smile.

Claris and Ari had been tight since meeting in second grade. The freckle-faced kid in pigtails had welcomed Ari, who only attended part time, while the other kids kept their distance. Even at that age, Claris was into holistic medicine and natural healing. Her pockets were filled with tiny bags and jars of herbs and ointments, which she freely dispensed to the scraped knees of anyone who would let her. Ari was a frequent but willing guinea pig over the years. In fourth grade Claris produced a green salve for mosquito bites that turned Ari's skin a rosy purple. Great-Gran eventually used a potion to take the itch away; after a long two weeks, the purple dots faded on their own.

But Claris got better at her craft as she got older, and her green thumb with herbs and medicinal plants eventually led her to open Basil & Sage almost three years ago. The shop squatted on the bank of the Oak River in the tourist portion of Olde Town, an area filled with quaint, wood-sided shops and small eateries. Since restoration nine years earlier, this attractive area reflected the glory of the 1800s when Riverdale had been a major river port. Today Olde Town, with its red brick pavement, overflowing flower boxes that lined the streets, and electrified old-fashioned lanterns, drew a steady tourist trade that provided Claris with a livable income.

The two young women were as close as sisters, except Claris was a full-blooded human.

The beaded curtain rattled behind her as Ari pushed into the small kitchen. The sunlit room was saved from drabness by a vase of yellow and blue flowers on the worn wooden table and the tidy arrangement of utensils and craft items throughout the area. A gleaming, silver coffee pot, which Ari had given her when the shop opened, dominated the counter of the small kitchenette on the right. The left side of the room held floor to ceiling shelves stacked with assorted jars of various colors and sizes. Sleeping quarters were upstairs. Behind the kitchen table a door opened into the greenhouse, where Claris grew her own medicines and special herbs, including many of the ingredients Ari used for her own potions and ointments.

"Comb your hair," Claris called from the front.

Ari clutched the coffee cup and ignored her friend. Half a mug later, she refilled and finally looked in the rectangular

mirror attached to the fridge door. Green eyes, red-rimmed from
lack of sleep, stared at her in dismay from the center of a
windblown tangle of honey-blonde strands. She had inherited
the hair color, so unusual for a witch, from her great-
grandfather, the human Great-Gran brought into the clan.

She snatched a brush from Claris's bathroom and tried to
tame the tangles. Leaving home with wet hair almost always
ended in a bad hair day. Admitting defeat, Ari grabbed her
coffee cup and wandered up front.

"Not enough sleep," she complained. "Up all night at a
murder scene."

"Murder? That's awful. Hope it was no one I know." It was a
rhetorical comment. Claris's tone said she couldn't possibly
know anyone who would be a murder victim. That she remained
so untouched by violence while living in Olde Town was part of
her charm.

"Well, in a way you do. Remember the redheaded girl at
Monday's class? The one who wanted the love potion?"

Claris sucked in her breath, almost dropping the herbs in her
hand. "Is she dead? Or did she kill someone?"

"She's dead. And the boyfriend's a suspect."

"The angry guy? That's not a surprise, but wow." Claris
stopped for a deep breath. "You're telling me I had a murderer
right here in my shop?" She stared wide-eyed at Ari.

"Relax. He won't be back. And maybe he's not guilty. We do
have another suspect. But I'd kind of like for him to be guilty. He
was so nasty that day."

"Well, yeah, but murder?" Claris studied Ari's face. "Why
are you involved? Aren't they both humans? Did it have
something to do with the class? Are the police coming here?"

"No one's coming here. Don't worry about it." Ari hesitated.
She'd already said too much, but this was Claris. They told each
other everything. "Yeah, they're human, but there's evidence of
supernatural violence. Claw and teeth marks." She didn't
mention the broken neck or the splattered blood. Claris couldn't
stand the gory stuff, even in movies. Maybe that's how she

managed to live and work in Olde Town; she simply shut out all the violence.

"Oh, an Otherworlder did this." Claris's tense shoulders relaxed a little.

At moments like this, Ari was most aware of the differences between them. Not necessarily a bad thing, but it surfaced from time to time. The term Otherworlder had been adopted by both communities, but it still defined a rift. Human vs Otherworlder. Ordinary vs magic.

"Maybe. We can't rule out anything at this point." Ari sipped her coffee and dropped the topic. "Thanks for the pick-me-up. I needed it. Can't keep my eyes open."

"You should go back to bed. Take a nap upstairs, if you like."

"Tempting, but I have way too much to do. Ryan should call any minute." Ari took another swallow of the cooling coffee. "Funny thing. I've known since Sunday that something was going to happen. One of those spooky feelings."

Claris flashed her a knowing smile. "You mentioned that on Monday. Something about having an interesting evening the night before. Then we got sidetracked by the class and the tour bus. Is this murder connected? When you brought it up, I thought you meant *good* interesting, not *bad* interesting. Nothing that would lead to dead bodies." Her hazel eyes lit for a moment as she added, "I keep hoping that one of these days you're going to meet some hot guy. Maybe a tall, muscled superhero type."

Ari grinned. Claris had harped on this theme since she and Brando, another childhood friend, *found* each other about six months ago. In spite of being a boy—and a wizard—Brando had shared in their exploits since elementary school. Luckily, he hadn't adopted the common wizard trait of arrogant superiority. Or Ari and Claris had beaten it out of him years ago. Either way, he was one of the good guys.

At the moment, Ari was a loner with no immediate prospects. Her job didn't leave much time or energy to date. A Saturday night now and then, but she hadn't had a steady guy since an abrupt breakup three years ago. Ari was fine with that, Claris wasn't.

"Not that kind of an evening," Ari retorted. "Although the vamp I met probably has his share of women drooling over him. Dark-eyed, sexy dude." Ari rolled her eyes. "Can you believe I said that? Never thought I'd think a bloodsucker was sexy. But he's also…" She searched for the right word. "Unpredictable."

"Who is he?"

Ari frowned. "Nobody you'd know. Andreas De Luca."

Claris put the last of the herbs in place, her fingers moving with practiced precision, and turned to Ari. "Actually, I do know who he is. He's a singer at Club Dintero. Voice like a dream. And yes, he is sexy. How'd you meet him?"

"Oh no, you first," Ari said, staring at her friend. "Since when are you hanging out at vamp clubs?"

"I'm not hanging out." Claris chuckled. "Blame Brando. He took me to dinner at Club Dintero last Thursday night. It's a respectable supper club. Fancy waiters, candlelit tables. And the music was sooo romantic." She lifted a melodramatic hand to her forehead and sighed. "He's good. It was quite a performance," she said, dropping the posturing. "Now you."

Ari gulped the rest of the coffee, gratefully felt her synapses start to fire, and told Claris about the meeting, complete with details.

"He bit you?" Claris exclaimed when Ari finished. She reached out a hand. "Oh my God, are you all right?"

"It was only a scratch." Ari downplayed the incident, even produced a chuckle. "If you're asking if I'll turn into a vampire, don't worry. It takes a lot more bloodletting than that, followed by an infusion of vampire blood. How could you not know that?"

"I guess I did. I try not to think about those things. But this time we're talking about my best friend." Claris went back to fussing with her arrangements. "So, why'd he do that? And what did you do?"

Ari lifted a dismissive shoulder. "Nothing much. I kept in

mind that I was the Guardian and tried not to overreact. He didn't really hurt me. And what else could I do short of killing him? Slap his face?" She wondered what he would have done if she had. "Don't know what his point was. That he's big, bad, and scary? Testing my abilities? Or maybe it was his warped idea of fun. He is a vampire, you know."

"Yes, I got that. And that means he's trouble." Claris deepened her frown. "I admire your restraint in the face of such provocation," she said dryly, "but you aren't fooling me, Ari. Maybe if I hadn't seen him. But I think you were at least intrigued by him. Sounds like a bit of flirting going on. Kind of dangerous though. Even witch fire can't save you, if you can't or won't use it."

"Oh, come on. Flirting? If I felt threatened, I'd burn him just like that." She snapped her fingers. Lethal crimson fire was forbidden to fire witches only if considered an unnecessary use of deadly force. Like overreacting to Andreas' provocation.

Claris ignored her protest. "Cute or not, he's still a vampire. I want you to find a guy, but not this one. Not a barely restrained predator. I hope you never see him again."

Ari was a little taken aback by her friend's vehemence. Not that she was interested in any kind of a relationship with a vampire. And she got Claris's point.

"You'll probably get your wish—unless he breaks the law. And then it might be fun to lock him up." Ari set her empty cup down and looked at the clock. "Surprised Ryan hasn't called. He likes to get going early. I'll step in the back and give him a ring," she said, scooting toward the beaded curtain. "Can't be scaring off your customers with talk of murder and autopsies."

"Help yourself to more coffee," Claris urged, giving her friend a worried look. "You need it. Might have another myself, if it stays quiet up here. By the way, nice boots," she said, pointing to Ari's feet. "They new?"

"You like?" Ari showed them off by doing a little side step. "Cost me a mint, but worth every penny." The coal-black leather boots, all shiny and wicked, had called to her last weekend as she passed the window of an exclusive shop two blocks over. In a weak moment, she'd turned into the shop. Still wasn't sorry.

Entering the kitchen area, Ari punched in the police department's number, learned Ryan was in a meeting, and left a message with the clerk. Resigned to more waiting, she refilled the coffee cups, took a seat at the table, and scanned the morning paper. *The Clarion's* headlines warned of continuing political unrest in South America. What else was new? Smaller articles condemned government corruption and reported suspicions about a financial merger. A two-column story from the crime beat caught her eye long enough for a quick read. The latest drug fad appeared to be a hallucinogen called Fantasy.

Angela's death made page two.

Woman's Battered Body Found

The body of 18-year-old Angela Raymond was found last night in her Olde Town apartment. The immediate cause of death was unknown, pending autopsy. Around 9:30 p.m. neighbors called 911 due to loud noises from the residence where Ms. Raymond lived alone. Police and Council authorities are investigating the death as suspicious.

Ari was surprised the press had gotten the victim's name so soon. Family notification and confirmation of identity hadn't been completed when she left at 5:00 a.m., well after print time. Somebody had slipped up. At least there was no mention of claw marks or speculation about an Otherworld killer. That would have been messy this early in the investigation. Public attention wasn't always helpful, and human panic was a real possibility in this type of case. Too bad the reporter had mentioned the Council. A careful reader would notice that.

Ari finished the article as Claris came through the curtain. She turned the newspaper face down. Enough murder talk.

"Seen Yana lately?" Ari asked.

Claris settled at the table. "We talked on the phone. That reminds me, if you visit her sometime soon could you stop here first? I have some seedlings she wanted for her garden."

"No problem. It's been a while since I've been there." Ari's face pinched with guilt. "Thanks for reminding me. Maybe later today or tomorrow, while it's still on my mind." She brightened at the thought of seeing her mentor and discussing the werewolf case. Maybe even learning about a certain vampire.

Ryan's return call interrupted their chat, and Claris exited to the shop.

Ari listened in silence as Ryan related the expected results of the autopsy: homicide due to traumatic severing of the cervical spinal cord; multiple fractures of both legs, left arm, four anterior ribs; multiple bruises, lacerations and abrasions; perpetrator unknown. Off the record, the ME voiced his opinion that someone, or something, with exceptional strength had inflicted the injuries. Confirmation tests for drug use weren't completed, but preliminary results were negative.

Not much new there. She set aside her disappointment and concentrated on the rest of Ryan's news. Based on the sketch artist's image, the computers had identified the human boyfriend as Wesley Simpson. The address on file was old, with no forwarding update.

"I'll track him down this afternoon," Ryan said, yawning into the phone. "Right now, I'm going home. I'm beat. I came here straight from the crime scene and started paperwork. Sleep is sounding better than sex."

Ari's voice held amusement. "That's pretty tired. While you sleep it off, let me look for Simpson. The suspect I'm after won't be up until dark. Plenty of hours before then."

Apparently too tired to argue, Ryan agreed.

Moments later, Ari stuck her head through the beaded doorway to tell Claris good-bye. Customers crowded the counter, so Ari waved, mouthed her thanks, and, well-fortified by coffee, went out the back door through the greenhouse. She had suspects to find and dragons to slay. Or maybe she was just too hyped on caffeine.

* * *

After numerous conversations with Simpson's former neighbors and employers, Ari wasn't feeling quite so revved. It had taken three hours to track down Wesley Simpson's current place of employment with a packaging firm. Now she faced an immovable object in the form of the firm's one and only secretary.

"I told you," the woman repeated. "He isn't here, his supervisor isn't here, and I can't give out the home address. I'd get fired. You'll have to come back another day." She looked Ari up and down suspiciously.

After the secretary's third refusal, Ari gave up. This sentry seemed convinced Ari was a disgruntled girlfriend hell-bent on stalking their employee. Ari had given her best, most disarming smile, but no go. She decided it must be the new kick-ass boots.

Deciding Ryan could handle this with less fuss, Ari called the police station and left the info with a clerk. The secretary would be putty in the hands of Ryan and his blue tell-me-all eyes. Not to discount his shiny badge. Ari had one too, of course, but she was afraid her Otherworld credentials would scare the woman more than the new boots.

Her promise to Ryan essentially kept, Ari considered Claris's request. Still time to see Yana before dark. She stopped briefly at the shop to grab the seedlings and left with eagerness in her stride.

Chapter Five

Ari had lived in Riverdale most of her life. She grew up in the area, considered herself a river rat, and returned to town about two years ago after her witchcraft apprenticeship in St. Louis. Riverdale was home.

Geographically divided in half by the Oak River and built on the banks of the lesser stream and the high cliffs of the Mississippi River, Riverdale was also divided by cultures. The old and the new, the human and the magical.

According to Great-Gran and her never-ending history lessons as Ari was growing up, the original city was built entirely on the Mississippi bluffs with the docks on the lower banks of the Oak. Over time, the human population drifted inland on both sides of the smaller stream. New developments flourished, often referred to as suburbs, and a modern city center followed the migration. Olde Town took on an identity of its own. Riverdale's 287,000 residents, sprawling across the countryside in haphazard fashion, didn't fit well into any scheme for division. In spite of or maybe because of its differences, the city remained under one municipal government, a fact ignored by local vernacular. Olde Town, downtown Riverdale, and the suburbs all meant distinctly different places.

A year before Yana was unsworn as a Guardian, she moved to the suburbs. Not the far suburbs, but the land just east of Goshen Park. Her home was no more than fifteen minutes from

Claris's shop, and that afternoon Ari hardly had time to stretch her legs before she was climbing Yana's front steps.

Yana spotted the young witch immediately. "Arianna! Come in and help me."

Ari opened the screen door. Yana Montrey was struggling to move a six-foot-long bolt of fabric, a tough task given her four-foot stature. At 114 years old, Yana was well beyond middle age for a wood nymph but not yet considered an elder. Her naturally silver hair, wound around the crown of her head in the honeycomb style favored by her people, showed traces of white. As expected, she had aged rapidly since the unswearing ceremony in June and the associated loss of her guardian powers, especially the enhanced strength and the rapid self-healing. Her step was a little slower, but the yellow-green eyes still sparkled, and her smile was just as inviting.

Ari set the bag of seedlings next to the door, grabbed one end of the bolt, and they wrestled it down the hallway and onto the dining room table.

"What is this?" Ari asked.

"New drapes. Something much more cheerful." Yana began to unfasten the bolt so Ari could see the colors, primarily white and sunshine yellow with what looked like red ribbons here and there.

Ari looked around the room, thinking Yana's curtains were fine. They fit in with all the knick-knacks and the vivid splashes of color. Cozy and whimsical. But what did she know? Her own sparse apartment didn't reflect any decorating skills.

Hernando chose that moment to swagger into the room. The snowy white Siamese paused to inspect Ari with huge, cornflower eyes. Yana adopted him as a kitten when she first bought the house. Now he owned it. After many twitches of the tail and a pointed stare, he wound around Ari's ankles, purring. When she didn't respond immediately, he began yowling as only the Siamese can do, until she gave in and picked him up.

Yana stood back and pointed to the new drapery material. "See? Cheery. I think it will look lovely."

"Perfect," Ari agreed, absently stroking the cat's fur. "If you want to work on the drapes, I'll help." Ari wasn't sure what she could do. Maybe cut something. But she was willing to try.

"Oh, goodness, no. I'll sew later, after you're gone. Time for everything these days. Let's have tea. I made fresh scones," Yana coaxed.

As if Ari needed encouragement. She grabbed two small plates and took a seat at the kitchen table. Yana's kitchen owned a view of the back yard. Flower beds overflowed with late blooms visited by multi-colored butterflies and the occasional flash of garden fairy wings. Birds swooped, chitting and chirping around the three feeders.

"Do you ever regret it?" Ari asked, studying the peaceful scene. "Giving up the guardianship?"

Yana placed steaming cups of buttercup tea and a plate of scones on the table. The aroma made Ari's mouth water.

"Not often," Yana said. "It was exciting, but it's a job for the young. My body grew weary. And my spirit too, I think. It was time." She appeared lost in thought for a moment. She looked up, suddenly smiling. "Tell me all the news. When you visit me, it usually means something's going on."

"Yana," Ari protested, "I don't always bring my problems. Sorry if it feels that way."

"Nonsense." The wood nymph laughed. "Wasn't meant as a criticism, only a reflection of the responsibilities you've accepted. But before we talk about that, tell me, how is Claris? When I spoke with her yesterday, she sounded tired. That girl doesn't have our strength, and she works too hard."

"Oops, thanks for reminding me. Claris is fine. She's one of the reasons I'm here." Ari got up and retrieved the bag from the front door. "She sent you these seedlings."

They chatted for a while about Claris and Brando, the gardens, even the weather. Eventually, the conversation turned to Guardian business, and Ari detailed the girl's murder, the murder scene, and the human boyfriend's angry confrontation at Claris's shop.

"When I leave here, I'm going after the other boyfriend, the unknown vamp. A more likely suspect. Ever hear of a Vince or Victor?"

"Doesn't ring a bell. But I never knew many of them by name." Yana frowned. "Take care. These domestic things are dangerous. All that raw emotion."

"So you think it's domestic? Maybe that's it, but I haven't told you what happened last Sunday. And, whether connected or not, I've had this weird foreboding."

Ari described the werewolf's attack on the teens in Goshen Park, especially the creepy way he looked at her, and the sudden appearance of the vampire. When Ari finished, Yana puckered her mouth in thought. Or maybe it was worry.

"Don't like any of this," she finally said. "If you hadn't been there to protect those children… We haven't seen such behavior around Riverdale in a long time. The local packs usually do a better job of policing their own. And no one's seen the creature since?"

"Nope. The packs have looked, but so far nothing. No one can think of a likely redhead or anyone who turns into a reddish wolf. A loner, maybe. A transient. Maybe he's gone."

"What will you do with him, if you find him? Relocation wouldn't be easy. Where would you put a predatory animal who can pass for and think like a human most of the time?"

"I don't know," Ari said, giving her an unhappy face. "Relocations are never easy. I helped Martin with one a month ago. Vampire bats that weren't satisfied with cow blood. Have you ever tried to round up bats?"

Yana's chuckle showed the dimples in her cheeks.

"How did you cover it all?" Ari asked. "Olde Town and the new city? I'm busy with just one district."

"I had two apprentices. That's why the Council has split the territory."

"There's still a lot to do, and a lot I don't know. Like now. Something's happening in Olde Town. I can feel it. At times, I can almost touch it, but I can't figure it out."

"You will. These things take time to sort through." Yana paused. "You're impatient, Arianna. Driven. Maybe too much so. Sometimes I wonder if Great-Gran and I did the right thing after your parents died. You were still so young, just starting school. Perhaps we should have suspended your training schedule. Broadened your experiences."

"Like what? Sending me to boarding school or on a grand tour of Europe? In all my spare time." Ari attempted to introduce a lighter note. When Yana frowned at her flippancy, Ari sighed. "What choice did you have? I was born with the crescent birthmark." Ari reached down and patted the spot on her right ankle. "Marked by fate. All future guardians enter training as toddlers."

"Yes, but your mother's ways were…gentler, I think. And if you had remained with your grandparents and siblings, instead of only visiting on holidays, perhaps they would have balanced your education, made it less severe. But Great-Gran chose to push the guardian skills. The martial arts, the weaponry. And I went along with her wishes." Yana peered at Ari anxiously. "Your witch skills suffered in the process. And maybe, so did the child inside. Did you feel cheated, my dear?"

"Oh, Yana. What's brought this on?" Ari reached over and gave her a quick hug. "I never regretted the time I spent with you and Great-Gran." Seeing Yana wasn't satisfied with her quick reassurance, Ari drew back and tried to give her a better answer. "I felt cheated of my parents, sure. I was six, and I didn't understand where they'd gone. And there were times when I'd rather be with Robbie or Sis or go fishing with Grandpa than training. Especially when I didn't get it right the first time." Ari remembered the long hours of repetitive practice. The perfection expected by her instructors. Lots of bumps and bruises along the way. Be tough, her Sensei said, and then, be tougher.

Why was Yana dredging up the past? Ari hadn't thought about the early years and early losses in a long time. Many of those memories she'd rather leave buried.

"There were good things too," Ari said, smiling now. "You and Great-Gran were always there when I needed you. Spoiled me, I think." Ari pictured the long walks and the evenings of storytelling. The hugs. Making potions. Baking cookies, or if she remembered right, mostly eating cookies. "I'm surprised you think the witchcraft was neglected. Besides what I picked up from watching Great-Gran, I had four years of witchcraft training."

"Yes, Moriana taught you the basic skills, but she couldn't give you your heritage. You must learn to trust your magic, Arianna. Perhaps if you had the Book..." Yana wrinkled her brow, turned her gaze out the window.

Ari shifted, uncomfortable, wishing they'd get off this subject. The family Book of Shadows had been missing since her mother died. All the spells, potions, and magical rituals of generations of Calin witches resided in that one leather-bound volume. Ari had hoped it would return by her witch initiation at age eighteen, but that hadn't happened. The Book's absence was a sadness she couldn't shake. Without it, her witch abilities would always be limited.

Ari returned her wandering thoughts to the conversation. Yana continued to reminisce. "Great-Gran was so happy when you were born. The family had blamed her for tainting the bloodlines by marrying a human. Then you came along with the birthmark, and she was determined to make you the best."

"Why the walk through history, Yana?" Ari interrupted, growing increasingly edgy. "Is something bothering you?"

"No, dear." Yana reached out and patted Ari's hand. "Just the ramblings of an old woman. And you're right, it is history. The past is behind us. We should leave it there." She smiled and withdrew her hand. "Now tell me about this meeting with Andreas. That is most unusual. And hardly a coincidence, I think."

Ari was taken aback. Not only by the abrupt shift in the conversation but by the certainty of Yana's conclusion. "You think he planned it? I accused him of tracking one of us. But why would he follow me? It must have been the wolf. Of course he denied it. *Claimed* he'd come to help."

"I didn't mean to imply he was stalking you. But I do think it was more than just being in the area. He had some kind of hidden agenda." Yana pursed her lips. "Talaitha wouldn't like this."

"What's Great-Gran got to do with it? Did she know him? He mentioned her name."

Yana shook her head. "She never told me. Only mentioned him once, a warning. There was something about his life before he became a vampire that worried her."

Before? That was weird. Interesting even, but Ari was more concerned about this hidden agenda. Had she missed some obvious clue? As if she hadn't already replayed the meeting with Andreas in her head a hundred times. "So, back to the park, are you thinking he was blood hunting?"

"No, no. Goodness, I would never suggest that." Yana fluttered her hands in protest. "Andreas is much more in control of his actions. He simply wouldn't do it. And if he did, he wouldn't reveal himself to you."

"Now you're talking like you know him." Ari's face made it a question.

"Met him," Yana corrected. "But I know quite a bit about him. Made it my business after your Great-Gran warned me off." For an instant Yana's face glowed with younger defiance, then she turned serious again. "You shouldn't underestimate him. He is more dangerous than most of the vampires you've met. Maybe than any you've met." Yana peered at her. "I don't like that he sought you out. Make no mistake, he did just that by revealing himself. Even if he was in the park for unrelated reasons, introducing himself to you seems quite deliberate." Yana tapped her chin with one finger as if sorting through some mental puzzle.

"I don't understand. Why are you so worried?"

"Because I don't understand his behavior. That's what worries me. He contacted me once in the seven years he was in

Riverdale." She raised an eyebrow. "And you've met him in less than three months on the job. Makes you wonder, doesn't it?" Yana gave her a sly look. "I assume you noticed his charm. It's hard not to notice. But there's more to Andreas than a handsome face. How old do you think he is?" Yana leaned forward to make her point and didn't wait for an answer. "Born to an Italian aristocrat in the late 1700s. Educated in Regency England."

Ari stared at her, realized her mouth was hanging open, and closed it.

"That's not all. Have you felt his energy? His power is advanced beyond his years. While rare vampires have inborn abilities, vampiric power is usually acquired through horrific acts of violence. I'm not saying that is Andreas's history, but the suspicion is there. We see the charismatic facade. I suspect he is more, and possibly less, than he seems. Did you know he was a favorite of the vampire court? Arrived in Riverdale with the current prince nearly seven years ago."

"I can't believe this," Ari protested. She was still stuck back on the age thing. "That makes him over 200 years old! Where's the cold, creepy look? Instead, he's got the laughter, the sexy eyes..." Ari stopped before she said too much.

"Proves my point. As long as I've known him, Andreas has moved among the human community. Perhaps he took care from the beginning to retain his human likeness. Or at some point he learned to mimic the behaviors of the living. In any case, it takes unusual ability that you cannot discount. He has all the cunning of two centuries of vampirism behind him."

Ari struggled to take it in. Andreas acted so alive. Her instincts had tried to tell her the animation and the power were contradictions—but 200 years! No wonder she felt the almost irresistible pull of his magic.

"A favorite of the local vampire court," Ari said, repeating Yana's earlier words. "What does that mean? Is it a political position? Is he a guard? An heir to the throne?"

"Maybe all of those or none. He's acted as a liaison to the Magic Council once or twice before Lucien was assigned. Some of the members trust him."

"So where's he been? Why am I just hearing about him?"

Yana gave her a shrewd look. "And how many vampires do you know?"

Ari counted them off on her fingers. "Lucien, Rita. I've seen Prince Daron on TV and several on the streets. Not many, I guess. Never thought about it before. Was he the vampire rep when you met him?"

Yana shook her head. "No. Before Lucien became the official representative to the Magic Council, Andreas approached me on behalf of Prince Daron. He offered to deliver a renegade vampire who had killed four humans. I accepted his offer, and the rogue was tried and executed."

"Why would he do that? Andreas, I mean. The vamps must have wanted something."

"Yes, that's what I thought, but when I asked, he said Prince Daron believed in a different kind of vampire society, less autocratic, more cooperative." Yana gave a dainty snort. "Maybe that was true, but they're still secretive."

"So, Andreas is some kind of spokesman."

"His authority has never been clear. But enough talk of vampires." Yana picked up the plate of scones, offered her the last one. "Let's finish up, and we'll go for a walk in the garden."

Ari grabbed the last pastry. She vowed to make tomorrow morning's run twice as long. As Yana puttered around the kitchen, Ari nibbled and considered everything she'd heard. A more detailed picture of the mysterious vampire was emerging—a picture with numerous warning flags. No matter how sexy or interesting he might be, Ari vowed to stay out of his way.

Besides, she had a murder to keep her busy.

Chapter Six

By the time Ari left Yana's, dusk had fallen. Olde Town was coming to life. As she approached the waterfront district, the excited voices of tourists and Gothic wannabes floated down the hill from the vampire bars and clubs. She began the climb in their direction. Time to hunt some vampires.

As Yana had pointed out, Ari didn't have many contacts among the undead, but she did know Rita. She'd met the vampire a year ago when Rita was a newborn and abandoned by her sire. Rita was in a bad way, starved and desperate, hiding in an alley, fighting urges that were alien to her. While abandonment was rare and illegal under both state and vampire laws, it happened from time to time, and shelters had sprung up to meet the need.

Ari had taken her new charge to one of these vampire shelters, where staff provided for Rita and taught her to control her instinct to hunt. At the time, Ari was mostly concerned with protecting potential human victims, but her intervention had saved Rita from certain execution. While they weren't best friends, Rita still spoke to her. Since Rita was a creature of habit, Ari knew where to find her.

Maurie's was an undead hangout on State Street, an unassuming bar with one asset: pinball tables. Rita liked to play, and she liked to drink. Maurie's had both. Ari read the sign on the front door advertising today's 2-for-1 special. Bloody Marys. Go figure.

"Guardian, are you lost?" Rita threw out the challenge from a back table as soon as Ari entered the door. "Need someone to show you the way home?"

Rita always dressed like a hooker. Hell, maybe she was one, but a lot of vamps dressed in that come-hither way. Today she was all in red, from the spike heels to the silk blouse that dipped dangerously close to her navel and the matching leather skirt that barely covered her thighs if she tugged hard. She lounged in a chair, one long leg crossed over the other, revealing a good bit of skin. She sipped a tall, reddish drink that Ari assumed was a Bloody Mary, vampire style.

"Now, Rita, be nice," Ari said without rancor. She felt the watchfulness of other vampires as she crossed the room. Ari swiveled a chair from Rita's table and straddled the seat. "Maybe I'm here to see how you are. Chat with an old friend. You taking a drink break from your hard play at the machine?"

Rita snorted. "Yeah, sure. What do you want?"

So much for small talk. "Know a vamp named Vince or Victor?"

Rita frowned, uncrossed her legs, and squirmed in her seat. "Know lots of dudes. Why you askin'?"

"Just want to talk with him. About his girlfriend, Angela."

"Don't know Angela."

"Didn't ask you that. I'm looking for the dude."

They wrangled back and forth a while. First Rita didn't know him, then she might, finally let it slip his name was Victor. Rita leaned forward, more guarded now. "I'm no snitch. It ain't healthy to be askin' about people. Why you buggin' me? Go bother somebody else."

"Just tell me where I can find him."

Rita got a mulish look on her face and stared across the room.

Ari knew how to play the game. "Got all night. I'll just sit here until you tell me where to look." Ari could tell Rita knew something, and she'd eventually give in. Just a matter of time.

The bartender, openly eavesdropping while he polished glasses, and probably anxious to avoid a disturbance, cut short their fun. "You don't find Victor, little lady, he finds you."

Ari cut her eyes to him and stood. "Fine. Then you can tell him he needs to find me — tonight." She crossed to the bar, laid a card with her name and cell number on the counter. "If not, I'll be back after midnight to ruin your business again." Ari swung her gaze around the room to make her point. During her visit, the room had cleared, except for three die-hards at the bar.

Ari made the rounds of a dozen other pubs on and near State Street. As usual, they were doing a brisk business; it was always party time in Olde Town. The barkeeps denied any knowledge of Victor, but she didn't believe them — too many furtive looks among the local patrons. After returning to the street from one of these unsuccessful stops, she stood on the street corner, deciding where to go next.

Her cell rang. Caller ID unknown. The time showed six minutes to midnight. He'd cut it close.

"You looking for me?" The male voice was deep, no inflection, unfamiliar.

"Depends. Are you Victor?"

"Yes."

A man of few words.

"We need to talk. About Angela."

He took his time before answering. "I heard she's dead."

"Why don't you meet me, and we'll talk about it?"

He ignored her question and posed one of his own. "What happened to her?"

"Murdered. Lots of blood and gore. Not pretty," she said. "Now can we meet?"

A tourist couple with cameras and maps edged past, avoiding contact, as Ari's words added to their night of cheap thrills in Olde Town. She wished Victor was half as intimidated.

"I don't think so," he said.

She gritted her teeth. "Look, Victor, I tried polite, but this isn't a request. You're wanted for questioning in a murder case. We can do this one of two ways. Meet with me now, or I haul your ass to the police station."

He barked out a laugh. "You think you can do that?"

"Yes." Ari examined her nails and waited. She heard a murmur of voices on the other end of the line.

"Club Dintero. Twenty minutes," he said. Before she could react, she was listening to a disconnect tone.

Fine. She could do this on his turf, for now. Club Dintero. Where had she heard…? Oh, damn. Claris's supper club with the vampire singer. This just got better and better. Ari didn't believe in coincidences any more than other cops. She was getting that itch between the shoulder blades that cops feel every time they walk into an unsecured scene.

Five minutes later she stood across the street from a one-story, white building set in a quiet area three blocks off State Street. Elaborate fixtures, clean lines, discreet sign in black script, a dark red canopy over the entrance. A doorman in formal black attire stood on the stoop. As Claris had said, fancy.

She called Ryan. He was off duty for the night but still in his car driving home.

"Ari, just going to call you. Reached our boy Wesley Simpson. He'll be at the PD by 9:00 tomorrow morning. You coming?"

She stifled a groan at the thought of another early morning. "I'll be there. Right now I'm going to interview our vampire suspect. Name's Victor. I'm at Club Dintero, one of the vamp supper clubs. Victor chose the location."

"Want me to come? I could be there in fifteen."

"Not this time. I wanted you to know where I was, in case things go south. Back me up or bail me out if I need it."

"You sure about this? If you're not comfortable, maybe there's a good reason."

"Yeah, but what's he going to do in a public place? If I bring a human cop, it would probably spook him."

Ryan's sigh came through the phone. "OK, I get it. Call if

you need me. And call when you leave too. Whatever time it is, call me."

"Will do." Picturing him taking that call from his comfy bed, bare-chested, in cute little boxers or less, put a smirk on her face.

She glanced at the club entrance, then down at her glossy, kick-ass boots. She nodded to herself. Yep, good idea or not, she was ready to make this happen.

She marched up the steps. The doorman opened the door without blinking an eye or asking for an ID. That put a kink in her bravado. She was expected by club management. Not a good sign.

She stepped inside, alert for any sign of trouble. The classy surroundings were reassuring. The interior of Club Dintero was as elegant as the curb view: rich, warm cherry wood and leather in every direction. The main dining room was filled with secluded booths and alcoves along the walls, tables in the middle. Every booth was angled toward a spotlighted stage. At the mic, a pretty blonde vamp in a green, sequined gown crooned a sultry love song. Lighting was muted, mostly candlelight, which ensured the guests had privacy and intimacy. The subtle fragrance of sandalwood, emitted by the candles, added a sensual touch. Definitely a date den.

A hostess approached. The vamp's jet-black hair hung straight to her waist. She made no attempt to hide the scowl that stated Ari wasn't welcome. The woman motioned for Ari to follow and proceeded to thread her way through the dining room without a backward glance.

Surprised once again, Ari followed her without comment. Even though Guardians aren't required to surrender weapons, she had expected them to ask somewhere along the way. It was standard in any club, human or magic. She took the lapse as further proof they already knew her identity. Victor had chosen a setting that was far from neutral. Ari grimaced. Probably the same conclusion the Christians reached at the entrance to the Coliseum.

Victor sat alone at a table for four. He was big. Six foot, 230 or more, and wearing expensive dark-brown leather from head to toe. He sat stiffly, staring straight ahead as they approached. The eyes he turned toward her were slitted, reptilian, until he chose to present a polite smile. He rose and pointed to a chair.

"Victor?" she asked.

When he nodded, she pulled out her badge. "Arianna Calin, Guardian." She moved to the seat directly opposite him, where a low partition partially protected her back. She began the interview as soon as they were seated. She went over the basics first, asking him to state his name and how he could be reached. When they came to his employment, Victor's answer explained her reception.

"Dining room host, Club Dintero."

Ari's head jerked up, and she met his flat, obsidian gaze. He smirked at her. She scanned the room, wondering if they were being watched. Hell, of course they were being watched. The staff would be protective of the boss.

Not that Victor looked like he needed protection. The rugged features and broad, athletic build might be considered attractive, in a dead guy kind of way. Unlike Andreas, Victor's predator side was barely hidden. She half expected him to flick out a forked tongue to smell her. Based on the age of the victim, he looked older than expected, probably forty or better at transformation. His lack of humanity told her that had been decades ago.

A waiter stopped to offer drinks, which they both declined. This wasn't a social event.

"Tell me about your relationship with Angela Raymond."

"What happened to her? You said she was murdered."

"You tell me," Ari countered. "Did you see her last night?"

"No. And I don't know what happened. If I knew, why would I ask? Don't bandy words, Guardian. Just get on with it." His voice had a biting edge.

Ari's back stiffened as she bit back just as hard. "She was beaten, her legs and arms broken. Covered with bites and claw marks. Her head was nearly ripped off. No human did that. It was someone very like you."

Victor sprang to his feet, slammed both hands on the table, and bent forward, looming over her. His chair crashed to the floor. "You bitch," he snarled under his breath.

At the first flicker of movement, Ari had shoved her chair back, out of his reach. Her eyes locked with his, and she eased upward, leaning toward him. It put them almost nose to nose. Close enough to inhale his citrusy scent. When Ari didn't shift her gaze from his, Victor's eyes widened at her boldness. She knew he would try to bespell her. This was a guy who wanted control.

Ari was prepared for the magical assault on her defenses. She simply stared at him, waiting for it to be over. His eyes slitted; the muscles on his jawline tightened. His magic grew strong, but she'd met stronger. "Sit down, Victor. This display isn't helping your case."

She felt the stillness in the dining room. How much trouble was she in? Not from Victor, but Otherworld power was all around her. The staff would be on his side, and regulars would know him. There could be a hundred vampires in the club, and an equal number of innocent humans. Fighting her way out wasn't a good option. She kept her eyes glued to the furious vamp and mentally inventoried the magic items in her pocket. Nothing helpful. No disguises or disappearing powder. Things were about to get sticky.

Chapter Seven

"Is there a problem?"

Ari froze, recognizing that compelling voice the instant he spoke. Andreas De Luca stood next to their table, his gaze moving lazily between them as if confronting two squabbling children. His distinctive magic brushed against her skin, raising her awareness. Could things get any worse?

Victor's reaction to Andreas was immediate. He stepped back, dropping his hands. "No, no problem," he said through his teeth. "Sorry, Andreas. She accused me of something I didn't do."

"Actually, I didn't. I said it was somebody like you."

Victor shrugged and put his public face back on. Obviously he wasn't going to fight with the other vampire present. He looked at Andreas again. "Guess I overreacted."

Andreas produced a slight smile. "Then I trust the interruption is over," he said oh-so-smoothly. He motioned to the stage, and the music that had stopped when Victor's chair fell started again. Guests averted their eyes and resumed their dinner or drinks. When neither Victor nor Ari moved, he added, "I assume this meeting is concluded."

"Then you assume wrong," Ari retorted. She heard how bitchy she sounded and tried to moderate her voice. "I need more than a simple denial from you, Victor. Like I said before, either here or downtown."

Andreas sighed. "Perhaps we should be seated if this conversation is to continue. And take a moment to, ah, regroup, so to speak. You will not mind if I join you?" He made it a question, but he didn't wait for a reply. He held Ari's chair, waiting for her to sit again. "Ms. Calin, it is nice to see you."

She couldn't figure out why he wanted to join them. Was Victor a friend? If so, maybe Andreas could keep him under control. He couldn't make things much worse. Either way, she was curious enough not to object. His reasons would surface sooner or later, and they might have some bearing on her case.

"Mr. De Luca." She responded to his civility with a short nod.

"You two know each other?"

Victor's tone struck her as suspicious. Weird reaction to a co-worker. "Not really," she said.

"We have met." Andreas continued to hold her chair.

When Ari sat, his fingers lingered on the back of the chair long enough to brush her shoulder. A warm quiver shot across her back. Damn him. Ari wasn't sure whether the contact was deliberate or not, but it certainly kept her aware of his presence.

Victor picked up his overturned chair and squared off like a prize fighter assuming his corner. Andreas sat between them and signaled the waiter.

"I have found that discussion flows more productively when you observe the social graces," he said to no one in particular. To the waiter he said, "Antonio, bring us a bottle of Chianti and whatever else my friends desire."

A little irked by his presumptuous manner, Ari ordered black coffee and resigned herself to something dull and tasteless. After all, what could vamps know about a decent brew?

"Have you been in our club before?" Andreas asked. When she said she hadn't, he launched into an explanation of its menu and nightly entertainment that lasted until the waiter returned with their drinks.

At least the coffee smelled good. Ari took a tentative sip.

Caught unprepared by its excellence, she shut her eyes for an instant and drank in the flavor and aroma. The smooth warmth of a tropical Jamaican sun slid down her throat. Catching herself, she shot a peek at Andreas and found him watching her with amusement.

"Special blend," he murmured.

Ari pretended not to hear him.

Andreas was different tonight. The playful, taunting guy in jeans from Goshen Park was gone. This evening, he was the elegant vampire, aloof sophistication and dark mystery. Black Armani suit, black shirt with the mandarin collar open and flipped to one side. He looked good enough to turn heads, and he did. Ari noticed the way women glanced in his direction, as if they couldn't help themselves.

While drinks were served, Andreas continued his light, one-sided chatter about the club, the singer, the crowd tonight. Victor worked on a dark drink with aromatic spices called Sweet Death.

Preparing to resume the interview as soon as the waiter left, Ari tapped an impatient toe.

Andreas beat her to it. "I understand why you're here, Ms. Calin. We heard about Angela's unfortunate death. I am sorry for it. I believe you have questions. How can we help?"

Ari wasn't about to let him control the questioning. He'd been playing lord of the manor for several minutes, and it was time to put his lordship on the sidelines. She set her coffee down. "That's a good question, Mr. De Luca. Since you chose to join us, I've been wondering why I've run into you twice in the last week. And both times the circumstances were…less than ideal."

"Fate, I believe." He tipped his glass in a slight toast. "Fate sometimes takes a hand in our lives, whether we welcome it or not."

"Smooth answer, but not very informative. What's your interest in this interview?"

"My interest? But, of course." His manners were unruffled. "Perhaps I should have clarified that earlier. I am the managing partner of Club Dintero. Victor is my employee, and Angela was a regular guest. My immediate concern, however, is preventing a repeat of the earlier disturbance. Does that qualify as sufficient interest?" He spread his hands as if offering his statements for inspection.

"Fine." She gave him a hard look. "You can stay if you like, but Victor needs to answer my questions. Without your help."

"Of course." Andreas gave her a single nod as his magic curled around her for an instant. "I will confine myself to the role of a referee, as you might say." He leaned back and crossed his arms.

Ari ignored him. Or tried. It was almost impossible when his energy kept seeping over her, like a feather brushed across her skin.

She turned her attention to Victor. "I still need to know about your relationship with Angela. Where and how did you meet?"

Victor dropped his gaze to his drink, as if the answers might be there. "She came to the club with a group of young human females about a year ago. Just more of the thrill-seekers we get. They sit down front, drink a lot of the fruity martinis, and talk with the performers. I keep them from interrupting the show or getting too noisy."

Ari got the picture. All the Otherworld clubs had their human groupies, teen girls like Angela, some as young as thirteen, dressed like they were thirty and carrying fake IDs. Underneath the veneer, they were unsophisticated, emotionally vulnerable, and all too available for sex. She couldn't quite see their appeal to an experienced vampire like Victor.

"I hardly talked to her before the night she came in with a black eye. Her face was all made up, but you could see it."

"When was that?" Ari interrupted.

"Six months ago. No longer." He glanced at Andreas for confirmation.

His employer nodded.

With an inward sigh, Ari turned to Andreas. "You saw it too?" She hated including him in the conversation, especially so soon.

"I did. Victor drew my attention to it." His answer was to the point, no more.

"Did she say who hit her?" Ari looked back at Victor.

"She denied she'd been hit. But when the club closed that night, she asked me to walk her home." Victor sipped his drink, set it down. "Her request wasn't unusual. These girls aren't shy," he trailed off. "Almost said I was busy. Young girls aren't my type."

Well, maybe. Ari decided she'd reserve judgment until she heard the rest of his story. They'd ended up together somehow.

"I thought she was afraid to go home alone," Victor continued. "So, I went with her. She spent most of the night talking about some loser named Wes. After that night, we kind of fell into a relationship." He stopped then added, "And before you ask, yes, it became sexual."

Didn't it always? So much for helping a young, vulnerable girl. She may not have been his type, but she was available. What predator can resist a willing victim?

Victor went on to describe the intervening months of his friendship with Angela. It boiled down to two or three date nights a week, ending at her apartment. He had little idea what she did when they weren't together.

"We had no claims on each other. Sometimes I didn't see her for a week or two."

"But didn't she talk about her life? What she did? Where she went?"

He shrugged, a stiff, calculated movement. "It wasn't my business. I didn't ask."

Hmm. Not much commitment in this relationship. She watched while Andreas refilled her coffee cup from the pot and mumbled a thank-you. "When did you last see her?"

"Last Monday night. She came in around 8:00. Early for her."

"Alone?"

Victor pursed his lips. "She was with another woman. Didn't

stay long. I thought she'd be back, but she never showed."

"The other woman, what did she look like? Did you know her?"

He shook his head. "She might have been in once before. Brown hair, older than Angela."

Well, hell, that probably described thousands of women in Riverdale.

Andreas leaned forward. "If I might interrupt…would it be helpful to know the woman was a werewolf?"

"Well, yeah. Are you kidding? Are you sure?"

Andreas frowned. "Certainly. I know a werewolf when I see one. I presume you would also like a description. Tall for a woman, nearly six foot. Dark brown hair that hung past her shoulders, athletic build, mid-thirties. Features a little too prominent for beauty, including the eyebrows. She was here a month earlier with a male wolf. Two or three inches shorter than the woman, bulky build, reddish-brown hair, middle-age." Andreas smiled and leaned back again. "They were not locals."

Ari stared at him a moment. "Uh, good eye for detail. How do you know they weren't local? Don't tell me you know every wolf in town."

"By no means, but I recognize our customers. And I notice newcomers. They stand out, especially when their speech is heavily accented and sprinkled with French vocabulary. I was at the front door when they arrived." He frowned in thought. "Might be European, but more likely Canadian."

Ari knew vampires had good recall, but you can't remember something you didn't notice in the first place. His observations were exceptional. She looked away, refusing to tell him how totally impressed she was. Instead, she spoke to Victor while she jotted the descriptions on a notepad. "Why didn't you mention any of this?"

"I guess I never noticed."

Really? Ari looked at him, but Victor sat stoically, awaiting her next question. She wasn't sure she bought his explanation. But he was a vampire, and who knew why they did anything?

"We're almost done. Tell me where you were on Sunday night between 6:00 and 10:30."

"Working. Here, at the club. All evening."

Well, damn. That seemed rather solid. And easily checked. She looked at his boss for confirmation.

For a brief moment, Andreas's composure wavered. "You want to know where I was?"

Ari hid a smile. "I wanted you to verify Victor's statement, if you could. But if you're offering your own alibi, fine. I'll take it."

Composed again, he didn't hesitate. "Victor worked at the club that evening, observed by close to 300 guests. I can look up the exact numbers if you wish. He served as our maitre d'." Andreas regarded her with a level gaze. "And while I do not believe I require an alibi, it is easy enough to provide. I was on the club stage most of the evening."

"I heard you were a singer," Ari said.

"Did you? Have you inquired about me?" He leaned forward, his lips parted in a smile.

She wanted to bite her tongue. "No, of course, not. I just hear things." Oh, so lame, even to her ears. Somehow he made Ari feel awkward, on the defensive, and that wasn't a feeling she had often. Not in a long time.

Breaking eye contact with Andreas, Ari caught Victor watching them with a little too much intensity. Like there was something to watch.

She gave Victor a cool look. "We're done, unless you have something to add." She waited, but Victor sat stone-faced, unresponsive. Then it came to her, in one of those sudden flashes of insight over something that's been under your nose all along. Angela didn't want the love spell for Wes. She wanted to break through this icy barrier, to touch the cold heart of a vampire. Unexpected pity washed over Ari. Angela had deserved better.

Knowing she wouldn't like the answer, Ari asked anyway, "Don't you feel something about Angela's death?"

Victor's social face didn't change, but his eyes flickered, then hardened. "What do you mean?"

"Grief. Regret. I don't know. Anything."

After a heavy moment, Victor eased his chair away from the table and rose. "I believe you said we were done. I have work to do."

Ari nodded with resignation. "Sure. Thanks for your time."

Victor left. Andreas and Ari remained seated. She wasn't sure what kept her from standing up and heading out the door. Maybe nothing. Maybe catching her breath. She shifted uncomfortably, drained the coffee cup and set it down.

Andreas was twisting his wineglass in his fingers. "You have much to learn, young witch. Not everyone is transparent, as you are. Do not bother to protest," he added, as she parted her lips. "Whatever pops into your head is written across your face. And regardless of what you believe, vampires are not devoid of feelings." His tone remained civil, but she sensed his disapproval. Or was it disappointment? "Victor saw your contempt for him, and it did you no credit."

A rush of anger flared and robbed Ari of words. This arrogant vampire had the audacity to criticize her for judging Victor, while he sat there smugly and did his own judging. At least she hadn't been rude enough to tell Victor what she thought. And here she'd decided Andreas had a social side. She'd certainly been wrong about that. He had no right to speak to her this way, even though she had an awful feeling he might be justified. That realization was more than she wanted to deal with. She rose abruptly, mindful of the chair, and scowled down at him.

"Good night, Mr. De Luca. I think we can agree it is past time I left."

"Allow me to accompany you to the door," he offered, once again the impeccable club owner. He gracefully unfolded his long frame.

"Don't bother. I can find the way." Ari turned toward the door.

"As you like."

She paused and looked over her shoulder. "Do you always

talk like that?"

He tilted his head, and a reluctant smile tugged at his lips. "You mean, as if I have lived in another country, another century?"

"Yeah, point taken."

* * *

Ari sighed with relief when she stepped outside, away from Andreas's unsettling presence and before she stuck her foot in her mouth again. She punched in Ryan's number. When he answered on the first ring, she grinned. He must have stayed awake and waited for her call. She liked that in a partner. His familiar voice began to unknot the tension in her stomach.

By the time she shared the information from the recent interview, Ari began to think things hadn't gone too badly after all. She'd gotten the interview. She'd learned Angela was a groupie, that someone had given her a black eye, and that their victim had been hanging out with a werewolf. It was too bad that Victor had a solid alibi, but all in all, not a bad night's work. She was still in one piece, wasn't she? She had entered the vampires' lair and escaped with only her ego bruised.

Chapter Eight

The Wesley Simpson who appeared at the police station the following morning wasn't the same cocky guy who'd disrupted Ari's class. Oh, it was the same face all right, but now his eyes darted around the room and nervous sweat streaked his temples. As Ari pictured Angela's troubled face during his outburst at the shop, his current state of fear gave her secret satisfaction. Simpson ducked his head when he saw Ari. Too bad.

Ryan didn't give the suspect a chance to relax but started the interview immediately. The cop whipped through the standard questions and spent the next twenty minutes grilling the subdued boyfriend about his contact with Angela. Simpson stuttered and stammered his way through the two-year relationship.

They'd dated regularly for the first year, then Angela's behavior changed. She began to hang out with Otherworlders and disappeared for days. Unlike Victor, Simpson had demanded an explanation. She'd refused to give one and often covered her activities with lies. He began following her, and at least twice when she said she was spending the evening at home, he'd seen her cruising the vampire clubs.

"Did you confront her about that?" Ryan asked.

Simpson hesitated. "Not until I heard she was sleeping with one of the fang guys. I told her I was leaving. She bawled like a baby, like I was the one who'd done something wrong. She promised she'd end it. And I guess I wanted to believe her, so I stuck around. But lately, she didn't seem to care what I thought." Simpson squirmed in his chair. "So, yeah, we fought a lot. I hated her cheating." He looked up again, his nose crinkled. "How could she do it with one of them?"

"That's pretty tough, Wes." Ryan voice was non-judgmental. "It's hard when your girl's screwing around. Hard to keep things under control. When did the fights turn physical?"

Simpson stiffened. "Never. I never hit her. Not once. Just a lot of yelling."

"She had a black eye."

"Yeah, I saw it, but I didn't do it." Simpson's face flushed, agitated. "Figured that was a present from fang boy."

Fifteen minutes later Ari didn't like Simpson any better, but she was convinced he wasn't the killer. He didn't have the stomach for it. And in some weird fashion, he had been more of a friend to Angela than anyone else. But that didn't necessarily make him a nice guy.

"So what was your problem when you came charging into Basil and Sage?" Ari asked.

Simpson had the grace to look uncomfortable. "I didn't know you were the Guardian. Just that you were a witch. A bad one, I thought." He swallowed hard when Ari scowled. "Angie and me'd been fighting, about everything. But mostly how weird she'd been. When I saw a pamphlet on your class, I thought she was into the occult."

"You said she changed long before that."

"Yeah, but I didn't know this was her first class. I figured she'd been going there every week for months." He hunched his shoulders. "I'd eliminated all the other explanations."

"Like what?"

"Drugs. I found some blue pills on her dresser. That Fantasy stuff. She gave me the old story about holding them for a friend. Yeah, like I believed that. I figured she'd been experimenting, but I never saw them again. And she never acted strung out, like she was using."

"Maybe she kept them hidden after that." Ryan had been listening quietly until Simpson mentioned the drugs. Now he was on point.

"I searched. Several times. Nothing."

What a creepy boyfriend, Ari thought. Follows her around, searches her apartment. She couldn't decide whether he was a misguided friend or a stalker.

"So go on," Ryan encouraged. "You must have had other suspicions."

"Only one, really. This vamp dude, I thought he might of bespelled her. But she laughed when I asked. And those people act like zombies, don't they? Or robots?" He glanced at Ari for confirmation. When she said nothing, he looked away. "Anyway, that's when I found the candles and some crystals."

"That's how you made the leap to black magic? Candles and crystals?" Ari's voice rose.

"Let's go back to the drugs." Ryan intervened to keep them on course. "Maybe you never saw drugs because Angela was quickly passing them on. A go-between. Did you see money? I haven't heard anything about a job. How'd she pay her bills?"

"I don't know," Simpson admitted. "She quit her waitress job almost a year ago."

The rest of the interview was pretty ho-hum. The morning of Ari's class was the last time he admitted seeing Angela. On the night of her death, he said he went to a movie by himself and might still have the ticket stub at home. He'd look. Not much of an alibi, but Ari didn't think it mattered. Given Angela's injuries, he'd never been a likely suspect.

Simpson left, and Ryan leaned back in his chair, stretching out his long legs. "Well, that was a waste of time. At least as far as identifying a decent suspect. The drug bit was interesting, but I'm not sure it's helpful. I'll follow up with the narcotics squad. But it looks to me like we're out of suspects."

Ari looked at him and shrugged. They'd have to start over, somehow develop new suspects. A knock on the door was a welcome interruption.

A harried-looking, twenty-something male, one of the couriers employed by the city, popped in long enough to drop a packet on Ryan's desk, the lab results from the crime scene. Ryan read the report aloud without much enthusiasm. As expected, it was unremarkable, until he reached the last item of evidence: twenty-six canine hairs.

Ari sat up straighter. Dog or werewolf? Angela didn't own a dog. And given Andreas's description of the woman at the club, werewolves suddenly seemed a real possibility. She knew DNA tests wouldn't hold the answer. Wolf and dog hairs were too similar to be distinguished without the follicles: an interesting fact Ari's forensics instructor would be surprised she remembered. He'd always complained her frequent looks out the window meant she wasn't paying attention.

"It doesn't have to be a wolf," she cautioned. "Maybe our victim had a dog in the past. Or she has a friend with a dog. Simpson would know."

Ryan made the call. Before he disconnected, he'd already given her the thumbs-up. "No dog. Not allowed in the building. I think we have a solid lead. Now what the hell do we do with it? How do we find a werewolf, Ari?"

"Let me work on that while you follow the drugs."

"Works for me. This Fantasy has been popping up all over the city. Heard it creates the illusion of anything you desire. Kind of like an internal virtual reality. Want to experience being a rock star? Want to know what it's like to date Angelina Jolie? You got it. Anything you can imagine."

"Angelina Jolie? Is she what you'd want?" Ari teased. "Your dream date?"

"What sane guy would turn her down? Hey, if I was into the drug scene, it might tempt me."

Ari laughed. "You're full of surprises. Just think of all those other secret fantasies out there. That translates into cash for the dealers, uber profits. Maybe Angela got in over her head. Or she ripped off a supplier."

"That'd get her killed, all right. I'll dig around. In the meantime," Ryan said, getting to his feet, "let's search her apartment again. Before we release the scene, I'd like another shot at finding drugs or drug money. Maybe we missed something."

* * *

They'd been in Angela's stuffy apartment for almost an hour with little to show for their efforts except a lot of dust bunnies under the bed.

"She sure had a bunch of face junk." Ryan was going through Angela's vanity. "What does this contraption do?" He held up an eyelash curler for Ari's inspection.

She pantomimed its use. "Don't you have sisters?"

"Nope. Three brothers. None of this girlie paraphernalia."

"More used to jock straps and smelly socks, huh? And Playboy mags under the mattress."

"What makes you think they're under the mattress?"

"Younger brother. You think sisters don't know these things?" Ari opened another drawer. "She liked expensive lingerie." She held up a red, lacy gown, tucked it back in, and gave the drawer a shove. It stuck. She yanked it out, and tried again. And again it stuck. This time she took the drawer out and looked in the back. Something was hanging from the top.

"Now what's this?" she said, catching Ryan's attention. She reached in, pulled off two strips of masking tape, and retrieved a solid bundle. No lacy stuff this time. It was a roll of hundred dollar bills.

Ryan counted twelve hundred. Quite a stash for a girl to keep in her undies drawer, but if she was selling drugs, shouldn't there be more? Thousands more. And where were the drugs?

As they talked it over, their elation faded. Finding the roll of cash hadn't gotten them any closer to a suspect. It raised more unanswered questions. Without anybody left to question, where did they go for the answers?

Chapter Nine

Sunday morning broke gray and cloudy, foreshadowing the storm about to crack open over their heads. Ari's first thought was to roll over and catch another hour. But Great-Gran's words to a sleepy child still played in her head, "Late in bed, early dead." Not exactly a suitable childhood rhyme, unless you were a Guardian in training.

As she woke her muscles with a brisk run through the park, Ari mulled over the leads they had, focusing on the two she needed to follow: contact Victor to see what, if anything, he knew about the money or drugs, and find the thirty-something woman who came to Club Dintero with Angela. If Andreas was right about the woman's species, and Ari had no reason to doubt him, Steffan, the werewolf representative on the Magic Council, topped the list of people to see.

As frequently happened, the werewolf's name brought a grin to her face. Steffan. Wolf. A word play too obvious to miss. Ari chuckled and lengthened her stride to match the tune now running through her head.

* * *

By mid-afternoon she'd cleared up some routine matters for the Council and left a message for Victor to call. Since the vampires wouldn't be awake for hours, she moved to her next task. Finding Steffan was easy.

Ari parked her Mini Cooper in front of Steffan's suburban home. When she heard laughter from the back yard, she found him sweating it out in a volleyball game with a mixed company of friends, including half a dozen shirtless guys. Her day was looking up already. A beer keg stood at the far end of the net. Judging by the level of laughter, the missed shots, and werewolves' great tolerance for alcohol, she assumed they'd been at this a long time.

"Hey! How could you have a party without me?" she called.

Steffan, one of the shirtless guys, turned at the sound of her voice. "Ari! Come join us!"

"Love to, but I'm a working girl today," she yelled back.

He tossed the ball to a buddy, grabbed a T-shirt from the ground, and pulled it over his head as he sauntered toward her. The casual observer would never guess Steffan was a werewolf. He was a cool, jazzy, redhead with burnished copper locks and beautiful long eyelashes. His sociable personality made him a people magnet. Women longed to marry him, or at least take him to bed, and guys sought him as a friend. A party person, a bender of rules, and the last guy you would picture involved with the serious business of the Magic Council. It seemed equally unlikely you'd find him howling at the moon.

Steffan wasn't a natural born. During college, he'd fallen in love with a werewolf. She also had a wolf lover who resented the competition; he attacked Steffan and left him bleeding in the woods. The girlfriend found Steffan in time to save his life, but he was infected with lycanthropy. Ironically, their relationship didn't survive his transformation, and the girlfriend returned to her original lover.

Somehow, Steffan hadn't turned bitter. He embraced his new strength, his self-healing, the pack life and even the monthly run in the woods. He'd quickly risen through the ranks of his pack and was elected to represent them on the Magic Council. Ari and Steffan met shortly after that and had now been friends for six years. He was one of the Council's hardest working members. He chaired two committees and was the chosen go-to guy for unusual or complicated problems that involved any of the lycanthrope families.

Ari and Steffan greeted each other with a hug of mutual affection. They hadn't had a chance to talk for five or six months except at Council meetings, so it took a few minutes to catch up. Finally Ari got down to business and asked about new wolves in town.

"French-speaking women," she specified.

"Well, that does narrow the field." Steffan pursed his lips. "Interesting you should ask. We've got our eyes on a possible pack right now. Canadians. Strangers pass through the area all the time. When they settle in but shun the rest of us, I get worried." He waved a hand toward the keg. "How about a beer while we talk? At the house. Where it's more private."

Ari waited on the wooden deck while he collected their drinks. She leaned on the rail, watching the wolves' festivities, a pack party to celebrate a member's promotion in his day job. Ari felt a brief pang of envy at their easy camaraderie. Someone always at your back. A Guardian's life was so often solitary.

Steffan returned and handed her a beer. Cold and bitter, just the way she liked it.

He leaned one arm on the deck rail. "About four months ago a pack, maybe ten or twelve men and women, moved in from Canada. They're staying in an old house at 13th and Vine. Leader's name is Louie Molyneux. Tough-looking thug. Pack's not friendly, at least not with us, but so far no trouble either. No visible employment. At night they hang out at the vamp clubs. It's off behavior but not necessarily bad."

"So why are you watching them?"

Steffan slowly shook his head. "Beats me. But I'm not the only one feeling uneasy. My pack mates are talking about it, asking questions. No one has seen this group on night runs or in furry form. Almost like they want to hide the fact they're werewolves. Can people in Canada be so naive they don't recognize a wolf?" He rubbed his nose and grinned. "It smells wrong. I've even wondered if the missing red wolf from Goshen

Park isn't part of the pack. Anyway, I'd bet money that's where you'll find your French-speaking woman." He downed the rest of his beer in one long swallow.

Ari's interest sparked when he mentioned Goshen Park. This was a pack she'd like to visit. "Any suggestions on how to approach them?"

"Don't go alone. Can't your police buddies call the she-wolf down to the station?"

"How? They have all these legal rules. And we don't even have a name. Besides, I'm beginning to think I need to get a look at the entire pack."

He shrugged. "Then some of us will go to the house with you."

Ari thought about it. She might get a foot in the door, but she'd sure spook the Canadians. She'd hate to have them run before she knew if they were guilty of anything. "Thanks, but it feels too early for a showdown. Now that I think about it, I'd rather not do this on their turf at all. Not if I can think of another way. I'll stay in touch." She reacted to his quick frown. "Don't worry, Steffan, I'll figure it out. But thanks. And thanks for the beer. Sorry I interrupted your game."

"We've got all night. Yard lights. Come back later when you're not on the job."

"I'll try."

Steffan cleared his throat in disbelief, and Ari laughed.

"I promise. I'll try," she repeated. And maybe she would. Someday. When she had the time to let her hair down.

She returned to the street, climbed into her dark green Mini Cooper, and gave the car a friendly pat before starting the engine. After rescuing the car from a salvage lot, Ari had bonded with Mini during restoration. Now when something bugged Ari, she often went to the garage just to talk it over. Not that the car talked back. That was the best part. Mini just listened.

So as Ari drove home, she and Mini hashed it over. And inspiration came to her. The Canadian werewolves hung out at vampire clubs. With a little help from Victor or Andreas…if she could talk one of them into helping her.

The idea had gained momentum by the time Ari reached home. On impulse she dialed the club to leave a message. It was still too early for the vampires, but she now had two reasons to talk with them. When a female voice answered, she asked to leave a message for Victor or Andreas.

She nearly dropped the phone when an unmistakable voice came on the line.

"This is Andreas. How may I be of service?" Suave, charming, magic tamped down.

"Hi," she said, a little tongue-tied with this unexpected development. They hadn't parted on such good terms. A little prep time for this conversation would have been nice. "This is Arianna Calin." How could he be up this early? It wasn't dark yet.

"How delightful to hear from you." He didn't sound delighted, but at least his tone was neutral.

OK, Arianna, your turn again. What in the world was she going to say to him? She'd expected to have time to work out the details before anyone called her back. Deep breath. Improvise.

"I know where the she-wolf is," she said. "The one who was with Angela that night at the club. At least, I think so. But I have a problem and need your help."

Pause. "I'm sure I should be flattered, Ms. Calin, but why involve me?"

"I need someone connected to the vampire bars and club owners. And you must want to get Victor off the hook." She ignored his less-than-welcoming tone and tried to establish a little rapport. "I'm sorry we got off on the wrong foot, but I could really use your help. At least hear me out."

"I fail to see the benefit for me. Victor has what I believe you call an airtight alibi."

"Nothing's airtight. He'll be a suspect until the killer is found. Besides, didn't you want this murder solved?"

"Indeed. On that we can agree."

"Then help me." Seconds passed without a response, and

Ari sighed. "Think of it like this. Once this case is solved, you'll be rid of me. No more trouble at the club. No phone calls. Life goes back to normal."

That got a chuckle. "An occurrence greatly to be desired. All right, Ms. Calin, I promise nothing, except listening. What would be my part in this plan?"

"It's simple really. You contact the other club and bar owners. I'll give them a police sketch of the she-wolf based on your description. When someone sees her, they call me. Or if they won't do that, they call you, and you call me."

"Why this elaborate scheme? If you know where she is, why not arrest her?"

"Can't. The victim's human, which means we have to follow human law. The she-wolf's staying on private property. Until we know a lot more than we do now, we have to snag her in public where we don't need a search warrant."

"And if you find her in one of the clubs, what do you propose to do?"

"Well," Ari filled in the details as she went. "If there's any doubt about her identity, maybe you or Victor could go along and point her out. Then I'll talk to her."

"You make it sound easy. And, in the event she does not wish to talk, what then?"

Hmm. Good question. Ari hesitated, weighing her choices.

"Or is that where I come in again? Please, tell me you don't expect me to hold her hostage until she complies." Andreas's voice held a strong undertone of amusement.

"Don't be funny. Let me think about it," Ari said, struggling to keep her annoyance in check. After all, she was asking for a big favor. "You know, I never expected you to answer the phone and ask all these questions."

"Then why did you call?"

His question was so reasonable she swallowed her irritation. "I was going to leave a message," she admitted. "OK, here's the plan. If she refuses, I'll take her into custody and put pressure on her at the police station."

"You intend to arrest this woman inside my club or some other owner's club?" Andreas wasn't amused anymore. Incredulous, maybe.

"Not unless I have to," Ari protested. "I think she'll talk to me. Give me some credit, Andreas. I don't intend to start a riot."

"You astonish me. I assumed that was exactly your intent, and that you expected me to put down the uprising. I'm relieved your expectations were not so grand."

"Cut the sarcasm," she said. "Unless you've got a better idea, this is my only chance."

"I cannot agree. Consenting to an arrest inside my club strikes me as a very poor business decision." He paused. "I am not unsympathetic, but Club Dintero is a reputable establishment. I intend to keep it that way. Come up with a better proposal, and I'll reconsider. And I will put some thought into it myself."

"This is urgent," Ari said. "The killer could get away. Or kill again." She wondered if he was brushing her off. Maybe she'd pushed too hard.

"Then you should move quickly to find a better plan."

That was the best she could get from him. At least he didn't say no. Not entirely.

Chapter Ten

O nce she was off the phone, Ari flopped on her couch and tried to come up with ideas to make her plan more acceptable to Andreas. When she finally realized that dusk had darkened her windows, she abandoned her efforts, began a kitchen search for food, and prepared to go on patrol. She'd just bitten into an apple, while contemplating the skimpy contents of her fridge, when Martin called. The elf served as Guardian for the rest of Riverdale, including the suburbs. Mostly wolf country.

Martin's voice vibrated with tension. "Ari, we've got a mess on our hands! There's been a vamp fight at Hartley Park. Two dead, their heads torn off. Third vamp got away. Probably headed your direction. Toward home. We're searching the streets, but no sign of him yet."

"A public fight? What brought that on?" She knew vamps sometimes settled disputes through violence, but never where the community could see it.

"Haven't heard. But this big vamp's really out of control, on a rampage. I notified the Council and the vampire court. Don't try to take him by yourself, Ari. He's over 250 pounds, built like a sumo wrestler, long black hair. His name might be Christopher. Here's Steffan. Maybe he can tell you something more."

She heard rustling on the other end, then Steffan's voice.

"He's right. It's a mess here. There must be two hundred lycanthropes milling around. An impromptu Were Fest. But I wanted you to know a couple things right away. The vamps in the fight were brought here by that Canadian pack. Strange coincidence, right? That's not the weirdest part. I'm being told the vamps were drunk. Is that even possible?"

Ari hardly heard the rest of the conversation. What Steffan had said made no sense. Vampires were resistant to spells and charms, even her stuns, and drank alcohol without visible effects. Prescription and recreational drugs were the same. Vamps simply didn't get drunk or high. Witnesses had to be wrong. But whatever was going on, she couldn't think of anything more dangerous than an Otherworlder who was out of control. Especially a vamp.

Telling Steffan she had to go, Ari strapped her ankle holster in place and slipped in the Cobra D22 derringer with its two rounds of silver bullets. It wasn't lethal to Otherworlders, except at unbearably close quarters, but it might slow a vamp or get his attention. She shrugged into her leather jacket, checked her silver dagger. The knife was specially made, modeled after the F-S Fighting Knife once carried by US Marines. She never left the house without it and trained with it regularly. Once she verified her bracelet and pocket pouch were stocked with spells, potions, and extra ammo, Ari hit the streets.

She made a fast call to Ryan. This wasn't his fight yet, but it would be if humans got in harm's way. He agreed to have his officers step up neighborhood patrols and notify Ari if anyone sighted the suspect. Given the vampire's size, he should be easy to spot.

Ari made the usual evening rounds, stopping in pubs frequented by vamps and a wine cellar owned and operated by wee folks, the unofficial town criers for Olde Town. Word of the fight was spreading, but slowly. Probably because it happened on the eastside. A quick sweep of Goshen Park turned up nothing. Ari backtracked to canvas more of the vampire strip. No rampaging vamp. No Canadian wolves. She listened for gossip about illegal magic or drug use but didn't hear anything on that either.

It was after one in the morning. Ari was on her second trip through the vampire bar district when she heard the screams and sirens. She sprinted toward the commotion coming from the Second Chance Saloon, a dive that catered to members from the roughest vampire nests. She arrived as Ryan's police cruiser squealed to a stop.

Yelling and shrieking, pushing and trampling over each other, panicked humans and Otherworlders jammed the bar's parking lot. Adding to the confusion, a crowd continued to pour out the pub doors. Ari jumped in the bed of a parked truck to see over the crowd. A solid mass of watchers encircled two male vampires and their victims.

The neon bar lights reflected from a dark pool of blood surrounding one of the victims. The body, minus the left arm, lay still, already beyond help. The other victim thrashed wildly to break free from the grip of his vampire attacker.

Ari leaped into the crowd, shoving and pounding her way toward the survivor. As she broke out of the circle, she heard a sharp explosion behind her. She spun quickly looking for some lunatic loose with a firearm. The crowd parted and began running. She lost sight of the bigger vamp, but the other stood fifteen feet away, his hands around the throat of his victim. Ari shot a stunner in hopes of breaking his death grip. The blue flame caught the vamp in the thigh. He turned toward her. Wild, rolling eyes, showing white, attempted to focus. When she hit him in the other leg with a second stun, the vamp dropped the victim, but instead of moving toward her, he crouched, snarling, defending his prey.

She inched forward. If she could get close enough to snatch the victim… The vamp hissed, spittle dripping from his fangs. He suddenly rushed toward her, long arms swinging. Before he could pin her in a death grip, she kicked up, catching him hard on the jaw. Knocking them both off balance, Ari fell on her side, rolled to her feet, and grabbed the dagger. The vamp hurled himself toward her, ignoring the weapon. No hesitation, no flinching. Momentum carried him straight onto the blade, and his body hit her as a dead weight. The blade pierced his heart. And a silver dagger is as good as a stake.

Ari shoved the leaden body away and looked for the other vamp. He crouched near the building, a line of police officers and drawn guns facing him. Big guy, long black hair, fangs and clothes splattered with blood. Christopher.

She scrambled to her feet, yelling "Stop!" and ran toward them, hoping to end this without another death. The big guy had other ideas. Or maybe he wasn't thinking at all. He charged the officers. They opened fire with a deafening roar. The vampire staggered and crumbled under the heavy barrage. Silver bullets. It was over in seconds. A heavy smell like burnt sulfur hung in the air.

Police officers rushed to tend to the victims. The human was dead; the other victim still had a faint pulse. The fur on the back of his hands indicated he was a weretiger, the only reason he survived. Paramedics arrived and transported him to the Otherworld hospital, but he'd do most of the healing himself. Fluids would help. Once he was strong enough to complete the change into tiger form, he'd mend quickly.

Satisfied the worst of the crisis was over, Ari grabbed the closest witness who wasn't screaming or yelling and asked what happened.

"It started inside," he said. "This big vamp comes tromping in a half hour ago, joined some friends. I guess they were friends. He was pissed from the word go. Someone started yelling back. Somehow it boiled down to these four, cussing and shoving. That's when the barkeep told them to take it outside. They did. Someone hollered 'fight' and we all headed for the door. Then it turned really ugly." He lifted his hands in a helpless gesture. "By the time we realized how bad it was, it was too late. Ain't nobody going to take on a pissed off vamp."

Ari took his name and number to pass on to Ryan.

The police strung yellow and black crime scene tape and

moved the crowd away from the bodies. Four officers worked the crowd, collecting names of witnesses. Ari spotted Ryan near the door of the bar and started toward him.

Someone grabbed her arm.

"Hey!" She tried to jerk away but her arm was held in an iron grip. She spun toward her attacker and came eye to eye with Andreas. "What are you doing here? Let go of me."

His face, only inches away, was frozen in a glare. Distant, alien. That predator look. Only his eyes sparked, searing her face as if he found something repulsive there. She felt the hot anger seething under the surface.

"Let go of my arm," she repeated. "What's wrong with you?" She was confused by his behavior. They'd just had a civil phone conversation. Surely this rage wasn't directed at her. Yet his eyes told her otherwise. Her witch blood surged in response, fingers tingling.

She forced the reaction down. Witch fire wasn't the answer. Not yet. Not this close, and certainly not in a crowd. What she needed was a clear head—and some answers. "Talk to me," she said through clenched teeth. "I get it that you're angry, but I don't know why."

"You reek of blood, Guardian. Vampire blood." Andreas's voice was low, but it vibrated with fury. His fingers dug into her arm. When his magic pushed against her defenses, she struggled to pull away. He released her, but stepped closer, crowding her personal space.

"You ask for my assistance," he hissed, "and then you turn around and murder my people? Did you enjoy the kill?" His words cut like ice, brittle shards of accusation.

"Andreas, stop this." Ari's pulse hammered. She felt his control slipping.

"Answer me. What was it like?"

She braced her hands against his chest, her magic meeting his, and absorbed the rolling anger. "Of course I didn't like it. But somebody had to—" she stopped. No explanations. He didn't want to hear them. Not now. She wasn't even sure he was listening to her. She stilled, willing his rage to cool.

Feeling the magic surrounding the pair, the Otherworlders in the crowd began to edge away. Ryan must have noticed something. Maybe her closeness to someone he considered a danger. Not such a far-fetched idea tonight. She heard Ryan's voice. "Hey, is everything OK over there?"

No one answered him.

She shoved her hands against Andreas's chest, demanding some space. He allowed the distance to widen without protest. Relieved at this headway, she gave him a hard look. "If you've got a point to make, now's the time."

"Don't bait me, Arianna." Despite the warning, his tone was neutral now. A definite sign of improvement.

"I wasn't. But I don't get this. The vamps were killers, and they left us no choice. I can explain if you'll let me." She didn't owe him an explanation, but failing to handle this right might end with one of them dead.

Andreas took a step back. The power level dropped, and the ants quit marching up and down her arms.

"Proceed," he said, settling back on his heels. "Explain this to me." His voice was cold, unyielding.

Before she uttered a word, Ryan stalked over. "Is there a problem here?" He stopped six feet away, a suspicious frown on his face. She noted his hand hovered at his side, close to his holstered weapon.

Andreas ignored him.

"No, no problem," Ari said. "Just a misunderstanding. This is Andreas De Luca. He's with the vampire court and concerned about what happened tonight." She waited to see if the vampire would confirm or deny his position with the court. He didn't.

She took a steadying breath. In an effort to ease the tension, she finished the introduction of the two men. After a noticeable hesitation, they responded appropriately. Ryan accepted the vampire court's need for information, and the moment of crisis passed.

Together, Ari and Ryan related everything they knew about

the fight and the events that transpired at the Second Chance parking lot. Throughout this recital, Andreas remained silent, not even asking questions. Ari had no idea what he was thinking; the vampire had wiped his face of expression and blocked his magical power.

When they finished, Andreas spoke only to Ryan. "If you allow me to view the bodies, I can provide positive identification, Lieutenant. And notify the nests."

"Appreciate the IDs." Ryan looked at Ari. "But the notifications are your call, Ari. This is Otherworld business."

"I've no objection. He can do it more quickly."

Andreas didn't even look at her.

Ryan nodded, and the two men walked across the parking lot. Ari didn't follow. With Andreas ignoring her, her presence would only add tension. She watched as they stopped briefly at each corpse.

When they returned, Andreas finally spoke to her. "Are you still convinced there was no other way?"

"Yes, I'm positive." She answered without hesitation, but she wasn't going to beg him to believe her.

He frowned, slid his hands into his jeans' pockets and walked away.

Ari stared after him, feeling somehow betrayed. He claimed she was easy to read, but if he'd seen the truth tonight, he wasn't acting like it. Why had he jumped to the conclusion that she was in the wrong?

"He's a strange fellow, even for a vampire," Ryan said.

"Yeah. Complicated." Ari turned toward the cop. She didn't want to talk about Andreas, didn't even want to think about him right now. She wanted to concentrate on the case. "I hope you handled the gunshot I heard."

To her surprise, Ryan chuckled. "Hank, one of our officers. He carries firecrackers in his pocket. First time I've seen him use one, but it busted up the crowd." He glanced around the crime scene. "What do you suppose set this off? Your vamp buddy ID'd the big guy as Christopher. That's the one you're looking for, right?"

Ari hardly thought Andreas qualified as her vamp buddy, but she agreed Christopher appeared to be the suspect from the eastside fight. She repeated what the witness had told her about this fight and added the details on the earlier incident: the Canadian wolves, the unlikely reports of intoxication.

"Sounds like the eastside fight carried over into this mess," Ryan said, eyeing the coroner's van. "But a lot of things don't add up. Any theories?"

"Don't I wish. I'm afraid something even worse is going to happen. And Molyneux's wolves keep turning up everywhere. I'd like to know if they were here tonight." She noticed the crew with the body bags. They were getting ready to load the vampires. She pointed toward them. "You realize the vampire corpses are useless as evidence, don't you? There will be nothing in the bags but bones and dust when they reach the morgue. Even if we took samples now," she said, anticipating his question, "there's no way to preserve them. Once a vampire dies, decay spreads rapidly until it's done. It's quick."

"Great," Ryan grumbled. "Didn't know it was that quick. Not many vamp deaths reported. What about the human? Will he rise as a vampire?"

"No, he's just dead. It doesn't happen by accident."

A uniformed officer called to Ryan and, muttering an apology, he went back to work.

While the police were busy outside, Ari stepped inside the Second Chance Saloon to speak with the barkeep. The lighting was dim. The air stank of beer, spilled on the floor and tabletops, and cigars, a favorite vice among werecreatures. A lone barmaid mechanically wiped tables with a rag and stacked dirty glasses on a metal tray.

"Hey, Miss, don't do that. Everything in here is evidence."

The girl jumped, the tray teetered, and Ari sped forward to grab it. The barmaid was short for an elf, pale and thin. Her shoulders slumped, and when she turned toward Ari, tears glistened on her cheeks.

"I'm sorry. I didn't know," the elf said.

"Careful." Ari set the tray on the table. "I didn't mean to startle you. I'm with the police. Can you tell me your name?"

"Feyla. Sorry I jumped like that. Just can't stop crying. I was so scared during the fight, and now they're dead."

"Did you know them?" Ari softened her voice. The girl's tears were real. Was she a friend of the victims? A girlfriend?

"Not really." Feyla sniffed, wiping her face with the back of a hand. "The vamps were at one of my tables. They'd been nice all evening until the big guy came. And the foreigners."

Ari pricked up her ears. "Foreigners?"

The elf bobbed her head. "They didn't speak very good English, so I figured they were visiting someone."

Feyla didn't know where the strangers were from, and she seemed unaware of their species, but she remembered there were two women in the group. And she was positive the trouble started at their table. "I know the Second Chance has a poor reputation, but it's never been this bad." The girl sniffed. "You're not going to close them, are you? I'd hate to lose my job."

Fearing an outbreak of tears, Ari assured the girl any closing would be temporary. She told Feyla to leave her name with the officer at the door and to point out the vamps' table before she left. Feyla pointed toward a table near the stage.

As Ari approached the table, she noted that Feyla hadn't gotten this far in her cleaning. Eight glasses. Two vamps and six companions. There was nothing else on the table surface except moisture rings, some spilled cigar ash, and used napkins. Maybe forensics would find some useful DNA.

Using a clean napkin from the bar, Ari pulled out each chair, checked the seats, and finally looked under the table. Two cigar butts, mud from somebody's dirty boots, a sticky patch from spilled beer, and a tiny speck of something blue. She dropped to one knee and leaned in for a better look.

"Do you have an evidence kit?" she yelled to the officer on the front door.

"Yes, ma'am." He brought it over.

"There, see that blue thing?" She pointed under the table.

"Sure do." He pulled a plastic bag from his kit and offered it to her.

Ari shook her head, "No, go ahead." She didn't see a reason to write a report for finding evidence if she didn't have to. Besides, the young officer would enjoy the experience so much more. His face creased into a wide grin when he retrieved what looked like a small blue capsule. "Looks like some kind of drug, ma'am."

Score one for the good guys. "Nice going, Officer. Take it to Lt. Foster," she instructed. "I guarantee he'll be interested."

As he scurried off to find his lieutenant, Ari wondered if they'd opened Pandora's Box. If that capsule contained a drug with a violent, intoxicating effect on vampires, Riverdale's current problems could morph into a nightmare.

Chapter Eleven

The following days were busy. Interviews, meetings, worrying. The community was on edge, and Ari had little time to spare for the freaky confrontation with Andreas. Efforts to stop the Otherworld violence demanded everyone's attention.

On Monday, Ari and Ryan, aided by a detective from the eastside unit and by Martin, the other guardian, interviewed witnesses from the two vampire attacks. From the dozens of bystanders, crime scene officers had recommended twelve for further interviews. The barmaid, Feyla Rains, was one of the twelve, but she didn't add much to her statement from the night before. That kind of set the tone for the day.

As often happens with witnesses, the descriptions of events varied from one person to the next, but there was nothing they hadn't heard before. Three facts remained constant: the fights had erupted with little warning and no apparent cause; the vampires appeared to be intoxicated, twice described as staggering and foaming at the mouth; and the Canadian werewolves had been at both events. Whether the Canadians had participated, instigated, or been bystanders was an issue for debate.

Surprisingly, witnesses denied seeing drugs or magic use at either crime scene. After talking it over, the four investigators concluded some witnesses must have lied about the drugs for fear of incriminating themselves. The blue capsule was indisputable proof. As predicted, the lab analysis identified the contents as Fantasy, the powerful hallucinogenic that had swept through the human community. The rest of the lab report was unexpected and more alarming. The drug formula was different than previous samples. It contained an additive that defied identification, causing the lab's computers to display contradictory readings and error messages.

Martin and Ari exchanged looks. "Magic," she said. "If this substance is affecting Otherworlders, magic is involved. The drug has been cursed or enchanted."

"You're joking, right?" This startled question came from the eastside detective. Ryan just shook his head.

"I wish we were." Martin's fair skin was paler than usual.

"Why isn't the crime lab telling us that?" The detective didn't want to believe them.

"Because they don't know. Human machines aren't set up to identify the changes that magic produces." Ari appealed to Ryan. "Let's send a sample to the Otherworld Forensics Lab. Maybe OFR can confirm our suspicions."

"How do they prove a drug's been cursed? On second thought, I don't want to know." The detective looked at Ryan. "Do you deal with this kind of stuff all the time?" When Ryan gave him a crooked grin, the officer stood. "Glad there's somebody who takes these cases. And I'm just as glad it isn't normally me. You let me know if there's anything I can do."

Ari doubted they'd see him again.

* * *

Two days passed without noticeable progress. Ari talked with Martin and Steffan frequently as community tension continued to rise. Rumors spread like wildfire. A lot of smack talk was going down. Name calling, finger pointing. The sale of firearms to humans jumped fifteen percent, the sale of silver bullets skyrocketed. Friends and family of the injured weretiger formed a night watch, announcing they would kill any vampires that came near their homes. The local wolves watched everyone with suspicion.

"Can you blame them?" Steffan asked during his latest call. "We've had two fatal fights. Tempers are running high. If we don't get a lid on this, the community's going to blow."

Ari tapped a pencil on her kitchen table. She'd been writing her reports to the Council. "I wonder if the situation is as bad with the vampires."

"Haven't heard from Andreas, huh?"

"Not since Sunday. Doubt if I will. He was pretty pissed, only I'm still not sure why." She'd already told Steffan about the parking lot confrontation. "I guess we have to assume Prince Daron's got things under control."

After they disconnected, Ari debated calling Andreas to break the ice. An update on the vampire situation would be good, but she had another, more pressing reason. With the crisis deepening, she needed to make contact with the Canadian wolves. An interview with the mysterious she-wolf seemed like the perfect excuse, and Ari still thought Andreas could make that happen. The vampire hadn't withdrawn his promise to help. Of course, he hadn't renewed it either. And his distrust of her couldn't have been more obvious. She put her phone away, not yet ready to have him refuse the call. Maybe if she gave him more time.

Too restless to finish the reports, she decided to pursue another angle. While Ryan talked with the narc squad, Ari wanted to tap community sources on the drug angle. She wished she'd paid closer attention when Fantasy was all over the media. As she recalled, *The Clarion* had printed a series of articles. She called the newspaper's general number. They transferred her to the crime desk to talk with reporter Eddie West.

When he answered the phone, Ari explained who she was and what she wanted. "I need to know everything you can tell me about Fantasy. Where it came from, who's selling it. Everything."

"Sure, I can do that," the reporter said. "It'll take a while, and I'm starving. Want to meet at the Daily Diner? I'll even let you buy. And maybe you can tell me why the Magic Council is interested in the drug traffic."

Ari chuckled. The guy had his own style. Half an hour later, she entered an unpretentious establishment that might have been situated in any small town, USA. A dozen booths. Half as many tables. Vinyl floor. A white-haired couple drank coffee at one of the tables. A forty-something female sat alone in a booth, her attention on the door. The only other occupant was a freckle-faced young man grinning at Ari from a corner booth. He looked seventeen. He waved.

"Over here," he said. "I'm Eddie."

He read her surprise, for as soon as she slid into the seat, he added, "I'm twenty-four. People always mistake me for a teen. Someday looking younger will be a good deal. Right now it's a drag."

She grinned at his boyish admission. "Sorry about that."

"Don't sweat it. Hope you don't mind, but I ordered. Haven't eaten since breakfast. You want something?"

She said a Diet Coke would be great.

His brown eyes gave Ari the once-over. A guy look. "You don't look much like my idea of a Guardian."

"No? What did you expect?"

"Big, tough looking. Lots of weapons. You're just a cute blonde."

Ari rolled her eyes. "Uh-huh. As you said, assumptions are such a drag."

Eddie laughed. "OK, you got me. My mistake. And my turn to apologize."

His rib sandwich, fries, and shake arrived. Ari ordered her drink and watched in amusement as he took the edge off his hunger. He put down the half-eaten sandwich and wiped the sauce from his mouth. "Sure you don't want some? Best rib sandwich in town."

"No, really, I'm fine. But about the drugs?"

"Are you going to tell me why you want to know?"

"We'll see," she hedged. Not if she didn't have to.

He shrugged, and in between bites, he began to talk about the articles. "First heard about Fantasy when this woman called me at work. About five months ago. Her son OD'd. He'd flunked out of college and brought the stuff home with him. She thought *The Clarion* should be warning other parents. I was curious, so I asked around. The drug had been in Riverdale two months and already caused three overdoses. That's when I started writing the series."

"Where's the drug coming from?"

"Both coasts, and now here in the Midwest. Her son was in a small college in Alabama."

"So, everywhere," she said. "New York, LA, Timbuktu. What about local distributers?"

He scratched his chin and eyed her. "Got some ideas. Maybe Otherworlders. No proof yet. Maybe you know something." He paused, as if inviting a comment, then continued. "I had an informant. Good connections, but her boyfriend killed her before we got that far."

"What?" Ari straightened in her seat and stared at him. "What informant?" Riverdale didn't have that many murders. Not the kind the public and press knew about. "Are you talking about Angela Raymond?" Ari scooted forward on the bench. "She was working for you, wasn't she? Why didn't you come forward and tell the police after she died?"

"Hey, calm down. Why do you care if she was working for me?"

"You're the source of the cash," Ari continued unabated. "You did pay her in cash, didn't you? Hundred dollar bills?"

"Yeah, I did." His brows drew into a deep frown. "Is that significant?"

"Don't you get it?" Ari stopped. She needed to be careful what she said to the press. "Everything about a victim is important," she finished, keeping it vague.

Eddie'd already caught the implication. He shook his head vigorously. "No, uh-uh. If you think she was killed because of her undercover work, you're wrong. It was the boyfriend. Some domestic thing. I talked with neighbors the night she died. And the PD didn't deny it when I asked for an official comment. I didn't mention she was a source, because…well, it's confidential. And it didn't seem to matter." His jaw set in a stubborn line, but his voice had lost confidence. "Nobody knew she worked for me. I swear. Nobody. I never mentioned her name. Not even to my editor."

"Let's back up a minute," Ari said. She'd rather have him helping the investigation than wallowing in unproductive guilt. "We're still investigating. No one's under arrest, but maybe you're right about the boyfriend. Everything we know about Angela will help us nail the right killer."

"Wow, I can't believe it." Eddie propped his elbows on the table, his head in his hands. "I sure hope the boyfriend did it. But I can tell you don't think so."

When he looked at Ari, she saw the doubt on his face. She was tempted to say something, maybe even something reassuring, but he'd already begun to talk again.

"Angie saw the first article I wrote on Fantasy. She called me, wanting to know how much I'd pay for inside information. She promised details. Users, dealers. I asked how she knew this stuff, and that's when she got really vague. Said she hung around the Olde Town bars and heard stuff. But her timing couldn't have been better. I'd used all my data on the one article, and my editor was salivating for more. Suddenly I had visions of an award-winning series."

"So you said you were interested." Ari tried to hurry the story along.

He gave her a rueful look. "You bet I was interested. Especially if she could lead me to the suppliers. Front page stuff. And the Otherworld connection was major headlines. Told her I'd pay $500 a pop for anything she got. And I did." Eddie signaled the waitress and had his Coke refilled.

"Frankly, Angie was a gold mine," he continued. "She provided the info I used in the rest of the series, from the street price on Fantasy to its availability in the local bars. Her interviews with users were priceless. Great descriptions of how the drug affected each of them." He glanced at Ari. "Your greatest dreams in a capsule. That's what they said. Angie was good at getting people to talk. She might have had a career in this field."

Eddie looked pensive but continued his story. "But she wasn't smart about how she did it. She got her information by hanging out in dangerous places, like the Otherworld bars. And with dangerous people. I warned her about the vamp boyfriend."

"Was the boyfriend or Club Dintero involved in the drugs?"

"Club Dintero? You think Andreas is part of this? That's something I never expected."

"Stop it, Eddie! No. I wasn't saying that. But her boyfriend works there. I just wanted to be sure the club was clean." Ari reminded herself again to be cautious around the reporter. He picked up on everything. "How do you know Andreas?"

Eddie gave her a quizzical look. "Everyone knows Andreas. He's a popular singer. *The Clarion* has run a couple of pieces on the club. And I can't believe he'd have anything to do with the drug trade."

Interesting. Andreas had a public face outside the magic community. She'd bet they'd never glimpsed the angry vampire who confronted her in the bar parking lot. But she wasn't going to think about him now. She shrugged, hoping to signal her loss of interest in the subject of Andreas and his club.

"You never gave me an answer about Victor, the boyfriend," she said. "Involved or not?"

"Don't know. Angie never came through with the names. I assumed he was. Although, come to think of it, he didn't give her the sample she brought to me. She mentioned a werewolf friend."

Ari probed for specifics on the wolf connection, but Eddie didn't have any more details to give. "So what happened to the sample? You still have it?"

Eddie shook his head. "It was all used. By the lab," he added hurriedly. "I'll do a lot to get a good story, but I don't do drugs. There were two capsules. A private lab used both in the confirmation analysis. It was Fantasy."

"We'll need a copy of the report. Can you get it to Lt. Foster at the PD?"

"Sure. No problem, but why?"

"To compare it with the drugs we have."

"Looking for…?" He let the question dangle.

Ari considered how much to share. If she didn't tell him something, he might start guessing. And nosing around. She didn't want any part of their conversation on tomorrow's front page, but maybe she could make a deal that would benefit everybody. Eyes and ears in the human community might come in handy, and he was familiar with the drug trade. "I'll tell you, if it's off the record. Can you handle that?"

Eddie wrinkled his nose. "When you can release the story, will you call me first?"

"*If* we can release it," she amended. "Yes, I don't see why not."

"I have your word?"

"As long as I have yours."

"OK, off the record for now. But I'll hold you to that phone call."

Ari sketched the history of the earlier Otherworld attacks. Eddie had heard most of the details. Except the drug connection. When she added that an altered form of Fantasy might be responsible for the vampires' violence, he jerked up straight.

"Holy shit." He barely breathed the words. "Someone has found a way to make drugs that affect vampires. What a story!" Ari could almost see the headlines running through his head. "But you won't find the proof in my sample. I read every word of the lab report. No unidentified substance. I'd have jumped all over that. Wow, has this ever happened before?"

"Not as far as I know."

"You wouldn't consider changing your mind about this

being off the record, would you?" He grinned at her, because he already knew the answer.

She said it anyway. "Not a chance."

"That's too bad. Story of a life time with my byline in big letters." He leaned back and looked at her. "The vamps were hopped up on Fantasy."

Ari sighed and played with the straw in her drink. "It's not confirmed, but, yes, it's a possibility. One I don't want to read in the paper."

"Kind of scary people's fantasies are killing them, huh?"

"Don't even say that. The violence might just be a side effect." She gave him her best cop face. "And don't even think about printing it."

"Hey, I got it. Don't worry. Much as I'd love to rush this into print, we have a deal." The grin returned. "I wouldn't jeopardize a huge story." He tilted his head to one side. "You know, the last time I spoke with Angie, maybe a week before she died, she hinted about something new she was checking into. I thought she meant a different drug."

Ari followed his train of thought. "But it could have been the altered Fantasy."

"And maybe that's what got her killed." Eddie picked at the last of his fries. "I guess it *was* her work for me."

"You're not responsible," Ari said. "Angela lived a wild lifestyle, took a lot of risks. She got in over her head this time. That's what got her killed. And whether you paid her or not didn't change anything."

Ari left him seated in the booth, staring into space, occupied by his inner demons. He didn't notice when she stopped and paid the bill.

Chapter Twelve

Ari couldn't wait to share the news with Ryan, but she caught him in a foul mood.

"Dammit, Ari. What's the matter with my department?"

He was putting in long hours and made no secret he felt harried about the vamp murders. He grumped that his superiors were pressuring him to close the case, stamped 'random vampire violence.' With both suspects dead, police officials didn't want to waste further resources. Ryan thought he had a duty to resolve the matter.

"If someone triggered the vamps, with drugs or whatever, I've got to stop them. Or this just happens again. Right? One human dead this time. How many the next? Command's making a bad decision."

Since Ryan was on the lower end of the food chain in the police hierarchy, Ari and Ryan both knew who'd win the argument. He figured they had another twenty-four hours before his chief ordered him to shut down the investigation.

Ari interrupted, hoping she could cheer him with the information on Angela's undercover work. He wasn't very enthusiastic.

"And how's this get us closer to naming her killer? We can't prove a damn thing. Victor, Simpson, the she-wolf, some unknown druggie or dealer...any or all of them could have been

Angela's source. And decided to keep her quiet." Ryan's frustration seeped through the phone. "I don't know, Ari. It could also be somebody we haven't heard of. I'm going home and have a beer. Maybe I'll feel different when I've thought it over."

* * *

When Ari didn't get a call from Ryan the next morning, she figured he was still in a funk. No biggie. She had plenty to do.

Finishing the written reports consumed most of her day. This was one part of the job Ari could live without, especially this week. The Magic Council required each Guardian to provide a written report whenever an Otherworlder in that district killed someone, especially humans, or was the victim of human violence. There had been five such deaths and the still unsolved Goshen Park attack in the past eleven days. Although two of the deaths occurred in Martin's territory, the suspect resided in Olde Town. Ari had the unhappy task of facing an inquiry on every incident.

Her hardest report was explaining the stabbing death at the Second Chance Saloon. It shouldn't have happened, wouldn't have, if the vamp had been the least bit rational. He had plenty of time to avoid the blade. The vampire, now identified as Lawrence, didn't have the history or reputation of a troublemaker. And although Ari was convinced Lawrence had been affected by Fantasy, she had no proof. Some of the Council members would want more than a written report. Based on Andreas's reaction, she expected Lucien, the vampire representative, would be especially difficult.

She made the reports as detailed as possible, and it was mid-afternoon when she delivered the documents to the Council's clerk. He went away shaking his head, dismayed either by the size of the reports or the lateness of the hour. Whatever his concern, Ari knew each member would receive copies before the day was over. The Council would have plenty of time to read them prior to the weekly Friday meeting.

Finished with desk duty, she turned her thoughts back to the Canadian wolves. Talking to them became more urgent by the moment. While she worried that Andreas's continued silence meant he'd withdrawn his pledge to help, she wasn't ready to give up. She'd figured out how her original plan could work. If she waited outside the bar until the she-wolf left, then any discussion with her or arrest would not involve the club. To set it up, she still needed to talk with Andreas. So Ari decided to take the initiative. He sang at the club on Thursday nights. If she was standing in front of him, it would be hard for him to ignore her.

She called Claris and Brando. After a lot of fast-talking on her part, they agreed to join her for dinner. She suspected Claris gave in because she was afraid Ari would go alone if she didn't.

* * *

Ari paid special attention to her attire. Green silk blouse to match her eyes, long black skirt with a slit to the knee, and spike heels. Not her usual jeans and casual top.

Brando started laughing when he saw her. "So there is a woman inside those jeans," he said. "And you don't intend to play fair with this guy. I see the plan."

"I don't know what you're talking about. It's a supper club. Isn't this appropriate?"

Ari's escapades had involved, and amused, Brando for as long as she could remember. He'd played Little John to her Robin Hood, always game for the next adventure. But Brando's square, open face, carefree laugh, and jovial demeanor concealed a very serious side. Born into a family notable for its powerful wizards, Brando had dedicated most of his life to science. He'd written technical journals with titles Ari couldn't pronounce. Tonight, however, he was that childhood sidekick again, prepared to be entertained, and his brown eyes twinkled as he escorted his companions through the entrance of Club Dintero.

Right away Ari noticed the visible security guard next to the door, a change from the night she interviewed Victor.

"Arms up, please," the doorman intoned as the guard

stepped forward and produced a security wand.

Ari's eyes widened. At a supper club? What was the deal? She shook her head and stepped back, digging out her ID. Claris shook her head at her friend's refusal. At least she was in a better mood, Ari thought. Claris and Brando followed instructions without protest. Just another unique experience to them.

When Ari produced the ID, the doorman scrutinized it with care before handing it back. "Guardian," he acknowledged, his tone flat, impersonal. She felt a tension from him that hadn't been there before. Maybe he didn't like cops. Or maybe he remembered her first visit.

Once a hostess seated them, Ari turned her focus to the stage. The comedy duo drew friendly laughter, a good warm-up act. She expected Andreas to take the stage soon and looked forward to hearing him sing. Her plan was to snag him during a break.

When the comedy team continued through appetizers, entrées and even after-dinner drinks, it was clear Andreas wouldn't show. Adding his absence to the increased scrutiny at the door, Ari started asking questions. When the waiter said he didn't know why Andreas wasn't singing, she was more curious than before. She watched for Victor. Finally seeing him across the room, she caught his eye and motioned him over.

Victor gave Ari a blank face when she asked about Andreas and delivered a canned speech he must have used all night. "I apologize for the inconvenience," he said, "Andreas was unexpectedly called away. If you return next week, I'm sure you will not be disappointed again."

"I noticed the security. Has something happened? Where'd he go?"

Victor's bland face hardened. "I believe it was personal. Now if you'll excuse me?" He gave their table a too-polite smile and walked away.

Well, fine. She'd just been told it was none of her business. Fair enough. But nothing could have piqued her interest more.

"He's Mr. Personality, isn't he?" Claris laughed softly.

Ari didn't care how Victor behaved, except she knew he was lying. An absent star performer. The security. The tension. She didn't need witch senses to recognize trouble.

"Now what was that about?" she mused. "Andreas is tight with the vampire leader, Prince Daron. I wonder if there's a problem at the court."

"Vampire politics," Brando offered. "I understand theirs are even messier than ours."

Ari smiled, allowing Brando to distract her. His comment led to jokes about the latest foibles in Riverdale city politics. Speculation about the vampires was dropped, and after another drink, they ended the evening early.

As they left, Ari watched for Victor again. She still wanted to ask him about Angela and the drugs. He wasn't around, but two additional security guards had been added to the front entry. Her witch senses stirred. Not just trouble, something really bad had happened, and Andreas was right in the middle of it. Ari wished she knew what *it* was.

* * *

The night ended on another down turn. A small white envelope had been slipped under her apartment door during the evening. Ari knew what it was before she opened it. An official summons to appear before tomorrow's meeting of the Magic Council.

Chapter Thirteen

Heads swiveled in her direction as Ari walked into the Magic Hall. The forty members of the Otherworld governing council, dressed in suits or other formal attire consistent with their race and gender, sat in three rows of raised seats, forming a semi-circle facing the massive south doors. The first row held the representatives of five of the six major magic races: sorcerers (including the witch clans), vampires, lycanthropes, elves, and nymphs. Demons, considered the sixth race, were not represented. There were no treaties with the devil's offspring.

In front of and facing the arranged seats stood a small podium, and behind that a glossy dark wood conference table which currently had two chairs. Ari was surprised to see Martin occupied one of them. Even though the fight at the Were Fest had occurred in his part of the city, the combatants had been vampires, Ari's problem. Martin nodded as she took the other seat.

Both Guardians were dressed in traditional white uniforms. No jewelry or accessories. Although rarely worn outside these halls, the uniforms were required for Council appearances. Ari smoothed her skirt a couple of times and waited.

The Magic Hall, unlike the modern offices and cultural center attached, was built of stone along grand lines. Its style was copied from 13th century cathedrals with statuary and elaborate adornments, many depicting magical events in history. It was a reminder of continuity. Ari usually enjoyed looking around, but this morning her thoughts were on the pending inquiry.

The gavel came down. The Council president called the meeting to order and asked Martin to approach the podium. Ari tried hard not to fidget.

Her counterpart was a lean elf of indeterminate age. Martin looked more like a philosopher than a keeper of the peace. The impression was deceiving. Like most of his race, Martin was strong and agile, highly skilled in martial arts. Ari had been content with a tie the one time they had sparred.

Martin's voice remained firm and confident as he gave his report, detailing the events from the Were Fest. He concluded with the good recovery of the weretiger injured at the Second Chance Saloon. The representatives sat quietly throughout his presentation, but Martin was just the warm up. Most of the Council's time had been reserved for Ari.

It was a rocky start. She'd barely reached the podium before Lucien, the vampire representative, began grilling her about the sufficiency of her guardian training. His clipped tone and manner put her on edge.

She assured him her instructors, including Yana, had been excellent. She could have elaborated, reciting her skills and abilities, but court protocol dictated brevity unless invited to continue by the questioner. Lucien scoffed at her conclusion, leading her through a recitation of various rules and mandates.

Ten minutes later, a broad smile stole across his face. "Excellent, Ms. Calin. I am surprised and delighted with the extent of your knowledge. Most admirable. So, you would agree that your primary mandate is to preserve and protect the magical races?"

"Yes, of course."

"Then can you explain why you chose to terminate a vampire named Lawrence? And," Lucien held up a hand when she started to speak, "let me finish, Ms. Calin. And why you allowed an overpowering police force to gun down another vampire, known as Christopher?" He stopped, his eyes flashing with scorn. "Now you may answer, if you can. "

"The details are in my reports, sir, but basically both vampires were dangerously out of control when I arrived."

"I've read these pieces of fiction you call your reports," Lucien cut in. He rustled noisily through the pages. "I find nothing that explains your appalling actions. You would have us believe Lawrence killed himself, throwing his body on your knife," he scoffed. "And not one word tells me why you did not diffuse the situation by negotiation or, if necessary, taking the two men into custody. For their own protection, if nothing else."

The white-bearded Council president interrupted with his usual unruffled, unhurried manner. "Lucien, you must ask her a question, not make a speech."

"Yes, Mr. President. Ms. Calin, how do you feel about vampires?"

The question caught her off guard. "I don't understand."

"It's a simple question. Do you like them?"

"I don't dislike them." Ari's answer was honest. When she heard it out loud, it sounded evasive.

Lucien heaved a long-suffering sigh. "Let me make this easy for you. Do you have vampire friends?"

Andreas's angry face flashed through her head. Rita's mulish pout. Victor calling her a bitch. "Not really. But I don't have close friends in many of the races I protect," she continued before he could cut her off. "It's a matter of duty, not friendship."

Lucien frowned at the uninvited explanation. "Answer the question only, Guardian. We don't need a soliloquy." He rustled through her reports again. "Didn't you, in fact, take the easy way out? The option that was popular with your human friends?"

"There was no easy way. In fact, there was no choice. Christopher had already killed that night. Lawrence nearly killed the weretiger. They were out of control, no longer acting rationally. Whether that was drugs or something else, I can't be sure. But I know what I saw."

Lucien leaned over his table and stared down at her. "If you must continue with these long, unresponsive statements, at least admit this is only your opinion. Are you aware that no vampires have come forward to support your claim?"

"No, but there were lots of other witnesses. A whole parking lot of them that could give you the facts."

"Humans?" Lucien nearly spat the word. "Apparently you value their word above that of the vampires. Perhaps they are also more worthy of your protection."

"That's not true," Ari snapped, unable to hold back any longer. "I would have saved the vampires if I could!"

The hall grew silent at her outburst.

Lucien sat back and smirked. "This Guardian is not only unfit for her position but disrespectful of the Council. Perhaps her services are no longer needed."

"Lucien," the president said patiently, "If you have no more questions for Ms. Calin, I think we should move forward. The elves have the floor."

Ari wanted to continue arguing with Lucien, deny his accusations, but she'd already pushed beyond the limits of court protocol. Further infractions might only serve to prove the vampire's point. And he wasn't going to listen. No more than Andreas the night it happened.

Ari relaxed her clenched fingers and turned her attention to the elf's questions.

To her relief, the rest of the members were more understanding and less accusatory about the vampire deaths. What alarmed most of the Council were the potential dangers from Fantasy, the unknown source of its alteration, and the part played in these events by the Canadian werewolves. Steffan, of course, was a staunch ally throughout the proceedings.

After more than an hour of questioning, Ari was excused to wait for the Council's decision. An attendant escorted her to the vestibule of the Magic Hall, just outside the thick arched doors. Now they would deliberate.

Expelling her pent-up tension on a long breath, Ari sank onto one of two stone benches. It wasn't unusual for Lucien to be antagonistic. He had that kind of personality. But today had been over the top even for him. Ari was still steaming over his accusations when Steffan slipped out of the Council room.

"I don't have long," he said, keeping his voice low. "Lucien made a motion to have you removed. Don't worry. It won't pass, but I want to be there for the vote. While he's still ranting, I wanted to fill you in on the latest rumor. If it's true, it could explain Lucien's nasty mood today." He glanced around to make sure they weren't overheard. "Someone tried to assassinate Prince Daron last night. I don't have details, except I believe Daron survived." He looked at the closed doors. "I better go. Tell Martin. See what else you can find out." Steffan ducked back into the Council chambers, leaving Ari staring after him with a thousand unanswered questions.

That would explain Andreas's absence from the club and the increased security. Stepping outside the building to use her cell phone, she wondered which side of this Andreas was on. Was he loyal to the Prince? Or part of an attempted coup?

Martin took the news in stride and said he'd try to gather the details. She promised to call as soon as the Council was finished. "If I still have a job," she added with an uncertain laugh.

For twenty long minutes, she paced the confines of the vestibule, fretted about the Council's decision, and chaffed against the inactivity. She needed to be on duty. If the vampire community became unstable, the entire city could suffer.

At last they summoned her to hear the Council's decision. Ari avoided looking at Lucien. In fact, she didn't make eye contact with anyone except the president until he read the decision. It turned out fine. Her reports were accepted and approved as submitted and her removal voted down upon a vote of thirty-nine to one. It was obvious who the dissenter had been. When she finally glanced at Lucien, his face conveyed nothing except disinterest.

Ari nearly sprinted from the room and had her cell dialing

before she hit the front door. Martin answered before she heard it ring.

"Prince Daron didn't suffer a scratch," he said. "The attacker was one of his guards and was captured immediately. Don't know what happened to the assailant, but I can guess. Either he can't talk or won't, because the court's in an uproar. It's assumed he wasn't working alone, and the vamps are looking for conspirators under every rock. No one's free from suspicion."

"Attacked how?"

"Details are sketchy, and that's one I haven't heard. But I think we're safe in believing Daron survived. If he was dead, the vamps would be tearing the city apart. The timing of this is suspicious, you know. Right on top of the vamp fights." Tension crept into his voice. "The Otherworld community is primed to react. Rumors are flying about mind-controlling drugs and outside invaders. I've even heard the Magic Council itself might come under attack."

"That's ridiculous! There's no hint of danger to the Council."

"You and I know that, but once rumors start, they spread swiftly. They don't have to be true."

An hour later, Ari was still wondering how they could stop the escalating fear and suspicion. It called for something drastic. She couldn't help the vampires, not unless they chose to involve her, but maybe she could get the drugs off the streets. That meant looking for the source. Which brought her to a confrontation with Molyneux and his Canadian wolves.

Ari considered her options. So far, this was primarily an Otherworld issue, and without sufficient evidence for the human legal system, Ryan and his cops were off the list. What she needed was Otherworld backup. Not Andreas. Whether he was still inclined to help or not, he had his own problems now. Steffan, on the other hand, would be the perfect choice.

Once again she drove to the suburbs. Steffan should be home from the Council meeting, and she wanted to talk with him in person. Outwitting Louie Molyneux and his northern wolves would require a lot of careful planning.

Chapter Fourteen

Steffan wasn't only willing, he was eager to help. He wanted to set out immediately, but after weighing the risks involved, they put off the confrontation until the morning after the full moon, about forty hours away. They hoped to avoid a bloodbath by catching the Canadian pack members unaware, when they were exhausted and less alert after a night of revelry, running through the woods.

The intervening time was tense. Ari haunted the Olde Town streets and parks, determined to stop further violence before it happened. Yet every phone call, every message was potential news of some new disaster. The final night was the hardest. Steffan's control over his inner beast was strong, but even he found it difficult to resist the call of the full moon. Ari worried that the Canadian pack might choose that night to commit further mischief. When dawn came with no new crimes reported, she breathed a sigh of relief.

It was nearly 6:30 a.m. when she met Steffan two houses from their destination. Steffan was edgy; staying in the night before had cost him. The five weretigers who accompanied him were in better shape. The moon's lure affected their species less than the wolves.

Ari turned to take a look at the house, a three-story built around 1910. Shingles curled at the edges; dingy white paint clung to the frame, chipped and peeling. The upstairs shutters were closed, except for one on the third floor that hung by a single hinge. The yard hadn't been mowed since mid-summer, and hostas in neglected beds had lost a battle to weeds long before the weather curled their leaves.

It looked deserted. An impression negated by the faint but steady pulse of Otherworld power seeping from the doors and windows. The wolves were home from their hunt.

Ari looked at Steffan and nodded.

They approached the front door unchallenged. Ari pushed the button and heard chimes inside. When no one answered, she tried again. More chimes. Finally the door opened a crack.

"What do ya want?" A bleary-eyed face looked them over, a scowl gradually forming.

"We're here to talk with Louie Molyneux," Ari said.

The wolf opened the door a few inches more, his body filling the space. His shoulders were so enlarged from weight lifting he virtually had no neck. His face held creases from heavy sleep. "Who are you?"

Steffan moved forward on cue. "The local wolf rep to the Magic Council."

"And the rest of them?"

"The Guardian, and the others are local weretigers."

"Why are ya here?"

The wolf was suspicious, but Steffan had experience in diplomacy. Ari let him carry the conversation.

"The Guardian and I would like a few words with Mr. Molyneux. The tigers are here to make sure it stays peaceful."

The wolf gave a derisive snort. "So what's the deal? What's this about? Can't you come back later?"

Steffan shook his head. "Our business is only for Molyneux's ears."

The burly wolf blinked at them. "Wait." He closed the door and left.

Steffan turned to Ari and shrugged. "So far, so good. We wait."

The group cooled their heels for almost ten minutes before

the door opened again. The big wolf was back with three sidekicks carrying guns. He motioned them in. "Stop right there." He pointed to a side table. "Now, your weapons go here." He grinned. "Or I can search you for them." Ari shook her head. "This is a peaceful visit, but I'm not giving you our weapons."

The wolf puffed out his chest and stepped toward her. A door behind him banged open, and an older wolf appeared. Forties, closely cropped reddish-brown hair, compact, powerfully built. His age showed in the small paunch at the waistline. Slightly rumpled, he looked as if he'd just gotten out of bed. Despite that, his dominance was obvious.

"What's the delay?" he demanded. The wolves signaled their submission with dropped gazes. Louie Molyneux had arrived to deal with the intruders directly.

"Weapons," the big wolf said. "The woman refuses to be searched."

Molyneux's nostrils flared. He leered at her body, finally gave a dismissive jerk of his head. "These two only," he ordered, pointing to Steffan and Ari. "The others stay here."

Molyneux led them into the back of the house. Ari and Steffan followed, urged on by the three guys with the guns.

Ari wasn't happy about leaving their backup behind. She was surrounded by an unseen number of hostile wolves. She opened her senses and immediately felt the Otherworld magic and smelled the wolves behind the closed doors. Memory surfaced, a rancid scent Ari recognized from the park. The teens' attacker was on the premises. Somewhere very near.

Walking beside her, Steffan sniffed the air. He must have smelled the hidden wolves. So far nothing they hadn't expected, although proof the Goshen Park attacker was in the house was an added bonus.

Molyneux opened a set of doors, and they entered a large library. Shelves of dusty books, a paisley rug, roll-top desk, wooden chairs. Shiny computer equipment covered the library table. He hitched his pants and dropped into a desk chair. Two wolves stood behind him; the others remained in the hall.

Once Molyneux was settled, he pointed toward the other chairs. "Have a seat."

Steffan lounged against the door frame without speaking.

"No thanks," Ari said. "This won't take long."

"Suit yourself." Molyneux lit a cigar, took two slow puffs, and leaned back. "So what's this all about? You said you wanna talk, so talk." He put his feet on the desk and crossed them at the ankles. His small beady eyes bore into Ari's. He puffed away. Ari decided he'd watched way too many American gangster movies. It sounded even funnier in a French accent.

Figuring he'd been told who they were, she dispensed with the formalities. "I understand you were at the Second Chance Saloon Sunday night."

"Is that why you're here? Heard it got crazy as hell after we left. The bloodsuckers killed somebody. Damn shame." He puffed again.

Smoke began to fill the room and irritated her nose. Ari fought off a sneeze. "You talked with the vamps before the fight. Any idea what set them off?"

"Nope. Not a clue. Can't help you."

"What did you talk about?"

"Don't rightly remember. Typical bar talk, I guess. Women, sports, beer."

Ari prodded him about the fights at the bar and at the Were Fest, but Molyneux continued to profess his ignorance. When she pushed to know what happened just before the outbreak at the festival, Molyneux answered with increasing annoyance.

"Look, sister, I can't tell you what I don't know. Who the hell can predict what vamps will do?"

"How about telling me what you do know? About a drug called Fantasy. I hear you're peddling the stuff all over town." Ari had to give him credit. His reaction was almost invisible. Almost—but not quite. Molyneux's eyes flickered for a fraction of a second.

"That's crazy. You don't know what yer talkin' about. And I

don't have time for it." He swung his feet down and stood. "I've got things to do…" He let the sentence hang.

Ari met his dismissal with a challenge of her own. "I'm not done with you, wolf. You're going to see me around every corner."

Molyneux bristled, his body snapped to attention, his yellow eyes gleamed with malice. Ari's heartbeat jumped with a spark of recognition. She had seen that predatory look once before.

"When were you last in Goshen Park?"

He hesitated. "Never heard of the place."

"No? Big park on the edge of Olde Town? There's a funny story going around about a red wolf who hunted in the park for children. One day a woman came along, whipped his ass and scared him away. Ever heard that story?"

Molyneux's face turned red. "A stupid story!" He caught himself and continued with less vehemence. "No wolf would run from a woman. Now get out. Or I'll have you thrown out." The two wolves behind him came to attention, and Steffan straightened in the doorway.

"I'll go," she said. "But one last thing — the tall, brunette she-wolf who's been seen in your company… I'd like to talk with her. Is she around?"

He showed her his teeth. "She's gone. Sheila got bored and went home. Local company's too tame down here." Molyneux looked at his wolves. "See they find the door."

"Sorry to hear she's not around," Ari said, not moving. "Maybe you can deliver a message. Tell her that her friend Angie died. You know the one, the reporter."

Yep, that hit home. Now that Ari knew what to look for, she saw the telltale flicker in his eyes. Satisfied, she turned, brushed by the wolves in the hall, and strode out the front door. Steffan followed. She didn't stop until they had collected the weretigers and were back on the street.

Steffan hadn't said a word since they'd left the library. Now Ari heard choking sounds that turned into a chuckle. He responded to her look of inquiry with a wide, wolfish grin.

"I thought you were going to get us killed in there," he said, his shoulders starting to shake with laughter. "He was such an arrogant prick. And you kept poking him. The drugs, the wolf who had his ass whipped. Almost lost it on that one. And when you brought up the reporter, he nearly turned purple."

Yeah, well, Molyneux had been an easy target. Steffan's amusement was contagious. It wasn't really that funny, but an adrenaline hangover does strange things. They stood in the middle of the street snickering like a pair of idiots. The weretigers watched in confusion. Steffan tried to explain, reciting parts of the encounter, but the tigers still looked bewildered. It was one of those times when you had to be there.

* * *

On the drive home from Steffan's, Ari called Ryan and filled him in. It didn't take long for him to check police records and identify Sheila as Sheila Montgomery, Molyneux's long-standing girlfriend. Assaults, disorderly. Ari was glad to put a name on their suspect. Ari was positive Sheila had been in the house today, and that they'd meet again.

Ryan's other news was not so welcome. The police department's case on the vampire attacks was officially closed. Unless she found new evidence that allowed Ryan to reopen, Ari was officially on her own. In anticipation of the order, Ryan had spent the morning calling around the country, talking with other law enforcement jurisdictions about Fantasy. And he gleaned some unexpected results.

"Say that again." Ari thought she must have misunderstood him.

"It's true. No one else has heard of the altered formula. The Otherworld hasn't been affected, except in Riverdale."

"That doesn't make sense. Why us?" Ari demanded. "What makes our town a target?"

"If we knew the answer, we'd have the case solved."

"Molyneux knows. The smug bastard. Maybe his next move will give us a hint."

* * *

Instead, as hour after hour passed, Ari became more puzzled. She'd expected a response from the wolves, but not the one she got. Nothing happened. Well, that wasn't entirely accurate; whatever had been going on, suddenly stopped. There were no fights, no new reports of drugs among the Otherworlders. The Canadian pack was laying low. The rest of Monday, then Tuesday, came and went. The Otherworld community stayed quiet, as if holding its breath.

Except for the vampires. In the wake of the attempted assassination, they were squabbling among themselves. Ari talked with Rita and heard all about the whispers of a secret rebellion. Negative propaganda about the Prince and his so-called democratic court warned of a fascist takeover. Rita said she was staying out of it, and Ari agreed that was a good idea.

Ari heard nothing from or about Andreas. She spotted Victor one evening at a rival club, talking with a big tattooed vamp. He didn't see her or pretended he didn't. Ari didn't approach him. She thought maybe Lucien was right about one thing: she didn't like vampires much. At best they were annoying.

During patrol Wednesday night, Ari thought about the events of the last few days. She realized she was driving her friends crazy. Obsessed with solving a case that seemed unsolvable, she'd bent Yana's ear twice and bored Claris over coffee and innumerable phone calls. Despite these mental and verbal gymnastics, she was no closer to an answer.

Ari reached the end of her normal patrol route and turned onto the tree-lined street that led to her apartment building. The case replayed in her head for the umpteenth time. The four attacks: Goshen Park, Angela, Were Fest, the Second Chance Saloon. The werewolf presence. And Riverdale's unique status as the only market with the altered Fantasy. She knew they fit together, in some way. In some mad scheme. And Molyneux was the key.

Alerted by a sudden breath of familiar magic, she spun around. Her pulse jumped as he moved toward her from the trees. "Why are you following me?" she demanded.

"My congratulations," Andreas said as he drew near. "My presence is not usually noticed until I wish it."

"That's not an answer."

"No," he agreed. "It was a compliment. Wasn't that what you wanted the night we met?"

Ari refused to be baited. And to show he couldn't intimidate her, she turned her back and walked away. He caught up easily and fell into step. A soft, feathery sensation slid over her skin, a distinctive energy that flowed from him like a seductive fragrance.

"I heard you visited the club."

"We came for the performance. My friends say you're good."

"You should return and judge for yourself. Any Thursday night." His voice was measured, impersonal. In spite of his civil words, or maybe because of them, this didn't feel like a social call. Something was up. Why was that always the case with Andreas?

"You weren't there last Thursday," she said.

"Unavoidable business. Not likely to happen again." The subject was closed.

They continued in silence for two long, uncomfortable blocks, until she couldn't stand it any longer. Ari stopped and turned to face him. "Why are you here?"

"Do you wish me to leave?" he countered.

"I wouldn't mind. But do whatever you want." She turned away. Why hadn't she told him to go? Every past meeting had been awkward, potentially dangerous. Yet something about him continued to interest her. Her magic stirred. Yeah, that too.

"A young waiter from my club is missing," he said, catching up with her again. "I thought you might be able to tell me what happened to him."

"Me? How would I know? I don't know any of your waiters.

Or anyone else at the club, except you and Victor."

"Marcus waited on you and your friends Thursday night. You were observed talking to him," Andreas insisted.

"About the menu or drinks, maybe. I don't remember him. What do you mean he's missing?"

"He disappeared. Hasn't reported to work or returned to his nest. Marcus is normally responsible, reliable. This is not like him."

"And you think something bad happened?"

"The thought crossed my mind."

She glanced at him then. "I still don't get it. Why ask me?"

"It was suggested as a…possibility."

"What kind of possibility? By who? I haven't been notified of unidentified remains, bones or otherwise, if that's what you mean."

"That is good to know. But not exactly what I had in mind."

"Then what?" She stopped and tried to read his face. She'd heard something *off* in his voice. "What are you trying to say?"

The vampire threw up his hands. "To be honest, I don't know. This has been a bad week, and now Marcus has vanished. I feel responsible."

Ari later wished she'd let it go, but she didn't. "And you thought what? That I'd killed another vampire?" she asked with sarcastic brusqueness.

When Andreas didn't respond right away, the truth hit her. Slapping one fist against her hip, she glared at him.

"That's it. That's exactly what you thought, isn't it?" Her face flushed with sudden anger. "Who would suggest such a thing?" Her voice had risen. "Damn you, Andreas. That's the real reason you're here. You've decided I'm some sort of crazy vamp killer. It's almost funny."

Even in her anger, she recognized the irony. While she'd been stressing about his dark side, he'd concluded she was a vampire hunter. Time had not improved his view of the incident at the Second Chance Saloon. Any hope for trust between them seemed to be slipping away.

Andreas started to answer, but, stung, Ari lashed out. "For the record, I don't know anything about Marcus. And I certainly didn't kill him. I don't go around indiscriminately killing vampires. Although you're seriously making me reconsider that. Get the hell away from me, Andreas. And take your freaking accusations with you."

She stalked off, and this time he didn't follow.

Chapter Fifteen

The days began to run together and most of the next week passed without drama. Molyneux's girlfriend, Sheila Montgomery, hadn't surfaced yet, and the wolves rarely left their house on Vine. The noticeable tension in the lycanthrope community settled down. Steffan and Ari met for lunch toward the end of the week to talk over the situation. The upshot was that anxiety still simmered under the surface, awaiting some trigger to set it off. That didn't help Ari's sense of frustration.

The young vampire, Marcus, was still missing. Ari heard Andreas had been all over the city asking questions without finding a solid lead. Even 200-year-old vampires had their limitations.

As far as she knew, there were no new attacks on Prince Daron, but the vampires were restless. Convinced the would-be assassin had not acted alone, vampire leaders were still questioning everyone, trusting no one. Rita said her friends were watching each other, afraid the enemy might be in their own nest. Vampire paranoia had reached a new threshold.

In spite of the tension in the city, or maybe because of it, Ari drove to her grandparents' home in the hill country on the night of Mabon, the fall equinox. Visiting relatives was a bonus, but she'd come to reconnect with the twelve sisters of her coven.

Mabon was a sacred night of ceremony, feasting, and

meditation. Over a harvest meal, served on Great-Gran's best china, they downed half a dozen bottles of vintage wine, offering thanks to the Goddess for their achievements and toasting the tasks unfinished. Afterward, with hugs and good wishes, each witch went her separate way, renewed by the assurance they were not alone. It was a reminder Ari had badly needed.

She spent the next day with her grandparents, relaxing, setting her responsibilities aside for just a few more hours. When her parents died, her grandparents had raised her two siblings, and Ari had visited whenever her training schedule allowed. Mostly holidays, plus four weeks in the summer. Next to Great-Gran and Yana, they'd been the primary influences in her life. Grandpapa walked with a cane now, and Grandma's hair had turned white. Ari vowed to call more often.

On the drive back to Riverdale that evening, she was still feeling mellow when the ring of her cell phone dragged her back to reality.

"Ari? You gotta help me." The voice on the phone was female, high-pitched with stress, somehow familiar. Ari couldn't quite place it.

"Who is this?" Then immediately, "Rita?"

"Yeah, it's me. Please help me. Somebody's got him!"

"Who? Got who?" Ari asked.

"G-G-Gordon." Rita's voice shook so badly she struggled to get out the words. She choked on a sob.

"Who's Gordon? Calm down and talk to me." Ari pulled to the side of the road and gave Rita her full attention.

Rita sniffed, hiccupped. "My man. Number one dude. He's missing."

Ari sat up straighter. Another missing vampire? Well, this had a familiar ring. At least Rita didn't automatically assume Ari had killed him.

"What makes you think he's missing?"

"He's not here. We've seen each other every night for two weeks, like regular. And his friends say he never came home Friday night. They got him, Ari. And I'm s-scared." She choked up again on the last words.

Ari's first thought was Rita might have overreacted, that the new boyfriend could be shagging with someone else. Two weeks did not make a lifelong commitment. But this was the second missing vampire, and Rita's voice held panic.

"Where are you?" Ari asked.

"I can meet you somewhere," was the response.

Which meant she was calling from her nest. Whatever their sleeping abode — apartment, cave, or crypt — vampires never revealed the home address for a logical reason: sleeping vamps were defenseless to attack. It was a rule so deeply ingrained that Rita had followed her instincts even in a crisis. They agreed on Maurie's Bar in an hour.

* * *

An unhappy Rita was still slutty. The yellow silk pants and matching top left nothing to the imagination. Ari rather liked the boots, but not in vivid lime green. A neck scarf, color-coded to the boots, completed the eye-popping outfit. Rita's face was deeply shadowed; lines creased her forehead; her shoulders slumped. A neglected drink stood on the table. Ari cringed. This wasn't going to be an easy conversation.

Ari pulled out a chair. "Rita?"

The vampire looked up. "I called his friends again. While I was waiting," she said in a monotone. "Still no show."

"Well, that's good you checked. Now, let's see if I've got this right. You met Gordon, another vampire, right?" Rita bobbed her head. "Two weeks ago, and…"

"No, months ago. We hooked up two weeks ago."

"So when did you last see him?"

"Friday. Well, Saturday morning, I guess. He left just before dawn. But he never got home. I didn't know that, until Saturday night." She looked at Ari. "Someone snatched him."

Or staked him, Ari thought. Only something drastic would keep a vampire from the safety of his nest when the sun rose. "What makes you so sure someone took him? Couldn't it be an accident or a fight, maybe?"

Rita started shaking her head before Ari finished. "Uh-uh. It's just like the other vamp. The wolves got him." Rita shivered.

"What other vamp?" Ari demanded, leaning forward. "Are you talking about Marcus? Do you know what happened to him?"

Rita nodded eagerly. "Gordon told me. Killer wolves are using voodoo to capture vampires. And making them slaves. Now they've got Gordon too," Rita wailed.

Ari tried to sort out the grains of truth. She suspected the tale had grown with the retelling. "Where did Gordon hear this?"

"His nest mates told him." Rita was positive on this part. "Two nestlings saw it happen. The wolves were after him, and Marcus never got home. Just like Gordon," she whispered, her eyes round.

"What wolves? Where?"

Rita's mouth turned down. "I don't know."

As Ari absorbed this unforeseen answer to Marcus's disappearance, she fired off follow up questions, but the young vamp had told all she knew. "What did Andreas say about this?"

Rita ducked her head. "Nobody told him. Bad things have been happening. Andreas could be part of it. We were afraid somebody else might disappear if he thought they knew too much." Confusion deepened the lines of Rita's face. "Gordon said to keep my mouth shut. But that was before…" She stopped, swallowed hard, and finished in a rush. "But I'm telling you. I have to trust someone."

In a way, Ari was flattered. Vampires didn't trust easily, and Rita's faith in her was rather touching. But Ari wasn't sure she could live up to the expectations. If Molyneux's wolves were behind this, Gordon and Marcus were probably dead.

They talked awhile longer; mostly Rita talked, about Gordon. Ari sipped a glass of seltzer, her head only half in the conversation. Why would anyone kidnap vampires? And almost as interesting, how would they even do that?

She stole a glance at Rita. Having unburdened herself, turned over the problem, the vampire was sitting a little straighter, sipping her drink. She'd quit sniveling and had noticed the cute guy who'd walked in the door. It was a distinct improvement in attitude, and Ari figured it was a good time to leave.

On the walk home, she considered her best course of action. Should she call Andreas and tell him what she'd heard? He was worried about Marcus. On the other hand, she didn't owe him anything. He didn't trust her, might not even believe what she said. And the potential fallout of repeating Rita's story was something to think about. She didn't want to set the vampires against the wolves. Not without proof. For the present, she'd keep the information close, confined to a select number of people. Which did not include Andreas.

A twig snapped, and Ari spun into a crouch.

"Who's there?" Her eyes searched both sides of the street. She'd been aware of the faint smell of wolf for five or ten minutes but not close enough to be alarming. She'd assumed it was a passing stranger. Now, she wasn't so sure. When no one answered, she walked on home. Maybe it was nothing, but she vowed to be more alert in the coming days.

* * *

Ari knew Rita's story might be another example of the paranoia sweeping the Otherworld community, but she alerted Martin and Steffan to the rumors. They'd heard nothing but agreed to ask their usual sources.

Ari nosed around Olde Town for two days on her own, talking with barkeeps, listening to chatter. She haunted the public vampire hangouts. Ari kept her questions casual, answers vague, not wanting to add fuel to new or existing rumors. She put out the story that she had important information for Gordon, that she wanted to speak to him or anyone who could deliver a message to him. She hoped she'd turn up a nest mate, but no one responded. It had been a long shot; the vampires rarely volunteered to talk with authorities. She didn't have the option of knocking on his door. Even if Gordon had a door, she'd never find the vampire's hidden base on her own. Besides, even she wasn't reckless enough to enter a private vamp nest alone.

By the third unsuccessful afternoon, she admitted she needed help. Vampire help. And this was beyond Rita's pay grade. Ari swallowed her pride or her fears, whichever was dominant at the moment, and called the club. Andreas was her best bet. He had a vested interest in any outcome that might produce Marcus.

The woman who answered the phone said she'd have to see if Andreas was around. Ari gave her name and waited to see what he would do. He didn't leave her dangling for long. Within seconds, the voice returned stating he wasn't available.

Ari considered her response and left a message. "Tell him I have news of Marcus." She wasn't above using bait.

Five minutes later, her cell rang.

"You told me you knew nothing about Marcus," he said without preamble. He was annoyed. Even annoyed, his voice sounded good.

"That was then," Ari said, nerves making her flippant, "this is now."

"Do you actually know anything useful?" he asked, his tone impatient, suspicious.

"Yes, but I won't discuss it on the phone. I want to meet."

"Why? I believe you told me to stay away from you."

Hmm, yes, she had. And apparently she'd pricked his male pride. He didn't intend to be agreeable about this. So, she told him the truth. "Yeah, well, something's come up. And I want you to hear me out without the option of hanging up."

He sighed. "Another scheme, madam witch?"

"Information. And a proposition," she countered.

"Could you possibly be more cryptic?"

"Probably." A chuckle escaped her. "But I'm not going to tell you anything else until we meet."

"You drive a hard bargain." He paused while he seemed to

be thinking it over. "Come to the club tonight. We can talk between sets, if that suits you."

She agreed and hung up. She knew he'd be singing, and she needed more than a few minutes to explain her plan — and a lot of convincing after that — but it was a start. And it couldn't hurt to put her best foot forward. That would take prep work.

Ari begged and pleaded shamelessly. Claris hated the whole idea. She didn't want Ari to go to the club alone. Definitely not after a makeover. She put the temptation of vampires in the same category as teasing venomous snakes. Probably a good analogy, but Ari didn't want to seduce him, just get his attention. They wasted an hour arguing. When Claris realized Ari wouldn't change her mind, she caved.

Ari lugged seven outfits from her apartment to Claris's kitchen. Some had never been worn. Most were things that had caught her eye, but the chance to wear them had never come up. Claris tried to reject them all. Too short, too tight, too red, too revealing. In the end, they matched a white, silky blouse with black pants, fitted over the hips and ending in flowing legs. Dressy but not too formal. With the addition of a silver chain belt, matching earrings, and black strappy heels that added four inches, the outfit was complete. Claris objected to the low neckline but admitted the overall look was rather striking.

The controversial decisions made, Claris turned her expertise to hair and makeup. When she stepped back, Ari snatched the mirror and hardly recognized the cascade of loose blonde curls.

"Are you sure?" Ari asked. She'd never tried the curly routine before. Not like this.

"Oh yes." Claris laughed. "I almost feel sorry for Andreas. How's he going to say no to that face?"

Ari knew her best friend was biased, but the effect wasn't bad. She studied her reflection again.

"Do you know what you're doing, girl?"

She sure hoped so.

Chapter Sixteen

Ari timed her arrival at Club Dintero for late in the evening, nearly 11:00 p.m. She hoped it would allow more time for conversation if the dinner crowd had cleared, but people were still in line at the door. Full house. For a moment she wondered if she'd be turned away. Then the doorman nodded and motioned for her to bypass the line.

As soon as she stepped inside, the magic touched her. The five piece band was good, but Andreas's voice dominated the candlelit room, holding the rapt attention of nearly 300 silent diners. Ari had barely noticed the audience before an irresistible urge drew her gaze toward the stage. A single spotlight framed Andreas's commanding figure. Solid black, from the silk scarf knotted at his neck, to the full length Armani suit jacket that fell to his knees, to the black shirt, vest, and pants. Temptation incarnate. His feet were planted apart, confidence and mastery in every line of his body. The haunting melody was in Italian. Even without translation, it captured the mind.

His coal-black eyes found her and silken threads of magic wrapped her in a soft web. The room faded away. She floated as in a dream, warm and safe. A place to linger forever. Her witch magic began to sing in concert with his, and Ari called it back to her. The effort brought her out of his web with a jolt.

Damn, how strong was he? She wrapped her magical aura around her. As long as she kept it in place, his magic was held at bay. Then, mercifully, the song was over. Andreas bowed to a wildly applauding audience and left the stage.

"Good evening."

Startled, she stared at him. "Uh, hello." How did he move so fast?

He produced a polite smile. "If you will come this way." He waved a hand toward a hallway on the left.

Ari hesitated. A meeting in private? She hadn't anticipated that.

His brows rose. "We have twenty minutes."

Swallowing her doubts, Ari preceded him down the hall. It was better this way, she told herself. Fewer interruptions. At least she knew her time parameters. He ushered her past four closed doors, not stopping until they reached an exit door at the end. He touched a security panel, the door opened, and they stepped into a paved lane leading to the rear parking lot. Dense trees lined the opposite side of the lane. Total privacy.

The night was pleasantly cool. The crisp cleanness of fall filled the air. Ari hung back and watched her companion as he stopped in the middle of the lane. Andreas arched his shoulders and threw back his head, breathing deeply. For a moment all Ari could think about was how sexy he looked.

"I hope you don't mind talking out here. It has been a long evening, and I needed the fresh air."

"Not at all. It's nice." She looked up at the stars, pinpoints in an uncluttered sky, to keep from looking at him. "What was that last song you sang?"

"An Italian love song. Did you enjoy it?"

"Amazing."

He turned to look at her. "It was, or I was?" His voice invited a broader interpretation.

She smiled. "Both," she said, not bothering to hedge. "But who's fishing for compliments now?"

"Touché." His familiar laugh came then, rich and intimate, strangely companionable.

He was so approachable tonight that Ari began to relax. A

dangerous frame of mind around a vampire, she thought, but then she hadn't planned to play it safe tonight. Mindful of the passing time, she began by coming straight to the point. "You haven't found Marcus."

"No. And I've run out of places to look." He arched a brow in query. "Unless you have a suggestion."

"I've heard the wolves have him."

He was suddenly standing before her, one hand on her arm. "This is true? How did you come by the information?"

Her witch blood sang at his nearness, sending shivers along her spine. "Andreas, you've got to quit doing this. Invading my magical defenses." Ari shook off his hand, and he stepped back. "You're giving me the heebie-jeebies, making my arms tingle." She wasn't frightened, and she'd lied about her magic's reaction. The singing wasn't a defense warning, but she didn't want him to remain so close to her. The greatest danger from him wasn't physical.

"Sorry, I did not mean to do that," he said, gliding away to stop next to the building. "Your magic speaks to me."

She shot him a brief frown, uncertain how to take that. She'd assumed the pull between them was something Andreas was consciously doing. She rubbed her arms. "Just don't startle me like that."

He nodded, his eyes unreadable in the darkness next to the building. "Please, tell me about Marcus."

"I don't know where he is, not yet. But I've got a good lead." She dropped her hands to keep from rubbing her arms again. Even from this distance, Andreas's intensity was distracting. She tried to ignore it and went on. "Another young vampire is missing and his nest mates may know what happened." She repeated her conversation with Rita, including Gordon's story about Marcus, reminded him of the Canadian wolves' connection to Angela's murder, and related her own suspicions about the other violent incidents.

"Molyneux's pack is involved," she said. "I know Gordon's nest mates could help me prove it, if I could find them. I've looked everywhere."

"Why didn't they come to me with this story?" Andreas asked, running his hands through his hair. "We have lost so much time."

"Rita says they're scared. After the attack on Prince Daron, they don't know who to trust. Or who's part of the conspiracy."

His eyes snapped to her face. "They thought I might be aligned against Daron?" He took a deep breath. "Well, there is a lot of suspicion going around. I've been plagued by my own." He bent his gaze on her. "And you, madam witch? Why did you delay so long?"

"You know why. But I'd like to put that behind us. I've got an idea to help us both…unless you really believe I'm the enemy." Ari held her breath. Everything depended on what he said next.

When he didn't respond right away, her heart sank.

Andreas crossed his arms. "The angry things I have said to you, the accusations, arose from frustration. They were inexcusable. I offer my sincere apology. And, to clear the air, I do not hold you responsible for whatever happened to Marcus." He hesitated. "Or even the death of Lawrence."

Surprised, Ari held her breath and waited for him to finish.

He dropped his arms, leaned bonelessly against the white brick wall. His hooded eyes grew even darker in the shadows. "Nevertheless, that does not entirely answer your question. There is a dynamic between us that lends itself to hasty words and misunderstandings. I am a vampire, madam witch, and you obviously are not. Doesn't that make us natural enemies? Getting beyond that point is not easy."

Ari paled, numb with shock. Natural enemies. She'd struggled with the concept of friendship with a vampire, but it never occurred to her that Andreas might be just as worried about trusting a witch. She was kind of embarrassed by her self-absorption. She wondered if the problem was insurmountable. She needed his help. Badly. Beyond that, she wanted…what? "I don't know what to say."

She watched his long fingers rake through his hair again. He glanced at her, looked away and back again. "You remind me so much of someone I once knew."

"So, where do we go from here?"

He shrugged, barely perceptible in the dark. "Despite the obvious pitfalls, I find myself unaccountably willing to listen and consider your proposition. If you still want to present it."

"Do you mean that?" She saw the flash of white teeth from his smile. "Here's the deal. We both need help. Let's make this a joint investigation. You know, work together. Share data. As partners."

Andreas straightened from the wall and burst into laughter. One hand on her hip, she frowned at his less-than-desirable reaction.

"Pardon me," he said, the moment of amusement wiped from his face. "But this proposal is more outrageous than the last." His forehead crinkled in mystification. "Whatever gave you this idea?"

Ari struggled with her temper. If they rubbed each other the wrong way, it wasn't always her fault. He wouldn't have been her first choice as a colleague, but she needed his access to the vampire community. If not, she'd be tempted to kick his ass about now.

"It makes sense," she said stiffly. "You want to rescue Marcus. My job is to find out if a crime's been committed. Working alone, we've gotten nowhere." Encouraged that he hadn't interrupted or started laughing again, she continued. "The two vamp witnesses need to be interviewed. If you can get me into Gordon's nest, they'll talk to me because I'm the Guardian. Not on either side of the rumored conspiracy. We both gain added credibility."

"Now that I know who to ask, I have the means at my disposal to obtain the information without you."

"Oh, sure. You could scare them or bully them, and they'd probably tell you," she said dryly, "if you don't mind making people more suspicious. Confirming they can't trust you."

Andreas's brows drew into a sharp crease. "I did not have torture in mind." He walked a few steps away, as though considering his options, then turned back. "But you could be right about the reaction to any form of influence right now." He studied his shoes a moment longer. "What do you intend, if I say no?"

"I'm not sure. I guess I'll find a way to go alone."

"They will kill you."

"I don't kill easy."

He laughed harshly. It wasn't at all pretty this time. "Have you ever been inside a vampire nest?"

"No."

"I didn't think so. Few outsiders survive the experience. The location is a closely guarded secret."

"I know that, but I'll find a way." She wasn't half as confident as she sounded.

"I think not. Unless I agree to help you." He slowly shook his head, as if arguing with himself. "You are correct that I very much want to find Marcus. Since you could possibly speed that process, I will take you to the nest. As long as you do exactly as I say." Spinning on his heels, he headed toward the door. "I am overdue for the last set. If you wish, we can continue the discussion when I finish."

"That'll be fine." Ari was dancing mental jigs and ready to agree to almost anything. Until she remembered that unexplainable moment of their magics intertwining when she first arrived tonight. A very dangerous moment. She didn't intend to spend the rest of the night fighting off his allure. "Uh, wait. When I got here, you knew when I entered the club, right?"

About to punch the security code into the door pad, he gave her a blank face.

"And you turned up the magic?" she persisted.

A corner of his mouth twitched.

"If I stay, you have to promise you'll tamp it down. Agreed?"

The smile reached his eyes. "Did you not tell me your magic

was strong enough to resist vampire…persuasion?"

"Agreed?" Ari repeated. She wasn't sure her magic would even try to resist if he really turned up the wattage.

"That would seem to give you an unfair advantage. But in the interests of our, ah, partnership, you have my word, on one condition. You too are bound by the same restriction."

"Me? I don't understand."

A frown touched his forehead, then smoothed away. "That is a problem, but nothing to worry about tonight. You still have my promise. For tonight only, madam witch."

She smiled at him. "I have a name. Have you forgotten it?"

"Arianna." He let his magic run over her as he reached out and touched a curl below her ear. "Nice hair."

Ari's pulse leaped as a shiver from his light touch raced through her. When his eyes dropped to her outfit, she felt her face grow warm.

"In fact, you look delightful. But it was not necessary. All you had to do was ask." With that cryptic remark, his smile flashed, and he opened the door.

Victor seated her at a table in the back as Andreas slipped behind the stage. Victor's stiff body language said he wasn't pleased to see her. Although Ari acknowledged she had a talent for annoying Andreas, she hardly knew Victor. Maybe he was the sensitive type. Didn't like being accused of murder. When the music started and her new partner began to sing, Ari forgot about the club's assistant host.

Andreas had a breathtaking voice. Masculine, powerful, and, at times, unexpectedly tender. Even though Andreas kept his promise and didn't try to breach her defenses, the performance held a richness of sensory experiences, his repertoire a mixture of English and Italian songs.

Ari sipped at a glass of white wine and watched the audience respond to his talent as much as his magic. She developed a quick preference for the songs in his native language, where unimpeded by words her imagination followed the meanderings of his voice. Images of warm, sunny skies, rolling hills, fig trees, and tangled vineyards stretching as far as the eye could see floated through her head. She sighed with regret when the last of the music faded. As the lights came up, she blinked, a sleeper snatched from a fascinating dream.

"You appear far away, young witch." Andreas stood next to the table, looking down with those laughing eyes.

Ari gave herself a vigorous, mental shake. "Sudden light change," she muttered. If they were going to be partners, she couldn't continue to be so transparent. He didn't need to know how much the music affected her.

"Come," he said, holding out his hand. "Let us leave here and find a place more appropriate for planning strategy."

Ari rose but didn't take his hand. Touching seemed like another thing partners should avoid.

They walked and talked, ending up seated on a stone bench at the east end water fountain in Goshen Park. The first moments had been awkward. What do you chat about with a vampire? But Andreas took the initiative and got down to business. Ari found him an easy conversationalist.

They decided to visit Gordon's nest that evening at nightfall, when the vampires would be up but not yet out for the night. With any luck, they also would have slurped a bag or two of O positive. Ari didn't want to conduct an interview while viewed as a potential witchburger.

Having made that decision, they tossed around ideas of how and why the two vampires were taken. Nothing made much sense. Ransom and other typical hostage scenarios were ruled out by the simple passage of time without any demands. The voodoo story didn't ring true, as Ari hadn't found any stirrings of black magic in the community. Using the dark arts left distinctive negative energy behind that tended to linger.

On the chance the kidnappings were related to the other attacks, Ari filled in any details he didn't already know. Andreas was a good listener: grasped things quickly, asked for clarification when necessary. Mostly he paid close attention.

At some point in the night, Ari realized they were mostly

just bouncing ideas around, as if they enjoyed the process. In fact, Ari was so caught up in the conversation that pre-dawn came as a surprise.

Andreas looked up at the lightening sky. "It is almost time for me to go."

"Before you do, will you tell me about the assassination attempt? Why did someone try to kill the prince?"

Andreas grew quiet. Ari knew she was risking their fledging relationship by asking about a vampire court incident, but it was something she needed to know. The timing of the attack had been too coincidental. There was a strong possibility it was linked to the other violence. Certainly it added to community tension.

"Somehow I perceive this is a test," he said.

Ari lifted her shoulders. He was right, in a way. She needed to know the limits of their new arrangement.

The corner of his mouth twitched. "It is no secret. The attempt was clumsy, easily thwarted. Too easy. I have trouble viewing it as a serious assassination attempt. Of course there are others who do not agree with me."

"But what happened?"

"A tradesman regularly admitted to Daron's court attempted to stab him with a knife. Since the prince is surrounded by guards at all times, there was little chance of success."

"So what was the point?"

"Exactly my thought. And I think the answer is complicated." He cocked his head. "What knowledge do you have of vampire politics?"

"I know somebody usually dies."

Andreas gave a careless wave. "Sometimes, but politics are never that simple. A prince's personal power must be stronger than each of his lieutenants, but he rules only as long as he commands the combined power of his court. Whether that command is based on fear or loyalty depends on the Prince. Daron rules by loyalty. I believe this was an attempt to penetrate that allegiance. To prove that Daron's inner circles could be breached."

"Something more than a security failure."

"Yes. If enough doubts are raised regarding the loyalty of Daron's vampires, community support will waver, and the throne will be open to challenge."

"A coup?"

"Something like that. This situation puzzles me." His forehead creased into thoughtful lines. "To mount a successful challenge a vampire would have to have great personal power — and the ability to hold the court. Such a person should be obvious. But I believe anyone who might fit that description is still loyal to the prince."

"Unless you're wrong."

"Yes, there is that."

Interesting. Was Andreas's name on the short list of the most powerful? Ari gave him a sideways glance. Yana had been right. Andreas was definitely more than he seemed.

"What's your part in this?"

An easy smile curved his lips. "Let us say I'm loyal to the Prince and leave it at that."

"Yana thinks you're a lieutenant in Daron's court."

"Does she?" The smile remained in place.

"Is she right?" Ari persisted.

"Leave it alone, Arianna. We're done with this topic. I've tried to answer your questions, but now you're getting into personal affairs. Further discussion of the court would involve vampire matters that have nothing to do with you."

Ari accepted the rebuff without offense. "I get the personal issue, but how do you know the attack on Prince Daron isn't related to the other violence? What if the same person or group, like the wolves, is behind it all?"

"Can you prove that?"

He had her there. "I'm just saying it's possible."

"Anything is possible." He stood and considered the sky again. "Dawn is close. Anything else you need to know?"

"One more question. That first night in Goshen Park—why were you there?"

Andreas looked down at her. "I was tracking the wolf. I had come across his trail and...followed a hunch. When I heard the scream, I assumed the wolf had attacked someone. But you were there." His eyes darkened to unreadable depths. "We would have met sooner or later."

Well, yeah, Ari thought. That was a no brainer. Riverdale wasn't a huge community. "What kind of hunch are you talking about?"

"A poor one, apparently. I wanted to see where he went, who he met. But as you know, his only contact was with the children."

Ari heard the reluctance in his voice. Not the whole story, but all he was willing to give. It was enough for tonight.

They parted at the park entrance. Ari went home to her apartment, and Andreas went wherever vampires go. She wondered if he slept in a coffin. Too creepy. She covered a yawn with her hand. It had been a long night, but she'd made a smart move bringing Andreas into the investigation. She hoped Ryan would see it that way. Wouldn't he be surprised to learn he had a vampire partner?

Chapter Seventeen

Even though Ari slept late, Friday dragged as she waited for the foray into the vampires' nest. She paced her apartment and jumped when the phone rang, edgy and eager to step into a world forbidden to outsiders. A copy of *Witches World* lay discarded on her kitchen table. After reading the same paragraph twice, she'd given up. She'd checked the clock at least a million times, but the hands seemed frozen in place.

Mid-afternoon she gathered the spells and potions for her pouch, selecting items that were most likely to affect vampires. Nothing in her arsenal would be foolproof or fatal, except the dagger and the witch fire, but she had lesser magics that could temporarily bind or slow a vamp. She wasn't kidding herself that these small protections would be enough against an entire nest though, and she knew she was placing her safety in Andreas's hands. The busy activity helped with the nervous edge.

She avoided calling Ryan. The vamps wouldn't allow a full-blooded human near one of their nests. He'd only worry, knowing she was going, and he'd try to stop her. She didn't want to have that argument. Or tell him about the partnership. Not yet. Not until she proved how useful Andreas would be.

* * *

Ari was early to the rendezvous point. Five o'clock, Goshen Park. She'd asked Andreas how he could meet so early, but he'd brushed it off, saying the ability to resist the sun grew over time. Ari knew it couldn't be that simple. She was betting others as old were still snoozing.

However he did it, Andreas strode down the path, precisely on time. He looked ready for a special ops mission in black jeans and a black, turtleneck sweater. The fabrics looked expensive, and she figured they were Armani too.

He looked her over and grinned. "My compliments."

He'd suggested she dress for the occasion, feminine but official. That meant her white Guardian jacket. Not a bad choice since it emphasized her lingering summer tan. She paired it with white skinny jeans, a silk blouse open at the throat, and ankle boots.

They looked like yin and yang, a symbolism she chose to ignore.

Before they left the park, he insisted she remove the silver charm bracelet. "The nest leader won't allow you to enter with a cross and holy water." He watched as she slipped it into her pouch.

"Why don't the charms bother you?" she asked.

"What makes you think they don't?"

"You haven't turned away or shaded your eyes."

"One develops a certain tolerance…"

"Yeah, yeah, I get it, over time. So don't tell me. Let's get on with this."

Andreas led the way through Olde Town's winding streets, gradually moving beyond the vampire clubs, beyond the tourist district, and into unfamiliar territory. The slope of the land grew steeper as they descended from the high cliffs to the lower banks on the southeast side, where the Oak River met the Mighty Mississippi. Within twenty minutes, they reached an area of thick brush. As Andreas pulled the branches aside, she saw crude steps fashioned from bolted logs that led over the edge and down the bank, disappearing from view. Vampire territory.

She froze for an instant, uncertain of her decision to be there. "Do you know where this ends?" she asked.

Andreas just looked at her. She climbed over the edge.

They reached the bottom and stepped onto a rocky area with pathways branching in four directions. A strong fishy smell saturated the air. The soft lapping of the river murmured nearby. Andreas chose a trail on the right, and they began walking again. Dusk had deepened into dark, and the path was becoming hard to see. Vines and brush encroached from both sides and grabbed at her jeans.

Andreas stopped. "Wait here."

When he disappeared into the shadows ahead, Ari glanced around, wondering what spiders or other creepy crawlies might lurk in the brush. She didn't like bugs. Brando had ruined their charm at age ten when he dropped a grasshopper in her shorts.

She shifted from one foot to the other, tired of waiting already. She'd almost decided to explore on her own when she felt Andreas return.

He held out a white bandanna. "You must wear this. Only vampires are allowed to see the paths beyond this point. Our friends are very nervous about this."

"It's fine," she said. It wasn't fine, but she knew her objections wouldn't change things and might be viewed as a sign of weakness. She didn't want to say anything that could be overheard by the wrong ears.

Andreas must have had similar concerns. He placed a finger against her lips. After tying the blindfold securely, he grabbed her hand, wrapping it with his long fingers. Ari braced for a flood of awareness at the physical contact, but it didn't happen. Andreas was blocking her out. He tugged on her hand, and she crept forward.

It was a long four or five minutes before they stopped. Ari tensed as her skin prickled with the Otherworld energy of other vampires. She battled an urge to rip off the blindfold when she heard movement around her. Andreas spoke softly with someone then took her elbow, and they moved forward.

"Watch your step," he cautioned. "The ground is uneven."

The surface sloped under her feet. Harder now, broken stone at first, and then smooth. A cool dampness coated her skin. The breeze was gone, the air stale. Ari suspected they'd entered a cave. The cliffs were riddled with hidden fissures. They navigated a series of turns, more voices, then Andreas pulled the blindfold away.

Ari blinked in the sudden light. Two hanging lanterns revealed a rocky passage with protruding surfaces, moist walls, and six unknown vampires.

Three vamps stood before them, three behind. A male vamp in casual blue jeans and a muscle shirt, transformed in his late thirties, looked Ari over. He didn't look friendly. Two female vamps, skimpily attired, one in red, the other in black, flanked him on either side. Neither woman looked at her or spoke. Maybe they were only eye candy.

The guy in jeans spoke to Andreas. "Why are you here? And with this female?"

"You appear to have misplaced your hospitality, my friend." Andreas's voice was cool but without censure. "Perhaps it will return if I introduce the Guardian, Arianna Calin."

"Her status doesn't explain the intrusion. Why are you here without an invitation?" The other vamp wasn't backing down.

Andreas ignored the challenging tone. "A vampire of yours is missing. A young man named Gordon."

The nest leader's jaw tightened. "What do you know of this? Is he being held by the court?"

Well, this wasn't off to a good start, Ari thought.

"Absolutely not." Andreas appeared unruffled. "A young employee of mine is also missing. I hope to locate both of them after talking with your nest members."

The other vampire snorted. "If we knew where he was, we'd have retrieved him. What information do you think we have?"

"I will know that when I've spoken with them. Two of your young men are acquainted with my missing friend. I will share everything with you once I have the facts."

The leader frowned and digested this. Clearly Andreas held some position that made the other vamp reluctant to disregard him. "Who do you want to talk to?"

Now that was a good question. Knowing Andreas didn't have the names, Ari waited to see how he would field this one.

"Young friends of Marcus, my missing vampire. They were with him the night he disappeared."

"These two have names?"

A little sarcasm always helps. Ari wondered when Andreas would lose patience. He never showed this restraint with her.

"I presume they do," he said pleasantly. "But I don't know them."

The two vampires stared at one another, then the nest leader blinked. "Find them," he ordered the female in red. She left without saying a word.

After tense minutes in which the leader and Andreas exchanged desultory comments on an upcoming vampire meeting and the rest of the group eyed them in silence, the female vamp returned, bringing two young men. The newcomers' body language telegraphed their desire to be somewhere else, anywhere else. They kept their heads down and shuffled their feet.

"Reno and Lorenzo," the woman announced and fell back into silence.

"You are friends of Marcus?" Andreas asked.

The boys glanced at each other and nodded, shuffled some more.

Ari nudged Andreas. "We need to talk with them alone."

"No," the leader replied, glowering at her.

She started to protest, but Andreas spoke first. "My friend, I understand your reluctance. We live in tense days. But you know me, and I give you my word, this will bring no injury to your nest. We wish only to find the missing men. We'll finish our business and leave more rapidly if you allow some privacy."

Scowling, the leader thought it over. In the end, he sent the guards back to the entrance and took the two women with him when he left. His parting shot, "You have ten minutes. Even you, Andreas, can't expect more."

Even you? Indicating he had some special privilege. She'd already figured that, but it was something more for her to think about at a later time.

Andreas spoke in her ear. "Your turn. Be quick."

He stepped away, leaning against a wooden brace at the turn of the passage. Ari knew he could still hear every word. The young vamps would know it too, if they thought about it. But his actions gave them their own space and the illusion of privacy.

Ari studied the boys, teenagers. Nestlings really, transformed within the last year. Awkward and lanky, never to outgrow those uncertain years. She shrugged off a touch of sadness. "Which of you is Lorenzo?" The skinny kid with his dark brown hair cut in a butch waved a hand. "Then you must be Reno," she said to the other.

Reno nodded, his eyes peeking out from a chocolate brown face.

She smiled to put them at ease. "Look, you're not in trouble. We're trying to find Marcus and Gordon, and we need your help. I was told you were with Marcus the night he disappeared. Is that true?"

"Earlier," Lorenzo admitted. "Didn't see anything happen to him. Honest."

"That's fine. Just tell me what you can."

The boys looked at one another, clearly intimidated with the situation. Lorenzo shifted his feet and stared at the ground. Reno stood stiff as a board.

"Lorenzo, look at me." Ari made it a gentle command. He was used to obeying orders. She added a little magical projection of empathy, and he slowly relaxed enough to give her a shy smile. "You could save your friend."

"We weren't supposed to be there," he blurted. "Not in a bar. It's not allowed for the first year."

"I don't care about that. Nobody's going to care if we save

AWAKENING THE FIRE 139

Marcus." She hoped that was true, that Andreas could protect
these kids from any punishment for breaking the rules. "Why
don't you tell me which bar, and we'll go from there?"

"The Bloody Stake," Lorenzo mumbled with a furtive glance
at Andreas. "Just that one night." Once the admission was made,
the rest of the story came pouring out, with Reno adding details
Lorenzo missed.

The three young friends had spent the night drinking and
playing pool. At some point a group of wolves joined them and
showed particular interest in Marcus once he mentioned
working at Club Dintero.

"Way too nosey. At first they were real interested in
Marcus's job. Asked a couple questions about *him*," Lorenzo
said, pointing his chin toward Andreas. "But Marcus blew that
off."

"They talked weird," Reno added.

Reno grinned. "He means they had an accent. Said they were
from Toronto, wherever that is."

Yes, Ari thought. There's the tie in.

"Can you describe them?"

"Sure."

It turned out not to be as easy as she hoped. Three or four.
One tall, some not so tall. No women.

"And one dude was pretty old," Reno said.

That could mean anyone over twenty, Ari figured. She gave
up on the descriptions.

"What makes you think the wolves had something to do
with Marcus's disappearance?"

The boys exchanged looks again, and Reno took the lead.
"They followed him. He left just before us, and they followed
him right out the door."

"I thought they called his name." Lorenzo shrugged. "Not
sure about that."

"And that's the last time you saw him?"

"Yep." Two nods of the head.

"Earlier in the evening, did the wolves and Marcus talk

about anything in particular? Besides his job?"

"Girls, sports. Asked Marcus lots of private stuff, like they were big buds. And they bragged about their partying the night before. Full moon and all."

Well, now. She hadn't realized that was the night Marcus disappeared. Right after she and Steffan had talked with Molyneux. Maybe she'd said something that forced the wolf to resort to kidnapping. Or it was already planned. But why? Drug dealing didn't normally involve kidnapping, did it?

"Are you gonna find him? And Gordon?" Lorenzo's questions brought her back to the conversation.

"I can't promise anything. But you've helped a lot."

The boys grinned and shuffled their feet again. They made Ari feel old.

The nest leader never came back. Andreas spoke privately with the young vamps before they retreated into the tunnels. Ari didn't hear what he said, but both kids were still grinning when he finished.

On the return trip to town, Andreas and Ari didn't talk much until they were back on the city streets, away from the caves and prying eyes. Maybe it was the euphoria of having a direction for their energies, but they seemed pleased with each other's efforts that evening.

"Nice job with the leader. I wanted to pop him," Ari said. "That probably wouldn't have gone over too well."

Andreas quirked his lips. "No, but the nestlings responded to you. Helped by a mind game or two." He cocked his head and gave her a shrewd look.

"A little projection," she admitted. "To establish trust. It wasn't like I told them what to say or think. What did you tell them before we left?"

"Mostly reminded them not to talk about this with anyone except the nest leader." He swung his head to look at her. "Where do we find the pack? Marcus and Gordon have been in their hands too long. I am anxious for their welfare."

"It's an old house in the human residential district. I know what you're thinking, but we can't go barging in there tonight. I've got to bring Lt. Foster in on this. If we're going to start a bloodbath in human territory, it needs to be legally sanctioned." She shook her head when it looked like he might protest. "We have to wait. I won't endanger the human community without Ryan involved. And that'll take time."

Andreas sighed in exasperation. "I know you are right, but I still don't like it."

"I don't either," she confessed. "I'll talk to Ryan in the morning. We'll arrange something for tomorrow afternoon when you're available. Agreed?"

She felt his reluctance, understood the inner struggle. He was used to being in charge and waiting for nobody.

"Tomorrow," he finally confirmed.

Chapter Eighteen

The Riverdale Police Department annex, where Ryan and his unit were housed, was a four-story, square, red brick building, built in the early 1900s, and frequently upgraded over the years. Once the seat of all police activity, the building had been superseded twelve years ago by a modern structure in downtown Riverdale. The annex still held a full contingency of offices and officers, and handled all crime in Olde Town and the west side of Riverdale proper.

Ari bounded up the steps to the front entrance with its massive double doors that opened onto the second floor. Information and Dispatch were just inside. Elevators would take you down to the first floor temporary jail and the police carport or up to the offices and conference rooms on the top two floors. Ryan's office was on the third floor. Ari swung into a side hall and took the stairs.

As she had suspected, Ryan and his unit were working Saturday morning. Her partner sat behind his desk in an old swivel chair. As long as Ari had known him, the chair had listed to the left, but Ryan refused to replace it, claiming it fit his butt just fine. A late-twenties officer in street uniform perched on the edge of Ryan's desk. The two men looked up when she poked her head in the door, and the uniformed officer stood.

"Am I interrupting?"

"No, not at all." Ryan waved her in. "Just admiring a picture of Tom's new baby boy. I don't think you two have met. Tom's new to the unit, transferred from patrol."

As soon as the happy father left, Ari sank into a chair and brought Ryan up to date on the call from Rita. She was deciding how to get into the rest of it when the door opened and Ryan's secretary brought in two cups of coffee. Temporary reprieve. Contrary to most police departments, RDPD had decent coffee, thanks to the ladies of the clerical staff who guarded the pot.

Ari had rehearsed the coming conversation in her head, but now it felt all wrong. She sipped her coffee and worked on a quick rewrite.

Ryan leaned forward to rest his hands on the desk. "Out with it, Ari. Something's on your mind, and I'd guess I'm not going to like it."

She nearly spilled her coffee, set it down.

Ryan grinned at her reaction. "You look like you expect to be sent to the principal's office."

"That obvious, huh?" Ari hid a flash of annoyance. Maybe she'd have to work on this inscrutable face thing. There was no easy way, so she just told him. "You know I talked with Rita, and that I've tried everything to confirm her story. Well, I finally gave up and called Andreas. You remember, the vampire you met at the Second Chance. I went to see him Thursday night."

"And? You're still in one piece, so I assume it stayed peaceful."

"Of course. And I asked Andreas to help us."

"Thought you'd already done that. And he didn't seem too eager after the bar fight. Did he agree to find the witnesses for you?"

"Sort of. I asked him to work on the case with me. With us. Like another partner." Ryan's brows shot up, but he didn't say anything, so she continued. "And I asked him to take me to Gordon's nest." She sipped from her coffee cup, peering at him over the rim, and waited for a reaction.

Ryan's body stilled, his face settled into a frown. "And what did he say?"

"He laughed at me."

Ryan relaxed and leaned back, a slight smile on his face.

Knowing she'd misled him, Ari plowed ahead. "But I didn't give up, and eventually he changed his mind. Said he'd take me."

"What?" Ryan exploded out of his chair. He shoved both hands through his blond curls, creating a disordered mass, and began to stride back and forth across the room. "Good God, Ari. You must be crazy! You can't trust a vampire. And you can't go into some vampire nest with him."

"I already did."

Ryan stopped, his feet glued to the floor, and stared at Ari as if she had turned into a two-headed frog.

"And I'm fine. Andreas went with me. We got what we needed and were back home in a couple of hours."

If Ari had expected their success would make him happier, he quickly burst that bubble. His face paled, then flushed in sudden heat.

"Of all the lame-brained, idiotic things anyone could do! I know you have this big-time, supernatural stuff going for you, but even you can't fight off a nest of vampires. How could you trust that…that creature?" He resumed his angry steps.

Ari didn't want this to end in a big fight, so she decided to keep quiet until he simmered down. That turned out to be a good decision. One of few, according to him.

"You could be dead," he ranted. "And I wouldn't even know it. You'd just be missing. Since you didn't bother to tell me, I wouldn't have a clue what happened — or where to look. Did you tell anyone?"

When Ari shook her head, he rolled his eyes. After another minute or two of verbal venting, Ryan dropped into his chair, still shaking his head back and forth. "Why? Just tell me why?"

"Because I couldn't do my job without him." Ari leaned forward, eager to make him understand. "He has access to places we can't go, places I can't even find."

"Maybe so. But no single case is that important." His jaw set in a stubborn line.

"I don't believe that, and neither do you. You put your life on the line every single day." Ari gathered her thoughts. "I pledged to protect every member of the magic community, not just those I like. Or think are worth it. I never forget that oath. Just like your responsibility to protect the humans, even the bad guys sometimes."

"I understand duty." Ryan spoke with resignation. "But I don't understand how you could trust him."

"What was my choice? There wasn't one. My brain hasn't gone soft, Ryan. I know what he is, but so far he's kept his word."

"Lucky for you. I hope you don't expect me to trust him." His tone was acerbic.

"No," she sounded resigned. "Not unless he earns it. But work with him. And we'll both keep an eye out for anything that doesn't seem right." She gave him a teasing smile. "Contrary to one person's opinion, I'm really not a lame-brained idiot."

Ryan's mouth twisted in a rueful grin. "Sorry about that. But damn it, Ari..." He stopped and regarded her with a worried frown.

"I know you don't like the idea. But fess up, Ryan, we can use his help."

He fiddled with a pen on his desk. "We'll see about that. I suppose I can go along with this for now. But you knew that when you walked in here."

"Oh, no. I wasn't that confident."

"But why didn't you at least call me? You shouldn't have gone into that nest by yourself."

This seemed to be a sticking point Ryan couldn't get past. She tried again. "I wasn't alone. And I didn't call because you'd try to stop me. So can we drop it now? We've got a good lead. A reason to go into the wolves' home, conduct a search, and start asking official questions."

Ryan still needed to vent, especially about including Andreas as an equal partner. As they argued through his objections, he gradually got used to the idea. Once he reached that point, they started planning the next move. Whatever was going to happen, it had to happen that night. Andreas wouldn't wait beyond dark. And Ari wanted to be part of any confrontation with the wolves, not mopping up the mess afterward.

* * *

Four hours later, Ryan held the necessary warrant papers and plans for a raid were in place. Ari recruited Steffan and a couple of his wolves to keep watch on the house on Vine and report any activity. Ryan arranged for four officers to assist in the search. Or the shootout, Ari mentally added. Molyneux didn't strike her as the compliant type.

Ryan wanted to move as soon as he had the warrant, but Ari convinced him to wait for Andreas. Depending on the condition of the vampire victims, they might need Andreas's help. And although she didn't mention it to her disgruntled cop, Andreas had earned the right to be there.

Around 4:00 p.m. Steffan reported Molyneux had left the house carrying an overnight bag. The wolf leader wasn't moving like he was alarmed or in a hurry, but the bag indicated he planned to be away for some time. Ryan and Ari talked it over and decided to let him go rather than blow the entire operation. The goal at the moment was finding the young vampires. If they found evidence of criminal activity, they'd locate and arrest Molyneux after the raid.

Another half hour passed before Andreas called. "Do we have a plan?"

"You bet." Ari arranged to meet the vampires in twenty minutes at Steffan's command post. She jumped in the van with Ryan and his impromptu SWAT team, and everything proceeded as expected, until they were only blocks from the rendezvous point. Ari's cell rang, and Steffan's excited voice could be heard all over the van.

"They're running! The whole bunch is piling into a black

van. What do you want us to do?"

"Nothing," Ryan shouted. "We're almost there."

"Were any vamps with them?" Ari demanded.

"Not that I saw. Just a pack of wolves. Dammit! They're pulling out."

Ryan turned on the lights, and the van skidded around the corner on two wheels. Ari spotted the house, but the wolves' black van was out of sight. Steffan ran into the street and waved.

"Which way they'd go?" Ari yelled.

Steffan pointed, and Ryan stomped on the gas. They careened around the next corner, tires squealing. Still no van. Ryan radioed the other patrol cars to be on the lookout for the fugitives. After driving around for another ten minutes, Ryan looked at Ari. "Shall we go back to the house?"

"The vampires weren't in the van."

"Yep, noticed that. We'll let patrol look for the van." Ryan swung back onto Vine and pulled over. Steffan and Andreas stood on the front walk, surrounded by a group of wolves and vampires. The two leaders appeared to be arguing. Ari and Ryan jumped out to join them.

"What's wrong?" she demanded.

"Nothing now," Steffan said. "A disagreement on whether we should enter the house before you got back."

Ari gave Andreas a quick glance, figuring he was ready to tear the house apart. In fact, she was surprised he'd paid any attention to Steffan.

"So what happened?" Ryan demanded. "What spooked them?"

"Damned if I know." Steffan's voice was sharp. "As I told Andreas, everything was quiet. Then all hell broke loose. They came pouring out like the house was on fire."

"They were tipped." Ryan said. "Either they noticed the surveillance or they were warned."

"We weren't seen. I'm sure of it," Steffan said. "We hadn't moved out of those trees in two hours."

"Could Molyneux have spotted you when he left?" Ari

suggested.

"No, he turned the other direction. Never came near us."

Ryan's jaw tightened, and he looked at Andreas. The vampire stared back. It wasn't hard for anyone to see what Ryan was thinking.

"We'll worry about it later," Ari said, before something got started between the two. "Let's check the house. See if we can find our vamps."

Ryan nodded once. He wasn't a happy man. Andreas started across the lawn.

Victor, one of the four vampires Andreas had brought, caught up with Ryan. "Shouldn't we be chasing the van? We can't be that far behind. If we lose them, we might never find Marcus."

Ryan shook his head. "They're long gone from here. Patrol officers will call us if they spot them."

"How likely is that?" Victor grumbled. "We should try."

"It's too late," Ryan said, not without sympathy. "Now, let's go get the evidence in this house before we lose that too."

Victor looked like he wanted to continue the argument, but Andreas shook his head. Victor subsided into a sulky silence as they entered the house. Ryan and his team began clearing the first floor, the wolves sniffed around the untidy mess, and the vampires charged into the basement. Ari started flipping on lights, until she heard Andreas yell. She dashed for the basement stairs, Ryan and Steffan close behind.

At first glance, the poorly lit basement looked like every other old cellar, damp and cluttered with junk. Ordinary, except for the smell. The faintly sweet scent of vampire mingled with a stronger stench of decay. Ari's witch senses recoiled, and she paused halfway down the stairs. A single dirty lightbulb revealed a gruesome sight in the far south corner. As she moved closer, she saw a nude male vampire wrapped in heavy ropes and secured to the wall by chains. On the far side of the room, a shrunken creature with leathery skin was confined in a similar way. For once, Andreas's still face spoke volumes. They'd found the missing vampires.

The chained victim whimpered intermittently, as if in great pain. The other creature sagged, limp, unresponsive, so mummified that Ari hadn't immediately identified it as another vampire. Andreas knelt beside the first victim. Puzzled that the other vampires weren't helping, Ari hurried forward. As Andreas started to unwrap the ropes, she shoved his hands away, finally seeing the problem. Over the ropes, both vampires were wrapped in thin, silver chains.

"Ryan, I need your help." She unwound the first layer as Ryan took Andreas's place. "Silver isn't strong," she explained in answer to the question on Ryan's face, "but it immobilizes vampires and burns their skin. The rest of this stuff — the iron chains and the ropes — is just overkill."

As soon as they'd freed the first victim, Andreas pulled Ari back and nudged Ryan to one side. "Stay back," he warned. "They've been starved. This one will be desperate for blood. Healing demands it. And you will smell like ambrosia."

Ryan jumped back, nearly tripping over a broken chair. The vamp's eyes flew wide open, his nostrils flared. An intense primal look focused on Ari. She backed out of reach, more than willing to let Andreas take charge.

Ryan and Ari moved to the second creature. The cop's face displayed his raw emotions at what he was seeing. Revulsion, yes, but also pity. His biases had limits. Even after they removed the ropes and chains, the vamp didn't move. His life force was so faint, Ari wasn't positive it was there. She was afraid they were too late.

Andreas crouched beside her. He reached out and gently touched the creature's face. After a moment, he told them there was still hope. "Where the life force exists, even a flicker, there is possibility."

Ari wasn't sure whether Andreas was being realistic or fantasizing the outcome he wanted. The emaciated creature was young Marcus.

"This kind of healing requires the blood of a master level

vampire," Andreas said. "Marcus and Gordon must be taken to our community for treatment. Gordon's recovery should be swift. At least physically. It is early to predict his emotional stability. Denial of blood is the worst torture imaginable for a vampire."

Ryan and Ari gave their approval to his plan, and the vampires prepared for departure. A big vamp cradled Gordon in his arms and carried him out the door. Ari watched as the remaining vampires wrapped Marcus in sheets from the linen closet upstairs. They worked slowly, with great care.

"Is there really a chance he'll survive?" Ari was finding it hard to believe.

"We can only try." Andreas's eyes lingered on the wrapped figure of his young friend. "The death process is well advanced. If his body recovers, it may take days, weeks, or months. I cannot even predict the rest."

"So he might never tell us what happened?"

"He may not be cognizant again."

Ari realized what pain those words must cause him. And that surprised her. Not so long ago, she'd have said vampires felt nothing, especially emotional pain.

"But the other one will recover," Ryan broke in. "How soon can we talk to him?"

"A day, perhaps two. As soon as he is fully fed, his system will rejuvenate during the sleep cycle. I will call when he is ready."

As the vampires left, Ari wondered what kind of treatment the vampires would receive. The Otherworld hospitals carried a blood supply, but she'd never seen a vampire there. Then again, how often did a vampire need medical treatment? Andreas said the victims needed blood from a master level vampire. Would that have to be Prince Daron or were there other masters? Like maybe Andreas?

Ryan's relief that the vampires had taken charge of the victims was palpable. Ari wanted to mention how helpful it was to have a vampire partner, but she held her tongue. There are limits, even in a healthy friendship.

Steffan and his wolves went home. Ari, Ryan, and the four police officers searched the rest of the house. The strong doggie odor left by unwashed werewolf bodies, mingled with the smell of dirty clothes and spoiled food, made the search rather unpleasant. They didn't find much beyond empty beer cans, cigar butts, and discarded takeout cartons. Ari took a quick look at the electronic equipment, a fax machine and two printers, all empty. The laptop she'd seen in Molyneux's office was missing, probably in his carry bag.

Ryan's grim-faced team carried the last evidence bags to the van. As Ari and Ryan followed, she leaned toward him, keeping her voice low. "Why such long faces? We recovered the vampires."

"An empty house. Junk for evidence. What do you expect?" He gave her a calculated look. "But you know what's wrong. The wolves should be in custody. Would be, if something hadn't spooked them." He shook his head. "I'd sure as hell like to know how that happened."

Ari watched him walk away, his body bristling with tension. She thought he was overreacting and hurried to catch him. She laid a hand on his arm. "We'll find them again. Maybe their escape wasn't all bad. It's a residential neighborhood, and they weren't going to give up without a bloodbath. And Andreas seemed relieved to get his vampires back." When Ryan glowered at her, she realized this had been the wrong moment to mention the vampire. "Yeah, it wasn't a perfect outcome. But this isn't over."

Chapter Nineteen

Ari woke at dawn, shivering. A cold breeze blew in her open bedroom window, rattling the blinds. But the real reason for her chill was the dream. She'd been looking in the window of Molyneux's library. A large, red wolf laughed as he dropped silver coins into the hands of a shadowy figure. Ari struggled to make out the other face but could never quite see it. The wolf counted the coins, one by one. She heard the metallic clinks. When he reached the thirtieth piece of silver, she woke, his laughter ringing in her ears, the face of Judas still unseen.

Ari closed the window and snuggled under the covers. She didn't feel nearly as complacent about last night's events. She'd had other dream fragments since childhood whenever faced with difficult or disturbing problems. In this case, her subconscious was searching for the traitor who tipped the wolves to the raid. While Molyneux's trip appeared to be an unhappy twist of fate, the escape of the pack was due to a last minute warning…one only a limited number of people could have given.

Ryan would blame Andreas. He trusted Ari, he trusted his cops, and he'd trust Steffan because Ari did. In Ryan's mind, Andreas and his vampires would be the only suspects left. Besides, Ryan found vampires the most inhuman. In his book, that translated to least trusted.

Ari didn't want Andreas to be the leak, but wanting wouldn't make it so. She kept remembering the first night in Goshen Park. Had he been tracking the wolf, like he said, or meeting him?

She turned over, fluffed the pillow, and drifted back into a restless sleep.

* * *

An hour later, Ari woke to the jarring ring of the phone. ID came up as Ryan. She groaned, not yet ready to deal with him and the inevitable accusations. But his first words brought her wide-awake.

"Molyneux crossed the border during the night. He's back in Canada. Border guards apparently missed our BOLO." He sounded exasperated and grumpy. "I don't know what happened to the rest of the pack. No one was with him. Sheila Montgomery is the only other name we've got, and it hasn't popped up anywhere."

"Then they might still be near Riverdale," Ari said.

"They could be almost anywhere."

Maybe, but Olde Town was where they had contacts. Someone in town had helped them. The way Ari figured it, they'd hide nearby until Molyneux got in touch with further instructions.

Ryan asked if she'd heard from Andreas yet. When she said no, neither of them pursued the subject. Ari was glad to delay a discussion of Ryan's suspicions until they had more information. The longer the delay, the better. Who knew? Something good could happen in the meantime.

To keep busy while she waited to hear from Andreas, she followed through on a promise to Claris. They spent the day cutting, separating, and tying medicinal plants and herbs to be dried. Claris acted a bit lonely with Brando out of town at a five-day conference on scientific wizardry. The busywork was a good chance for the two friends to catch up on gossip and indulge in girl talk.

On the way home late that night, Ari smelled the presence of werewolves. She took a meandering route through Olde Town, not wanting to lead them to her front door. She doubled back three times, hoping to catch them, but she didn't see a single wolf. When the smell and tingle of their Otherworld energy finally dissipated, she went home. Ari was determined to put an end to this soon. The wolves were becoming far too bold.

* * *

When the night passed with still no word from Andreas, Ryan called first thing in the morning. His suspicions had taken root and flourished over night.

"If Andreas is working with the wolves and tipped off Molyneux, he wouldn't want us to know what Gordon and Marcus have to say." Ryan's voice dripped with accusation. "Now that I think about it, he was very anxious to take them away. How do we know we'll ever see them again? Hell, they could both be dust by now."

"Come on, Ryan. Andreas isn't going to harm Marcus. He was worried about him. Searched every night for him."

"Or that's what he wanted you to think," Ryan countered. "Makes a good cover."

"Cover for what? What's this big conspiracy about?" Ari thought Ryan was letting the stress and frustration get to him.

"I don't know…yet."

She didn't share his suspicions. Not really. But he'd planted the seed. Or maybe watered it. The rest of the day, Ari replayed recent events in her head, searching for logical explanations. Something to prove Ryan was wrong — and that she hadn't made a big mistake by trusting a vampire.

What would Andreas gain from an alliance with Molyneux? The werewolf could be interested in the money, but the vampire? Ari didn't think so. Not judging by the decor of the club and his expensive clothes. Power or revenge, maybe, but not money. Damn, why didn't he call?

When the phone finally rang shortly after dark, Ari snatched it, hoping to hear Andreas's voice. Her tense shoulders relaxed. Gordon was awake and talking.

"What did he say? Does he know why they took him?"

Andreas hesitated. "It would be better for everyone to hear the words directly from Gordon. So there is no question of interpretation. Where can we meet?"

"What's wrong with the police station?"

He hesitated again. "I'm not certain Gordon is ready for such an intimidating atmosphere."

And maybe Gordon wasn't the only one who didn't want to be surrounded by human cops, Ari thought. Vampires weren't real keen about outside authorities. In this case, Andreas didn't trust the police anymore than they trusted him. She racked her brain for some place to meet that was neutral territory. Eventually, it dawned on her that she had an office. She'd only been in it once, but she had an assigned space at the Otherworld Cultural Center attached to the Magic Hall.

As soon as Andreas consented to the location, she called Ryan, and he approved. At least she'd found something they could agree on.

Ari arrived early at the Magic Hall in order to track down a set of keys. The white-haired custodian blinked at her request. His rheumy eyes peered at her from under bushy white eyebrows. After she explained who she was and showed him her ID, he placed two keys in her hand.

"You're responsible for any guests," he said sternly.

Ari produced a smile meant to reassure him, but she wasn't sure it worked. The ancient custodian frowned, shaking his head as he shuffled down the hall.

Maybe the ponytail didn't inspire confidence, Ari decided. It made her look too young. She pulled out the band and shook her hair loose. She'd need all the authority she could muster during the next hour or two.

Her office was a roomy rectangle, with an oak desk, leather chairs and a conference table that seated six, eight in a pinch. The well-worn chairs looked relatively comfortable and had that pleasant smell of old leather. A bookcase with two books, a Cultural Center Manual and an English dictionary, stood against one wall. Overhead lights and a gold-plated desk lamp with a green shade provided adequate lighting. No dust. Somebody must come in and clean. Who knew?

Ari picked up the manual, selected a chair on the far side of the table, and prepared to wait. As she thumbed through the book, the other participants trooped through her open door in one large group. Everyone was dressed casually in jeans and jackets. Andreas's sleek leather jacket appeared to be his usual brand.

Ryan's lips were drawn in a tight line. Grumpy, she concluded. Andreas was wearing his polite mask. Ari sighed. Resigned to the inevitable, she ignored the animosity of the two men and focused on the witness.

Without the feral stare from blood deprivation, Gordon was a nice looking vampire. A little too punk for Ari's taste, with the head bandanna and the heavy jewelry, but she could see why he appealed to Rita. The attitude didn't match his style. Gordon was twitchy; his throat bobbed up and down as he swallowed repeatedly. She wondered if this was typical behavior or a side effect of his recent captivity. He stuck close to Andreas.

Ryan chose the seat next to Ari, back against the wall, forcing the vampires to sit with their backs to the door. She hid a smile at Ryan's maneuvering.

Andreas introduced the young vamp and encouraged him to speak freely. "Just tell them in your own words what happened after you left Rita's place."

Gordon took a deep breath. "I was running home. It was late, almost daybreak. This black van drove by, twice. Wolf dudes inside. Offered me a ride, but I could get home faster on my own, so I blew them off. Next thing I knew, a couple of them were running beside me, asking if I knew some chick I never heard of named Sherry. Told 'em no. Figured they'd leave then, but they kept at it. 'Get in the van. Help us find her.' When I said no again, they jumped on my back, and I felt a prick in my neck.

That's it, till I woke in the cellar."

"And then?" Andreas prompted.

"I couldn't see, because of a hood. I smelled wolves and a vampire. My hands and legs were chained. After a while, a she-wolf made them take the hood off. She gave me a packet of blood, said if I answered questions they'd let me go. She left, and another wolf asked a bunch of really bizarro questions. I asked if I could go now, but they laughed and put the hood back on. They beat me with silver clubs." He stopped talking, his shoulders hunched.

Andreas put a hand on his shoulder. "Take your time."

When the young vamp had composed himself, Ari jumped in before he finished his story. "These questions—what did they ask?"

Gordon looked at her for the first time. "Stupid stuff. What foods I used to like or hate. Movie ratings. Stuff about girls. Sex. Music groups. Like they were taking a poll. They wouldn't tell me why."

"Did they seem to be looking for a particular answer? Like they wanted you to say you liked red-haired girls, for example?"

"Not then, that came later."

"What do you mean?"

Andreas intervened before Gordon answered. "This might make more sense, if you let him tell it in order."

Ari shrugged. "I can wait. Tell us what happened after the hood went back on."

"Somebody stuck a needle in my arm. The next time I woke up my skin felt like it was on fire. I was wrapped like a mummy with the ropes and silver chains. My head hurt." He touched his forehead, as if remembering the pain. "Everyone was gone. I still smelled the vampire, so I tried to talk to him. He never answered. Another wolf came, or maybe the same one, I don't know. Jabbed me with a needle again." Gordon stopped. "That's all I remember clearly. After that...just little bits." His voice faltered. Gordon's left hand trembled, and he hid it under the table.

"What kind of bits? Did you learn what they wanted?"

"Nothing made sense. Voices. Needle pricks. Funky smells. Everything was hazy. Inside my head, I mean. Couldn't get it clear." Gordon frowned. "Questions. Over and over. I finally started trying to give the answer I thought they wanted. Sometimes I wasn't sure the voices I heard were real. Maybe just inside my head. Music. Smells, like flowers and cologne. And cooked cabbage. Smelled rotten." He wrinkled his nose. "Someone told me I liked cabbage. I gagged and got hit with the club."

"Are those the same questions the first wolf asked?" Ari probed.

Gordon looked surprised. "Maybe. Yeah, now I think about it. Only now they'd hit me if I didn't answer right. I think." His face pinched in confusion.

"Tell them about the second packet of blood," Andreas said.

"I hadn't fed since I came. Had the belly cramps. The she-wolf came that last night. Held a packet to my nose, put a drop on my lips. Then she left."

"I'm sorry." Ari didn't know what else to say. She imagined how bad that had been for a starving vampire. "Anything else you remember?"

Gordon frowned, concentrating. "Laughing, joking about me." Gordon showed the first sign of anger over his captivity. "Something about rats. Some dude named Pavlov. Remembered his name so I could tell someone. If…well, so you could find him." Gordon heaved a big sigh. "Can I go now?"

"Enough?" Andreas asked, looking at Ari and Ryan. "I don't think further questioning will be helpful."

Ari nodded. Gordon had given them plenty to talk about.

Andreas rose, placing a hand on Gordon's shoulder again. "Friends are waiting to take him home. As soon as they're on the way, we can discuss this." He glanced at Ryan but didn't wait for a response before ushering Gordon out the door.

Ryan had maintained an ominous silence throughout the interview. As soon as the vampires were gone, he leaned back and crossed his arms. "What do you make of his story? Presuming it's true."

"What do you mean?"

"Sounds pretty bogus. Polls, music, cabbage, for God's sake. I wonder if he was deliberately vague. Maybe the vampires have a reason for not wanting us to know what happened."

"What reason? You walked in here mad at the world, and now this. These conspiracy theories are starting to sound crazy. You think they're making it up? Sure didn't look that way to me." Ari shoved her chair back and stalked around the table. She leaned across it to fire another comment when she felt Andreas walk in behind her.

"Am I interrupting?" he said, looking from one angry face to the other.

"No," Ari said.

"Yes," Ryan said.

Andreas's lips tightened for an instant. He pulled up a chair and sat. "So," he drawled. "What next, partners?"

Andreas emphasized the final word, and Ari thought Ryan would jump across the table. She choked down a startled laugh at the vampire's audacity. She wanted to treat it as nothing, diffuse the situation, but knew it was too late for that. Still, she had to try.

"We were talking about what the wolves did to Gordon," Ari said, returning to her seat.

"Pardon me for contradicting you, Arianna, but I don't think so." Andreas's eyes locked on Ryan. "That was not your last discussion."

"Andreas, don't go there," Ari began, but Ryan interrupted.

"No, he's right. Let's get this out on the table."

"Fine," she snapped, fed up with both of them. "We don't have time to squabble among ourselves, but by all means, get it over with." Ari sat back and put her elbows on the arms of her chair. The testosterone levels in the room were too damn high. If they wanted to fight, she wasn't getting in the middle.

"Since I'm the one with the problem, I'll start," Ryan said.

"This story of Gordon's has holes big enough to drive a tank through. It smells phony. As if you made it up."

"Interesting." Andreas was at his most arrogant. "Why would we invent such a tale?"

"To throw us off the track. To cover what's really going on."

"Which is what?" Andreas's brows lowered. "What do you believe is going on?"

Ryan gritted his teeth. "You and Molyneux are hiding something."

"So," the vampire leaned forward, "you think I'm conspiring with the Canadians. What gave you that ridiculous notion?"

"Is it so ridiculous? I know and trust everyone who participated in that bungled raid. Except you and your friends. *Somebody* warned Molyneux's pack that we were on the way."

"I agree. They were most certainly warned. But not by me." Andreas focused on Ryan's face. "Nor am I working with or for the wolves. And Gordon's story is his own. Tell me, Lieutenant, if your wild accusations had any truth to them, why would I help Arianna to confirm Rita's story? And why wait until the last minute to warn the Canadians? After all, I had all night. They could have safely dispersed, taking or disposing of Marcus and Gordon, and you would know nothing. If you want to ignore those discrepancies, prove I did this. And tell me what I would gain." Andreas's voice was controlled, but the muscles across his shoulders were strung tight.

"If I had the answers, you'd be safely behind bars."

"And that is exactly what you want, is it not?" Andreas emphasized the last three words in a voice grown soft and cold.

"I wouldn't lose any sleep over it."

Ari tensed. If they kept on like this, the joint investigation would be down the tubes and somebody might get hurt.

Andreas placed his forearms on the table and leaned toward the cop. "Is this about me, Lieutenant? Or a bias against vampires? You closed the case from the bar without solving it. It makes no sense that two previously inoffensive vampires turned murderous. But perhaps the truth doesn't matter when it comes to vampires."

"Wrong on both counts," Ryan fired back, leaping to his feet. "I don't trust you."

Chapter Twenty

Deadly silence. The two men stared at one another, and Ari held her breath. Trust was the heart of the matter.

"At least that is honest. Personal animosity, I can handle." Andreas spoke in a normal voice and leaned back, lowering the tension.

Ryan ran a hand through his hair and sat down. "I don't have to explain anything to you. But just to set the record straight, I was opposed to closing the Second Chance case. I was overruled by my superiors." He took a deep breath before he went on. "I'm just trying to do my job, Andreas. Right now, I want to know who helped the wolves get away. I admit some of what you say makes sense. But if it wasn't you, then who? We have a leak somewhere."

"Indeed. That would appear to be the case. I am making inquiries on my end of this. Rechecking every staff member that could have known. I trust you are doing the same."

Ryan's face flushed, then he acknowledged the logic. He gave a reluctant nod. "I will, but I know my men. It wasn't my side."

Sides? Uh-uh, Ari had had enough. "Is this about over? There are other possibilities neither of you mentioned. Steffan doesn't think his wolves were seen, but maybe they were. Or it was police scanners. An intercepted cell phone call. We don't know what kind of sophisticated surveillance equipment they might have. Or maybe someone was watching the PD and followed us. I know someone's been tailing me. Until we—"

"Someone's been tailing you? Why haven't you said anything?" Ryan interrupted. Both men stared at her.

"I haven't seen anyone. I smelled wolf, but it might be a coincidence."

Ryan looked at Andreas. "Do you believe that?"

"Not for a moment. These wolves are aggressive."

"Hey, I can handle the tail." Ari wished she'd never brought it up. "Let's get back to the point. If we keep the details of our investigation among the three of us, there shouldn't be another leak. If there is, then we start pointing fingers. In the meantime, we declare a truce. How about it?"

No one spoke. When she looked at Andreas, he shrugged. "Ryan?"

He scowled but said, "I'll go along."

"Good. So let's talk about what happened to Gordon. He heard the name Pavlov. Isn't that out of a science book? Experiments on dogs, not rats."

"Conditional reflex," Andreas said. "Pavlov was studying the reactions to stimuli."

Well, that was kind of specific information. Ari wondered if it was book learning or firsthand knowledge. The vampire had been around a long time. Someday, when he was in a better mood, she intended to ask him things like that.

"Yeah, I remember. And you're right, Ari. It wasn't rats. When the dogs heard the food dish, they got excited," Ryan added. "Or something like that."

"Close enough," Andreas said. "His work eventually resulted in attempts to control the responses, such as the aversion therapy used in some addiction treatment."

"Are we talking mind control?" Ari asked.

"Aw, don't do this to me," Ryan protested. "First voodoo, now mind control?"

"Might not be so far off." Andreas steepled his fingers.

"Experimentation of some kind would fit the facts. Unless the Pavlov reference was just a crude form of ridicule."

"It's got to be significant. Who throws around the name of some guy from a high school biology class unless it's important?" She turned to Andreas. "Has conditioning ever been turned into full mind control?"

"With humans? Limited. Brainwashing, like in certain cults. To my knowledge, never with vampires." Andreas shook his head. "It is almost inconceivable."

"Wish we knew what drugs they used," Ryan said. "The CS techs didn't find drugs at the house, but I could have them look again."

"Not necessary." Andreas drew an insulated packet out of his leather jacket pocket and handed it to Ryan. "The sample was extracted before we gave Gordon new blood. Whatever was in his system should be here. I added...a special preservative and kept it cool. But the fluid still has a short shelf life."

Ryan opened the packet wide enough, and Ari saw the small vial of blood inside. "I'll run it by the night lab. Put a rush on it. We should have results by tomorrow." His voice held a note of grudging approval.

"I believe it is the altered Fantasy or a similar drug," Andreas continued. "Gordon was more expansive when he was not under pressure. He described images, impressions really, that sounded like hallucinations. I am concerned the wolves are trying to alter or at least have a temporary effect on the vampiric neurological system."

"But why?" Ryan asked.

Andreas shrugged. "Any number of things, I suppose. Control could be one of them. Perhaps a biologist or Otherworld lab tech could hazard a better guess."

"Good idea. I'll talk with the OFR lab. But whatever they're doing, it hasn't gone well," Ari said. "Unless death or violence was the goal. Their hostages were a mess. Gordon's recovering, but what about Marcus? He was nearly mummified."

"Yes, decaying," Andreas said. "It is the same process as any dying vampire, except in painfully slow motion. Without sufficient blood, the vampire body loses its fluids, shrivels, mummifies, and without intervention, turns to dust."

"My God," Ryan said. "How could anyone sit by and watch that happening?"

Ari didn't have an answer. Considering parts of history, like the Nazi death camps, this wasn't the first time a similar question had been asked. It was still unanswerable.

Ryan ran a hand through his hair again. "Here's the deal, Andreas. Ari thinks we need you on this investigation. I'm going to trust her judgment. Don't have to tell you I have my doubts, but no one should be treated the way your friends were treated. If we work together, maybe we can stop these guys."

Andreas looked at him from hooded eyes. He nodded. "Agreed."

Ari watched the simple exchange. Some sort of understanding had passed between the two men, something she hoped she could build on. She stood and stretched cramped muscles. They'd been talking a long time.

"So what next?" she asked. "It's hard to anticipate what they'll do if we don't know what they want. Can we put all the pieces together? What's their end game?"

Ryan drummed his fingers on the table. "Drugs and money are a long-standing combination. But I can't imagine how that ties in with kidnapping and mind control. Are they drug dealers or mad scientists?"

"Perhaps they are both," Andreas suggested. "With one side supporting the other."

"Explain." Ryan looked interested.

"Let me see if I can." Andreas cracked a smile. "I was thinking out loud. What if the original Fantasy is all about money? And they use that money to fund the experiments on the altered drug? With an ultimate goal of obtaining total control over a vampire."

"And the violent incidents were bad side effects," Ari said, drawing the logical conclusion.

Andreas stood and strode across the room. "That would make Olde Town's vampires the guinea pigs. The lab rats."

"Until my visit to Molyneux forced him into scaling down his experiments to two," Ari said, not looking at Andreas. Damn, she didn't want to carry around the guilt for what happened to Marcus and Gordon.

"Aren't we getting carried away? This is all kind of far-out theory. And it still doesn't tell us why someone picked Riverdale. Or why somebody would go to such efforts to control a vampire." Ryan stopped in exasperation.

Andreas and Ari exchanged a look. If you could program a vampire to do your bidding, take control of his supernatural powers, the potential for misusing the magic was tremendous. And if you could program several...well, Ari didn't even want to go there.

Ryan caught their silent exchange, thought about it. His next words were subdued. "Yeah, I guess the control stuff is obvious. Nothing good, that's for sure."

"The formula's not perfected yet," Ari reminded them. "We've still got time to stop this. I just don't know how. Or where to start."

She was relieved when her phone rang, delaying the inevitable admissions from her partners that they didn't know either.

Ari smiled when she heard Brando's voice. "I thought you were out of town. How was the trip?"

"It was good. Got home this evening, and Claris told me about your drug case. I might be able to help."

"Really? What do you know about Fantasy?" Ari shrugged as Ryan and Andreas turned to look at her. Stunned, she listened while Brando presented a huge break in the case. Five minutes later, she relayed the information to her partners.

"Brando heard this wizard, Daniel Dubrey, speak at a conference. Um, I think he said three or four years ago. Anyway, Dubrey's work was based on combining chemicals and magic. He was doing lab trials on medicines enhanced by spells and potions. Brando says it's really specialized stuff. One of a kind. And here's the kicker—he lives near Toronto, Canada." She gave a double thumbs-up. "That can't be a coincidence."

Ryan broke into a grin. "So there's our starting point. Whether he's the manufacturer or not, he's got to know something. You should go to Canada. Talk to this wizard, and while you're there, see if Molyneux's been around."

"You think Molyneux is in Canada?" Andreas asked.

"We know he is. Sorry, forgot you hadn't heard." Ryan told him about the border crossing. "Don't ask me how they missed our BOLO." He turned back to Ari. "While you follow the drug trail, we'll keep searching for the pack."

"Nobody wants to come along?" she asked.

"My department won't approve a trip without consulting the local PD in Toronto. And that takes time." He glanced at Andreas. "Unless I'm mistaken, his travel is defined by the sun. You can slip in and out without anyone being the wiser. Besides, this wizard is more likely to talk with a witch than either of us."

"You are the logical choice," Andreas said. "It might be a good idea for you to be out of town for a day or two to confuse whoever has been tailing you. While there, don't approach Molyneux on your own. He will be among friends. The same goes for Sebastian, the vampire prince. He is a brutal dictator and no friend of Prince Daron."

Ari brought her chin up. She hated it when someone told her what to do. Or even worse, what she couldn't do. "You keep forgetting I can take care of myself."

"So you've said before. But it would be better to stay out of situations where you might have to prove it."

When Ryan didn't come to her defense, Ari realized her partners had found something else they agreed on. "Hey, no ganging up. I'm not going to do anything stupid. I'll visit Dubrey, and if I have any time left, I'll see what the locals say about Molyneux and Sheila. But I'm not going after the wolf or some evil prince. Satisfied? 'Cause that's the best you're going to get."

With Ryan's threats of dire consequences ringing in her ears if she wasn't back the next evening, they parted near the steps of the Magic Hall. Wondering if her elusive tail was watching, Ari headed for the airport.

Chapter Twenty-One

Modern air travel made Canada just a short nap away. At 6:35 a.m., Zoe Vesper, one of six Guardians assigned to Toronto, stood outside baggage claim with a placard and a wide grin. Ari soon learned that was typical Zoe. The woman was tall and lanky with short, brown, bouncy curls and eight ear piercings. But most interesting to Ari, she was half witch. Her witch clan had bred with elves, accounting for her nearly six-foot height.

"I have the address you wanted." Zoe beamed at her. "Programmed it into my GPS. He lives out in the boonies. Expressways will help, but it might take an hour."

Morning traffic was heavy. Once they hit the outskirts, Zoe sped up. She kept up a constant stream of chatter, pointing out turnoffs to local sites, once relating a multiple homicide by a dwarf with an axe. Considering Ari had gotten little sleep, Zoe was rather perky, but at least she didn't require frequent responses. Ari leaned back, letting the words flow past. When Zoe began to talk about Dubrey, Ari started paying attention again.

"He's a hermit. Lives on an old estate that once belonged to wealthy French émigrés. From the description I got, it's one shade this side of condemnation. Dubrey rarely leaves the property." She honked at a driver in her way but kept on talking. "I'm not sure he'll let us in."

"I'll get in somehow." Ari yawned, covered her mouth, sat up straighter. "Sorry about that. Short night. I have to talk to him. He's my only chance to learn about the drugs."

"If he's making Fantasy, like you mentioned on the phone, why haven't we seen it in Toronto?"

"I don't know. In some ways that's even more suspicious. The original formula is everywhere else. Why not here?"

"It does seem strange. Rumor says there's a secret lab. Might explain why he doesn't want anyone snooping around."

"Especially if he's doing something illegal," Ari said. "Wouldn't be the first or last time a magic user crossed the line."

"That's true. Otherwise humans wouldn't fear us so much."

Zoe finally lapsed into silence. She seemed to have run out of morning chatter, and they drove for miles in silence. Ari had nearly dozed off when they left the main roadways, followed a deserted road for a couple of miles, and pulled into a narrow private lane.

Zoe peered through the windshield. "I think this is it. Just down here a ways."

The dirt drive was lined with bushes gone wild. Branches scraped at the sides and top of Zoe's VW. After two quick turns, they saw buildings through the trees and stopped, covering the rest of the way on foot. If they surprised Dubrey before he realized anyone was near, they might avoid a greeting that involved weapons—magical or otherwise.

Their approach to the house went unchallenged. The old mansion stood forlorn from decades of ill-use and lack of repair. Withered weeds poked through the wooden porch floor; windows frames were empty; the front door sagged open.

Ari drew her jacket a little closer. Evil had visited here. Shrugging off that thought, she motioned to Zoe. They edged across the porch, testing each board, and entered the house. The musty smell wrinkled Ari's nose, and she stifled a sneeze. Huge cobwebs hung in the corners. A layer of grime coated the shabby furniture. Dubrey hadn't used this area for some time. No footprints in the dust. Near the back was the kitchen area with windows overlooking a weedy garden, servants' quarters, a guesthouse, and a large storage shed.

Ari crossed to the garden door. Zoe followed her outside.

The servants' quarters were also empty of life or activity. No furniture, no rugs. A trail of scuffed footprints across the dusty floor lead to a stack of clean, white packing boxes, dust free and recently packed. Zoe pried open a box corner. Test tubes. This must have been the lab.

As they approached the guesthouse, goose bumps raised along Ari's arms, a prickle at the back of her neck. A heaviness hung over the building. The front door was a gaping hole of freshly splintered wood.

Zoe gave her a wide-eyed look and flattened against one side of the door. Ari took the other, edging forward and going in fast. The smells hit first. Ozone. Blood. Charred wood. Walls and ceilings displayed black gouges and deep burns. Magical fire. The lethal kind. It had been one hell of a fight, Ari thought.

They picked their way past the debris, the smashed lamps, and overturned furniture. Only two or three steps inside, Ari picked up another telltale odor — decomp. They found the wizard's body in a back bedroom.

Daniel Dubrey's body had been brutalized. His limbs were shattered, bone poked through the skin, slashes and bites covered much of the body. Buzzing flies coated the eye sockets and open wounds. Whatever Dubrey had been in life, his uniqueness was gone, marked only by a mass of stringy, black hair.

"Mon Dieu," Zoe muttered, recovering after a moment. "What did this? Zombies?" She moved in for a closer look. "His neck is broken. That would be enough to kill him. But it looks like someone or something went into a frenzy."

"Except there's not enough blood." Ari pointed to a bone protruding from his upper arm. "That should have bled a lot. And there's no splatter on the walls." She centered herself and tapped her witch senses. "I don't feel the rage."

Zoe walked around to the other side of the body. "Look at

the board on top of his leg. Placed there after he was dead. This scene has been staged. So what were they trying to hide?"

"Maybe this," Ari said, crouching beside the body. "Fang marks. Here. And here. Not jagged like a wolf. Vampire."

For a brief flash, Ari wondered where Andreas had gone after he left her last night.

"How long do you think he's been dead? Couple of days?" Zoe's words brought her up short, and Ari looked again. Of course. This wasn't a fresh kill. She was letting her doubts about Andreas mess with her judgment. He couldn't have done this.

"Blood on the floor is dry. There's insect and rodent activity." Ari touched the corpse with her toe. It moved slightly. "Rigor must be leaving the body. I'd guess twenty-four hours, possibly longer, if your weather's been cool."

"At night. Could put his death as early as Sunday morning."

Ari stared at what was left of the wizard, but her thoughts went beyond him to all the failed leads in this case. Dubrey had been their best chance for answers. At least it wasn't a leak this time. Dubrey died before Ari and her partners knew he existed. That should have made her feel better, knowing Andreas wasn't involved and that she couldn't have prevented the death. But damn. Once again, someone was a step ahead of them. And Ari was getting damned tired of it.

She studied the room. "Let's search this place. Dubrey can't talk to me, but his death confirms he knew plenty. He's got to have records. Maybe they'll hold some answers." She looked at Zoe. "Do you agree with putting off a call to the local cops? The body's not going anywhere. Scene's already cold."

Zoe snorted. "Out here? In this dinky jurisdiction? They won't have a clue about Otherworld evidence. Don't think we need to worry about the police case."

Ari started with a quick walk through. The wizard had led a Spartan life. No TV, no sound system. Nothing recreational. The only modern convenience in the kitchen was a small microwave. Minimal fuss. Everything they found said this man was obsessed by his work.

In the front room, Zoe fiddled with the elaborate computer system while Ari opened and looked behind every book on the shelves. Zoe thought someone had already been through the wizard's computer and deleted incriminating files.

"Even his e-mail is empty," Zoe complained.

The elf-witch continued to click away as Ari moved on to search stands and table drawers. She opened the zippers on pillows and tapped the walls for hidden panels.

"Nothing," Zoe said, abandoning her efforts on the computer.

Ari straightened from looking under the rug. "Same here. But I can't imagine a researcher who wouldn't keep extensive notes. Maybe the killer took them."

"Here's a bunch of CDs." Zoe dug into one of the desk drawers. "It'll take hours to go through them, but I can look at a couple." The clicking of the keyboard started again.

Ari checked the wall clock. The hands had crept past noon. Her flight home left in three hours. With more than an hour drive to town, they'd have to leave soon. But Ari wasn't ready. They still had the storage shed and grounds to search, and the packed boxes in the lab would take at least an hour. She glanced at Zoe hunched over the keyboard with a tall stack of disks beside her.

"How about taking a break for lunch? Wasn't there a burger joint a couple miles back? I'll change my flight. We can finish after lunch. Besides," Ari rubbed her arms, "I need to get out of here for a while."

Zoe nodded in sympathy. "Know what you mean. Creepy place, isn't it? Bad vibes." Zoe's stomach growled, and she chuckled. "Guess my stomach just voted too." She pushed her chair away from the computer, and they heard a metallic crunch. Zoe picked a small object off the floor. "A thumb drive. Looks like somebody took a hammer to it or a boot heel." She looked at Ari. "Destroying evidence?"

"What's a thumb drive?"

Zoe smirked at her. "You really aren't a techie, are you? A

flash drive? You know, to transfer data back and forth between computers."

"Oh." Since Ari had one laptop, used for writing and printing reports, transferring had never been an issue for her. So no thumb drives. She shrugged. "Can you fix it?"

"Not a chance. An IT tech might pull off some data." Zoe sounded doubtful. "But I wouldn't count on it. I'll keep it, just in case." She stuck it in her pocket. "Ready to go?"

* * *

It was close to 2:00 p.m. by the time they finished the search of the guesthouse and the shed, where they found the wizard's herbs and potions. While Zoe continued to work on the computer, Ari walked the property. It smelled weedy, too dry. The area needed rain. Heavy brambles and drought-resistant weeds barred some areas, leaving her picking burrs from her jeans. The only evidence of interest was a set of partial shoeprints near the back door of the guesthouse. If this was the killer or one of the killers, he'd been in human form. Still consistent with a vampire. She left the prints undisturbed for the police.

"Anything?" Ari asked, returning to the guesthouse.

Zoe looked up from the computer and sighed. "A bunch of meaningless formulas. No notes. But I've got a long way to go."

"So leave it for now. Let's get to those packing boxes."

Zoe and Ari tackled the dismantled lab with renewed energy, glad to be away from the guesthouse and the oppressive presence of the wizard's body. They sat on the floor with boxes and contents scattered around them. For the first hour they worked in assembly; one person opened and sorted, the other repacked. So far, they'd found nothing more exciting than petri dishes, glass slides, small bottles of liquid chemicals, and sterile gloves, which they started using immediately. It would be awkward if they had to explain to local cops how their fingerprints got inside the boxes. Other containers held microscopes, vials for blood, and an assortment of measuring equipment and stirrers.

Ari's hands were hot and sticky. She ripped off the gloves and reached for a fresh pair.

"How many more boxes?" Zoe asked wearily.

Ari glanced over her shoulder. "Looks like eight. It's taken longer than I thought. Unpacking and repacking. But we're almost done. Let's divide the rest."

Zoe brushed a sweaty lock of hair to one side of her forehead. "I'm ready to get out of here." She sneezed. "Don't you wish we could snap our fingers and be done? The boxes would unpack and repack themselves?"

Ari shot her a quick smile and wiggled her nose. Myths and movies.

Zoe regarded the boxes with a dubious eye. "We still need to wipe down any evidence of our search. And get you out of here before I can call the police."

Ari was grateful Zoe had suggested over lunch that Ari's visit remain secret. It would save her a lot of time and questions. "I've tried to be careful, so they shouldn't find any unexplained prints."

"Not sure they'd care you were here, but it would complicate things. I'll just say you called from the States and asked me to interview Dubrey."

Their hands bumped as they reached for the next box. Ari grinned, handed it over, and took the next in line. Six more to go.

"Ari, look!" Zoe's voice was excited. "Notebooks. At last. Here, take some." She shoved two black journals at Ari.

Ari flipped the first one open. A small, spidery scrawl, sometimes drifting into uneven printing, filled the pages. Many words were technical; other cryptic entries appeared to be in a form of speed-writing, but enough was in standard English that Ari picked out the general meaning. The references to herbs and potions confirmed her conclusion. Dubrey's work notes. But the book she held was dated more than ten years earlier.

"See if there are more recent dates. This is too old."

"Nothing here." Zoe's voice had lost enthusiasm, and she

dropped the journals back in the box. "Don't see anything from recent years."

Ari ripped open the box she had just set aside and dumped the contents. More journals. Two years ago. That was better. Last year. May and June of this year. Aha! They were in business.

Heart pounding, Ari scanned the wizard's notes. After a moment, she scrunched her forehead and passed the book to Zoe.

"Can you read this? Why couldn't he use simple English?" Ari complained.

Dubrey's abbreviated writing and technical language made the process difficult, but gradually they put it together—enough to realize the secrets about Fantasy were in their hands. The long years of research, hoping to combine magic and science into magical cures. The early deaths of local lycanthropes and vampires who had been purchased as test subjects from unscrupulous Otherworld leaders. Sold like slaves. Dubrey's original goals might have been worthy, improving modern medicine, but he'd always been an evil man.

They repacked everything except the most recent notebooks and took those back to the guest house. Zoe accessed the Internet, searching for a key to decipher the abbreviations. If they could read the full notes, maybe they'd confirm the goal of the recent experiments. Dubrey wasn't motivated by money. But having total control over a vampire? Ari thought that was something that would intrigue him.

After forty-five minutes of muttering at the computer, Zoe slapped her hands on her knees. "I can't find a thing. This shorthand must be his own invention. Maybe somebody in your FBI could do it."

After noting Zoe's growing frustration, Ari wasn't surprised by her lack of progress, but calling in the FBI was out of the question. "Listen, Zoe, we can't turn this stuff over to any human authorities, here or in the States. What if the latest formulas got into the wrong hands…?"

"I know. That FBI comment just popped out." Zoe rose from

AWAKENING THE FIRE 177

the desk. "It already occurred to me that we can't trust humanity to protect it. I'll contact my Magic Council, tell them everything. They'll know what to do."

Ari nodded in relief, satisfied they were on the same page. "Good idea." She picked up the newest of the journals. "Let's take these with us, just to be safe. You can hand them directly to the Council." Ari hesitated. "But I need a favor."

Zoe cocked her head. "Name it. And I'll see what I can do."

"The broken thumb drive."

Zoe pulled it from her pocket, turning it over in her fingers. "What about it?"

"Forget you saw it." Ari stuck out her hand. "Maybe it's useless, but my PD's cyber crimes guy is very good. And I trust him."

Zoe tossed it into Ari's outstretched palm. "What thumb drive?"

Chapter Twenty-Two

It was dusk by the time Zoe and Ari made their way down the overgrown drive. Zoe carried a box of journals. Ari hurried to push back the encroaching branches. She sniffed and rubbed her nose with the back of her hand. It felt stuffy from dust. A shower would be good. She glanced over her shoulder, relieved to get away from the overwhelming gloom of the decaying mansion and the dead body. As they reached the last bushes, Otherworld energy set Ari's witch blood racing. She stopped so abruptly that Zoe bumped into her back, pushing them through the brush and spilling the journals on the ground. Recovering quickly, she stared at the two vampires leaning on the hood of Zoe's car. Ari wiggled her fingers at Zoe and stepped forward, away from the precious notebooks.

The vampires straightened, watching them with cold eyes. The burly, dark-skinned bruiser with silver chains on his vest kept his arms crossed in a show of male dominance. The older vamp, a Caucasian with every visible inch of skin covered in tattoos, grinned, showing his fangs.

"You know these guys?" Ari asked, making no attempt to lower her voice.

Zoe took the cue. "Sebastian's goons. Get away from my car," she said, stopping in front of the guy with the chains.

He didn't move.

"Sebastian sent us to get you," said his tattooed partner,

staring at Ari. He sounded tough. He *looked* tough.

Ari turned her head to Zoe, pretending ignorance. "Who's Sebastian?"

"Local vampire prince. Not a very friendly dude."

Heeding Andreas's warning, Ari shook her head. "Sorry, guys, no time for a visit today."

"Make time." The guy with the tattoos, obviously the spokesman, flexed his shoulder muscles. "Sebastian wants to see you."

"About what? I have a plane to catch. The airlines don't wait."

"Neither does Sebastian." His tone was surly now, and he ignored her question.

Ari debated what to do. She was pretty sure she and Zoe could take them, but she hated to start trouble she couldn't finish. When Ari was safely in the States, what trouble would Zoe have with Sebastian's court? Besides, Ari couldn't help but wonder why Sebastian wanted to see them, or how he'd known to find them at Dubrey's estate.

She tapped her watch. "My plane leaves in two hours and fifty minutes. I intend to be on it. Until then, I might be willing to chat, if we can be quick about it."

"Are you sure about this?" Zoe had dropped her voice, making Ari wonder how often Zoe dealt with vampires and their superior hearing.

Ari shrugged. "I don't have anything better to do between now and then. And Prince Daron would want me to pay respects on his behalf."

She wasn't ignoring Andreas's warning, but there was something to learn here. No matter what Andreas said, she couldn't let the opportunity get away. So what if Sebastian and Daron weren't friends? How big a deal could that be?

The vamps reached for Zoe's car doors.

"Hey, guys. This isn't a done deal yet. I need your boss's assurance I'll make my flight." Ari crossed her arms. She wanted Sebastian's agreement, but she was also stalling for time. Time and an opportunity to get the notebooks out of sight.

The vampires looked at her as if uncertain what to do next.

"Well, call him," she said.

"You don't call Sebastian." The dark-skinned vamp blurted the words.

"Why not? Doesn't he have a phone?"

"'Course he has a phone." The guy with the tattoos again.

"Then call him or give me the number. I'll talk to him."

Still looking uncomfortable, the tattooed guy pulled out a cell phone and walked several yards away, motioning for his buddy to join him.

Ari turned to Zoe, pointed to the notebooks and then the trunk. Zoe nodded. Hoping the vampires were too busy to pay close attention, Ari whispered, "This is your opportunity to bail. You don't have to come unless they insist. I'll take care of this. If we split up, you'd be available to mount a rescue."

"That was a very nice try, Ari, but forget it. I'm sticking. Can't let you have all the fun."

"That's fine. But remember that I offered." Ari gave her a brief grin. "Now tell me about your badass prince."

While they picked up the notebooks and filled the trunk, the vamps watched from a distance, absorbed in their phone conversation.

"Never met Sebastian," Zoe confessed, "but he's one of the older vampires that migrated from Europe, and everyone's scared of him. He's into torturing people, even his own. You cross him, you disappear. Regarding his ties to the drug trade or Molyneux, I can't even guess. Nothing would surprise me. Wish I had more for you, but Sebastian doesn't allow me any contact. Not even through the Magic Council. I rarely see the vampires."

The prince was a real charmer, Ari thought. But not so unusual for what she knew of the old ones who hadn't adapted to modern society. Made Prince Daron seem like a saint. Ari stole a quick glance at the two vampires. They were arguing. Maybe setting up a meeting hadn't been such a good idea.

"So how do you do your job," Ari asked, "when your

Council has no authority over the vampires?"

Zoe shrugged. "This is a large Otherworld community. Believe me, I have enough to do without them. Sebastian is chief judge and executioner in his own territory, and he keeps his people away from the human population. Mostly." She turned away to put the last journal in the trunk. "I've heard they use human blood donors. I just hope they're willing."

Ari frowned, still watching the vamps argue. "It's a different world up here. Almost like the vampires don't exist."

"Until something like this happens." Zoe followed Ari's gaze to the argument. "That doesn't seem to be going well."

The tattooed guy broke away and stomped toward them. It struck Ari that he seemed familiar, but maybe it was just the scowl on his face. He wasn't happy with whatever decision had been reached. He stopped in front of Zoe. "You. Get in the car. Pierre will go with you. You," he pointed a finger at Ari, "come with me."

"No way. Not until I hear what's going on." Ari wasn't about to let these underlings take control. It would be bad enough once they reached the prince.

"That goes for me too." Zoe folded her arms.

He was really pissed now. The veins in his throat bulged, but his voice stayed flat. "Sebastian will meet you near the airport. You can make your flight if you don't keep wasting time."

Zoe and Ari exchanged looks. This didn't sound like the Sebastian they'd discussed. Too accommodating. He must want something really bad.

"Need to make a call first," Ari said, waving her cell phone. This rushed meeting was giving her a bad feeling. Not a witchy kind of feeling, just that stirring in the gut, that hunch that told her something wasn't right. She wanted to alert Ryan. If she didn't show up later, he could at least call out the Mounties to look for bodies.

"No calls. Sebastian said no calls or the meeting is off."

"Well, your boss is the one who's so anxious to meet."

The vamp gave her the same stone-faced look.

Non-negotiable, huh? She pocketed her phone. Ryan was too far away to help anyway. What did she care if they found the bodies? "Fine, but the Toronto Guardian and I go together or not at all. We'll follow you in our own car."

The tattooed vampire frowned but offered a compromise. "You can go together, with Pierre in the backseat. No calls. Let's go now. Prince Sebastian is waiting."

* * *

An hour later, they pulled into the rear parking lot of a modern twenty-two-story hotel. Zoe parked her VW next to the vampires' black sports car. As they entered the hotel rear entrance, additional escorts arrived to take them to the top floor. VIP suite. Vampire guards stood at every entry.

Once inside the suite, the tattooed vampire directed them toward a seating area near the large bay window. The drapes opened to the night sky, and Ari looked out on a spectacular view of Toronto's lights. Zoe chose the nearest chair and made herself comfortable, casually crossing her legs. Ari elected to stand.

Double doors opened on the left, and five vampires glided into the room. Even though the haughty demeanor of the vampire in the lead identified him as Sebastian, Ari had to stop herself from gaping. The Toronto prince was the most underwhelming vamp she'd ever seen.

Squat, stubby, but it wasn't his diminutive size that drew her attention. She didn't dare look at Zoe. Ari swallowed hard to force down a wayward giggle and peeked again at the very weird mustache dominating his upper lip. History book pictures of Hitler came to mind. The same black, bristling scrub-brush. Only larger. It couldn't be real.

Sebastian suddenly focused on her, and she forgot the mustache. A sense of malevolent loathing slithered over her. She clamped down her magical defenses. Too late. Sebastian's power pushed through her outer walls like they weren't there. Blinding pain sent her collapsing on her knees, and she squeezed her fingers to her temples.

She dropped her hands to call the witch fire, but muscled arms grabbed her from behind, trapping her hands to her sides. Throwing her body against him in a frantic attempt to break free, she knocked them both to the floor, but her hands remained imprisoned. Curling in against the pain, Ari teetered on the edge of panic.

A sudden rush of heat flared in her head, a mental door slammed shut, and the pain lessened. Sebastian's intrusive magic battered unabated against the barrier. She couldn't push him out, but the certainty grew that he wasn't going any farther.

The pressure seemed to last forever. In reality, it was only seconds. Then Ari was able to think clearly again. She relaxed her struggles, and as soon as the guard let go, she shot to her feet. Five vamps formed a circle around her. Zoe's arms were held by two others, a knife at her throat.

Sebastian stared at her with cold, calculating eyes. "Interesting. Have a seat, Guardian. I am sure you would be more comfortable." His words, even recited in a soft, singsong voice, were not a request.

She sat. It was a minor issue, and Sebastian had made his point. By some miracle, Ari had blocked him, but she had no idea how she'd done it. Or how to do it again.

"Tell me, Ms. Calin, how do you like our city so far? Is it not fabulous? I believe this is your first visit."

Well, hell, now he wanted to chitchat? "I find it…overrun with dead things."

"How unfortunate. I thought we provided a rather lively nightlife. What would you say, Ms. Vesper?" A benign smile beamed at Zoe.

Released by the restraining guards, Zoe stretched to her full height. "You can leave me out of this, Sebastian. And in the future, if you have anything to say to me, do it through the Magic Council."

He barely spared her a glance. "I was merely being polite,

my dear. I have absolutely no interest in you or your Magic Council."

"So what do you want?" Ari asked, grabbing the offensive. "I have a plane to catch. If there's a reason for this meeting, beyond your obvious power demonstration, let's get on with it."

The guards watching her stirred, but Sebastian kept a smile painted in place.

"So impatient. Part of your American manners, I suppose. Very well. We shall *get on* with it. What brings you to my city? We rarely have foreign visitors, especially from the States. And never from Riverdale." His smiled broadened, displaying yellowed fangs.

Ari shrugged. "Nothing that concerns you."

"But everything concerns me. You visited the wizard. Why?"

"How did you know we were there?" she countered.

Sebastian giggled, an unexpected sound that made her skin crawl. "I know everything." He spread his hands in a wide arc. "Or I will when we are finished." His reptilian eyes focused on Ari. "Would you like to answer my question now? Or do you need further persuading?"

No thanks. Not the kind of persuasion he could deliver. Besides, what did she lose by telling him? Maybe she'd learn something useful if she dropped a hint or two.

"I wanted to talk with Dubrey about drug trafficking. Do you know anything about his drug experiments on vampires?"

Sebastian studied an invisible speck on his sleeve. "Experiments? On vampires? It sounds highly unlikely. Enlighten me."

"A drug called Fantasy. That Louie Molyneux is busy distributing to the vampires in Riverdale." Ari watched closely, but Sebastian gave nothing away, except by his silence. And that could mean something — or nothing. "Do you know Louie?"

Sebastian smiled. "You tell me. You seem to have all the answers."

"I think he works for you," she said boldly. "Or maybe you

work for him," she added, seeing if she could prick his pride. "And you're both connected to the wizard. Did you order Dubrey's death? I can't help but wonder why. Afraid he was going to control your mind?"

Sebastian giggled again. "How accusatory you are. It all sounds so fanciful. I have no knowledge of such matters. I am very distressed that you believe me capable of such bad behavior." His singsong voice rang with insincerity.

Ari snorted. Bad behavior? More like evil. Zoe stirred beside her. Anticipating more action? Reminding Ari to tread lightly?

"How is my old friend, Prince Daron?" Sebastian asked abruptly, a jovial smile creasing his face.

Ari chose her words with care. "I wouldn't know. I'm not personally acquainted with Prince Daron."

"No? Did I misunderstand?" The prince cocked his head. "I thought my people said you were bringing a greeting from his court."

"I lied."

Sebastian covered his giggle with a lace handkerchief. "A pity. But you know his lieutenant, Andreas, I believe. Another very old friend of mine."

"Isn't that nice. I'll be sure to tell him you said hey."

Sebastian's eyes slitted. "You are a disagreeable witch, and you have involved yourself in matters that do not concern you. If you hope to live a long life, Guardian, stay out of my affairs."

"By affairs, do you mean the drug traffic? Or the murder of the wizard? Your old friends in Riverdale will be so disappointed that you threatened me." Ari knew she should stop pushing. Sebastian had already proven he could breach many of her defenses. She braced for his reaction.

A wicked smirk crept across the old vampire's thin lips. "If Daron or Andreas object to my behavior, tell them to come see me." His nostrils flared above the bristles as he waved an imperious arm. "Get these females out of my sight. I have heard more than enough." He left through the double doors, another giggle escaping his lips. His departure left behind a power vacuum in the room and a dry taste in Ari's mouth.

The guards hustled the guardians down the elevator. The tattooed vampire's face twitched, obviously disappointed Sebastian had let them go. As soon as Ari closed the passenger door of the VW, Zoe floored it. She was as anxious as Ari to put distance between them and the vampires before someone had second thoughts. They didn't speak until they were more than half a mile away.

"What the hell was that about?" Zoe demanded.

Ari swore under her breath. "I don't know, Zoe. Way too weird." Ari clasped her hands together to stop the post adrenaline trembling. "If he wanted to scare me, he succeeded. Beyond that, I'm not sure. Did they hurt you?"

"I'm fine." Zoe glanced at her passenger. "But how about you? For a minute there…"

"Yeah. It was close."

Zoe drove straight to the airport. Once Ari was safely in the air, Zoe intended to take the whole story to the Magic Council. The wizard's death, the notebooks, the confrontation with Sebastian.

While on the drive, Ari remembered to ask about Molyneux and his wolf pack.

Zoe started nodding right away. "I know the perfect wolf to ask." When she pulled into the airport parking, she used her cell phone for a few minutes, then flipped it closed.

"Molyneux's in town all right. Or he was. Seen in a local bar late Saturday night. My contact Pepe says Louie works for anyone who pays. And he's worked for Sebastian before."

"And the others? Sheila and the pack?"

"Not seen around here for weeks. According to Pepe they have their own small pack. Sheila, Louie, their various siblings, and a couple of cousins. I'm familiar with most of them. Lowlifes."

"How big a pack?"

"Three Montgomerys, five of Louie's family, plus the cousins. Ten at least."

"Sounds like we have the entire clan in Riverdale." Ari opened the VW door and stepped out. She leaned on the window frame and made eye contact with Zoe. "Sebastian was fishing back there. Wanted to know how much we knew. In my book, that says he's guilty as hell. Watch your back."

"And you do the same. What do you think he'll do next?"

Ari didn't know what to tell her. Events were rushing forward faster than she could figure them out.

Chapter Twenty-Three

Once she made it home, Ari slept until noon. She finally crawled out of bed, made the coffee, and found two messages on her cell phone: Ryan and Zoe. She called Zoe first.

"Is there a problem? Something went wrong?"

"Not in the way you mean. The Magic Council took it well—even your part—and thought it was an excellent idea you had returned to the States. They felt Sebastian might take some action if you stayed." Zoe chuckled. "The Council already has the computer, CDs and journals in custody. Somebody on our staff was very busy last night."

Ari let out a breath of relief. That was one major concern off her shoulders.

"But that isn't the reason I called," Zoe said. "Louie Molyneux's body washed up on the beach near Lake Shore Blvd this morning. Coroner says he's been dead less than eight hours. Thought you'd want to know."

Speechless, Ari sucked in her breath. She hadn't seen that coming. His death wasn't so surprising, but the timing brought her up short.

"Ari? Did you hear what I said?"

"Yes, Zoe, I heard. How'd he die?"

"Neck snapped. No other marks."

"Quick and clean. Vampire."

"Like Sebastian?"

"Well, not him personally. But he ordered it. Isn't that how you said he handles things? People disappear? I mentioned the wolf last night and now he's gone. If Molyneux wasn't such a dirtbag, I'd feel bad about it."

"Yeah, I hear your sorrow," Zoe said dryly.

In a strange way, Ari *was* sorry. The witnesses in this case, anyone who could explain what was happening in Riverdale, were being picked off, one by one. And whether Sebastian was eliminating competition or covering his ass, the sneaky toad was involved in this right up to his funny mustache.

* * *

The rest of the day was a lost cause. Uncomfortable or unpleasant, often both. When she stopped to let Claris know she was back, her best friend became alarmed, almost to tears, about the meeting with Sebastian—and Ari had cut out most of the details.

Even Yana scolded her for going to Canada alone. Ari would have received a longer lecture if she hadn't mentioned the strange phenomenon, the mental gate that had blocked Sebastian's magical assault.

"Oh, my dear, you must have been in such grave danger for that to happen! If only your Great-Gran was here to explain this." Yana's voice broke.

Appalled, Ari thought her mentor was going to cry. She could almost see Yana ringing her hands on the other end of the phone. "I don't get this. You sound more concerned about this gate thing than about Sebastian. What's wrong?"

"Wrong? Everything. No, that isn't what I mean. It's really good news. It was the fire spirits that came to your rescue. A fire shield. A rare protection that usually accompanies other abilities that haven't surfaced. At least not yet. It is as I hoped or feared. Since you're witch powers weren't nourished in childhood, they're emerging as you need them. Oh, dear, this isn't how it's supposed to happen. You need training to control these things.

Do be careful, Arianna."

How could she be careful about something she'd never heard of? Ari hadn't heard Yana so flustered before. She demanded a better explanation, but the nymph refused until they could meet in person.

"I need time to think, Ari, and do some research. I'm not a witch. Oh, why couldn't this have happened years ago?" Yana promised to visit Ari tomorrow evening and explain everything.

The conversation added to Ari's frustration. She was tired and discouraged. Now her friends were ganging up on her.

When she met with Ryan at his office, he disapproved of almost everything she'd done in Canada. Like she'd planned for it all to happen. He wasn't even happy she'd brought back the thumb drive, claiming she'd tampered with evidence. Ari had sighed but said nothing. She wasn't looking for trial evidence, just information. They both knew this case wouldn't be settled in a human courtroom. Ryan still had a scowl on his face when he took the thumb drive to the lab for data recovery.

And Andreas. Ari didn't think he had any room to complain. He'd warned her about Sebastian, but just barely. Not enough. She wondered if he'd suspected Sebastian from the beginning. When she stopped at the club to ask him, he chewed her head off the moment she mentioned Sebastian's name.

"Trust you to go off and do exactly what you were warned against." His dark eyes flashed with annoyance.

Ari stood her ground. "Maybe if you'd told me Sebastian was behind the drugs and violence in Riverdale, I wouldn't have met with him. Although, I'm not sure we had a choice. You suspected him, didn't you? From day one."

"No, Arianna, I did not. Don't try to put me in the wrong. You broke your promise and could have gotten yourself killed."

They were standing in the middle of his office where she'd found him going over the club receipts. Ari had her hands on her hips.

"Maybe that's because someone didn't share. Unlike you, I've told you everything I know. So what's going on? Some private vampire war? Coincidental, isn't it, how everything seems to be about the vampires?" She glared at him.

"Your suspicions of me are tiresome — and wrong." Andreas walked away from her.

"Really? Sebastian said he knows you well. Have you talked to him recently? He made a point of saying he knows you and I are friends. "

Andreas swung around; his gaze sharpened. "Did he? Now that is the first interesting thing you've said tonight. Very interesting. He must have a spy in town."

"Well, duh. Molyneux was here." Ari knew she was being bitchy, but she was more than annoyed by the way her friends and partners had reacted to her trip. She hadn't gone looking for trouble, but if she hadn't talked to Sebastian, she still wouldn't know who was behind this whole drug scheme.

Andreas paid no attention to her attitude. "The spy has to be someone else. I was not with you when you visited Molyneux. That was Steffan."

"Fine. Maybe Molyneux saw us somewhere else. It doesn't matter. And don't try to change the subject. I still think you're hiding something."

Since the conversation had deteriorated to bickering, Ari went on patrol.

* * *

Thursday morning she woke in a better mood. A full night of sleep had improved her perspective. Although her friends were overly protective, she decided they meant well. She patched up the disagreement with Claris by phone, then she called Yana. They talked for an hour. Ari said she was sorry; Yana admitted she'd overreacted. Her mentor even laughed when Ari described Sebastian's mustache. Yana still wouldn't talk about the fire shield until they met that evening, but today that short delay seemed acceptable. Satisfied two parts of her life were back in sync, Ari made early rounds throughout Olde Town, stopped at her office in the afternoon to write a lengthy report on the Toronto trip, and started home.

She glanced at the setting sun and hurried her steps. It was late, near dusk. The report had taken longer than she thought. She didn't want to keep Yana waiting. Her mentor was bringing dried herbs for a new potion, and Yana would insist on explaining the details of its various applications. Ari wanted to allow plenty of time for dinner and a long discussion regarding the mysterious fire shield, an ability Ari had never heard of before yesterday. She was making a mental checklist of restaurants they might try when she turned onto her street and saw the first of the flashing red lights.

Emergency vehicles crowded haphazardly around her apartment building. Her first thought was fire. Then a horrible premonition hit her, crushing out rational thought. She started to run, shoving through the onlookers. A uniformed officer grabbed for her arm, but she pulled away.

"Miss, you can't go over there! This is a crime scene."

Ari saw cops near the front steps and a mound of rumpled clothing.

She heard calls for her to stop. Ryan stood near the entrance door. He heard the commotion and turned to intercept her. Ari tried to push past, but Ryan grabbed both arms and held on.

"No, Ari. You don't want to see this."

She looked at his face, a sudden rush of fear constricting her throat. "Yana?"

Ryan's face was ashen.

Anguish punched her in the gut. "No! Oh, please, no!" She struggled to get loose, and another cop came to assist Ryan. Her self-defense training must have kicked in, as she delivered sharp blows to bodies and shins until she broke free. Scrambling away, she dodged the reaching hands of the evidence techs.

By the time Ryan reached Ari again, she had Yana's body clutched in her arms, rocking back and forth. Two cops tugged on Ari's arms in an attempt to remove her from the crime scene, but Ryan waved them off.

A strange keening sound penetrated Ari's pain. When she

realized it was coming from her, she made an effort to stop. Ryan squatted by her side. He was talking to her, but somehow she couldn't comprehend his words. The world was a red haze, confined to Ari and Yana swaying back and forth. And the metallic smell of blood. Everywhere.

After a while, Ryan pried her fingers loose. When she didn't resist, he pulled her to her feet, and others moved in to place Yana on a gurney. Ari rode with the body on the way to the morgue. She spoke only once, her voice lifeless, saying she'd wait for the family.

As she sat by her mentor's body, Ari stared at the savage, gaping wounds. She didn't need an evidence lab to tell her what happened outside her apartment. Yana had been ambushed — attacked and mutilated by werewolves. The Canadian pack had come looking for Ari, found Yana instead, and left a terrible message. Ari should be the body on the slab.

Ryan returned to his investigation as soon as Claris and Brando arrived to sit with her. After a while Ari sent them home, promising to join them soon. She needed to be alone, needed to get her head wrapped around this.

Another hour passed before the clan arrived. An hour in which images floated through Ari's head in a continuing slide show. Yana and Great-Gran. Yana and eight-year-old Ari having tea. Yana in her garden, walking through the woods, appearing before the Magic Council in her white uniform, calming a drunken dwarf. A million pictures, but Ari wanted a million more. Yana had been an anchor in her life as long as Ari could remember. She couldn't imagine a world without her.

Yana's wood nymph family took her body home to be prepared for burial. Tonight was for them alone; tomorrow, a small number of close friends would witness Yana's return to the earth. Ari faced a long night ahead with nothing more to do, except think.

She wandered out the morgue doors and crossed the hospital parking lot. As she approached the grove of trees at the end, Andreas stepped into the streetlight.

At first, Ari just looked at him. "Why are you here?" she asked, her voice flat.

The vampire hesitated, seemed uncertain, and Ari cut off his explanation. "Let me guess, before you start making up some excuse. Ryan called you. And the two of you decided I need protection from the bad guys. He's busy with the...investigation." Ari couldn't yet say the word *murder*. "So you got guard duty."

"Something like that. Why else?" he agreed levelly, watching her face.

"I wish they would come after me. Settle this now. Here, tonight."

"Not the time, Arianna. You are not yourself. Perhaps an escort is warranted, under the circumstances."

And Ryan sent a vampire, instead of a cop? Or had Andreas volunteered? Ari tilted her head and thought about it. Her magic stirred and, without conscious effort on her part, reached out to touch his. Finding strength, even reassurance. She raised questioning eyes to meet his.

"I am sorry, little witch."

The simple words breached the last of Ari's defenses. She moved toward him, Andreas opened his arms and wrapped her inside. She sighed against his chest, safe, secure, for the first time in hours. Not needing to be the strong one for a while. And then the tears came. The grief bottled inside poured down her face. They stood like that for a long time.

Eventually, Ari started talking about what happened, about her love for Yana. Andreas listened without comment to her emotional freefall. Then they walked. Ari didn't pay much attention to the route, but along the way they stopped at Yana's home to get Hernando. Near dawn, Andreas left her outside Claris's door. Ari hugged her best friend, handed her the cat, and fell into an exhausted sleep.

* * *

Yana's cleansed body was wrapped in layers of white lace.

Following wood nymph tradition, the clan carried her through
the woods to a site chosen in secret and prepared during the
night. Claris and Ari were among a small band that walked with
the family. They were barefoot, and the ground under Ari's toes
was hard and cool. A young wood nymph male followed the
procession sweeping a branch of pine needles across the ground
to obliterate their passing; he'd also follow them out. Claris cried
softly, but Ari's eyes were dry. She'd run out of tears, leaving
only an overwhelming emptiness. The family sang quietly in an
ancient tongue, rejoicing for the time they had her spirit with
them, grieving now that she was gone.

When the procession reached the gravesite, each mourner
dropped white flower petals into the grave and the body was
lowered. As it disappeared from view, Ari had a sudden urge to
snatch her back. Then the moment was gone, and more petals
dropped into the grave. The nymphs' song was different now,
comforting, like a mother's lullaby to a sleeping child.

The first dirt was spread by Yana's father, the closest
relative. The others followed his lead. The smell of moist earth
and the fragrance of the lilies drifted around Ari as the dirt
trickled through her fingers. Yana's clan finished covering the
grave. Once the service was complete, branches, dried leaves
and pine needles were scattered over the site until the new grave
was invisible. The nymphs would not visit again. They had
returned Yana to the woods.

* * *

Ari spent two days holed up in her apartment, alone in her
grief and with her guilt. Guilt that she hadn't come home sooner
that day, that she hadn't been there when Yana needed her. That
she hadn't saved her friend — or died instead.

Claris and Brando tried to talk with her; Ryan left a message
each day. She didn't answer them. She knew her friends were

worried, but she didn't have the strength to reassure them. Andreas, an unexpected and curious source of comfort that first night, was giving her space. He had good instincts.

On the third day, Ari went back to work. She wasn't over the loss. She might never put it behind her, but she was ready to hunt down Yana's killers.

Chapter Twenty-Four

The bell jingled over the shop door, and Ari paused in the doorway. Claris let out a squeal, rushing to grab her in a tight hug.

"I am so glad to see you. Coffee's made," Claris said, releasing her hold and searching Ari's drawn face.

"How's the cat?"

"He's adjusting, but he misses her. He sits in the greenhouse and watches the birds from the kitchen window. He doesn't come up front much."

Ari ducked into the back room. Claris frowned, watching her, but Ari was glad her friend didn't follow. Hernando lay curled in the sunny window. He lifted his head, considered Ari with listless eyes, then tucked his head back under his tail. She patted his head.

"Buck up, old fellow. We'll make it."

When Ari carried two mugs of coffee into the shop, Claris was helping a customer. Ari pulled up a stool and looked around, sniffed the fragrant herbs. It was all so familiar. She'd been here often enough; it was like a second home. Yet today it felt different. Then again, maybe it was Ari that was different.

The sound of the front door closing as the customer left nudged her attention, and Ari shifted her gaze to Claris. The puckered brow said her best friend was still worried.

"How are you...really?" Claris asked, perching on another

of the tall stools behind the counter.

Ari handed her a mug of coffee. "I'm angry." Her voice was flat, emotionless.

"You don't sound angry."

"When I'm not angry, I don't feel anything."

"It's part of the process, I suppose. My mood's all over the place. Sometimes I feel fine for a while, then I remember. I know we'll get better."

"I don't want to get better. That's the problem." Ari didn't bother to hide the confusion she felt. "I want to stay angry. Need the anger. I'm going to find them and kill them." Ari looked at her friend's shocked face. "Does that make me as bad as they are?"

Claris reached out a hand and grabbed Ari's fingers. "No, not at all. There's nothing wrong with feeling angry, or even hating them. It's what you do with it. You're one of the good guys, honey. You know — white hat, white horse." She gave Ari a soft smile. "You'll do the right thing."

"Will I? I'm not sure I know what that is."

"You will." Claris slid off the stool when the shop bell tinkled again. "You'll figure it out." Claris turned her attention to the customer; Ari took the empty mugs to the kitchen.

She stopped just inside the kitchen to lean against the wall. This was the first time she and Claris had been seriously out of step. Claris didn't get it. Ari didn't want to be a white hat, the good guy. Or the one who did the right thing. She wanted vengeance. Her friend's words only made her feel more alone.

Hernando chose that moment to bump against her leg. Perfect timing? Cats have a way with that. Ari picked him up, cuddling his soft fur against her cheek. He rewarded her with a rhythmic purr. She wished she could take him home, but with her hours, Hernando would lead a lonely life. At the shop he was surrounded by company. Besides, he fit the cozy atmosphere.

Before leaving the shop, Ari stuffed her pockets with ingredients from Claris's shelves. Last night's hours of mixing potions and spells had depleted her supplies. Whatever happened next, Ari would be ready this time.

* * *

As Ari climbed the steps of the police station annex fifteen minutes later, Ryan exited the double doors. He stopped, questioned her with his eyes, and then continued down the stairs as she turned to walk with him.

"Tell me what you know about the attack," she said before he had a chance to ask the inevitable questions.

"You sure you want to know?"

"Of course I'm sure." Ari sounded irritable. No surprise. "We have a case to solve."

Ryan's sigh conveyed his doubts, but he answered her question. "At least five assailants. CS techs found trampled footprints behind the bushes, where they must have waited. Looks like they took her by surprise, but we found two patches of lycanthrope blood. Recovered a silver stiletto."

"Yana's stiletto," she said. "She would have fought back."

"Yes," he agreed. "Canine hairs all over the area. We're trying to match DNA, checking against the names you picked up in Toronto. But Sheila Montgomery's profile isn't in the system. They compared hairs from this scene with those from Angela Raymond's apartment. Found color matches. No proof yet, but, of course, the Canadian wolves are our primary suspects. I reissued the BOLO, upped the charges and priority." Ryan stopped next to his police cruiser and stared across the street as if he didn't know what to say next. "I'm headed to the eastside. Want me to drop you somewhere?"

Ari shook her head. "No, thanks. Wrong direction." She planned to head deeper into Olde Town, waiting for the vampires to wake. She could think of only one person who might help her in a no-holds-barred hunt to eliminate the wolves.

"OK, catch you later. We'll find them, Ari. I promise." He shuffled his feet, suddenly uncomfortable. "It's possible this was a reaction to your trip."

Ari nodded dully. She'd already figured that out. "Yeah, they blame me for Molyneux's death. I suppose they're right. I dropped his name to Sebastian. The bastard must have thought we'd already linked them."

"If it's revenge they're after, they won't quit now. And I bet the girlfriend's leading the charge."

"Yeah, Sheila. But damn, she needs to come after me — not my friends." Ari blinked back sudden tears. Not from grief, but a flash of overwhelming rage. For a moment, her body felt on fire.

"Ari, are you all right?"

"No, Ryan, I'm not," she snapped. "I just lost one of the most important people in my life, and I'm pissed." She took a deep breath. "Let's not talk about me. I just want to find her killers."

"Sorry, but I —"

"Don't be," she interrupted. "Just drop it." Ari knew she shouldn't take it out on Ryan, but being bitchy felt better than being empty. "I know you're worried, but you have to stop. What I need is to solve this case. Have you heard from Andreas?"

"We talked once or twice."

"And? What did he say?"

"Not much." Ryan looked away.

Guess that meant they'd mostly talked about her. How she was coping or not. Great.

"Anything about the cases?" she prompted. "Marcus or Gordon?"

"Nothing new. Marcus's recovery is slow, and I guess Gordon's doing fine. Andreas hinted about problems at the vampire court. He's not very talkative. Seemed on edge, but I don't know him that well. He's been out of touch so much, I finally got his cell number."

Ari's lips parted in surprise. She didn't have Andreas's personal cell number. The boys had certainly gotten chummy in the few days she was out of commission.

Ryan smirked at her obvious surprise, dug in his jacket

pocket, and pulled out a slip of paper. "Here, he said to give you the number if you asked. I won't need it now you're back."

* * *

It was still too early for the vampires, even Andreas, so she headed for her office at the Cultural Center. She kind of liked the idea of her own place to conduct business and make private calls.

The custodian smiled when he saw her unlock the office door. She must have passed some test when they didn't destroy his building that first night. He nodded as if her presence was a daily occurrence, which might not be such a bad idea.

She looked at the office with a different perspective than before. Her world had changed: scarier, more serious, maybe more grown up. Those terms weren't quite right, but close enough. Ari knew she'd changed. And the things around her needed to change too.

The desk currently stood under unprotected windows. Bad idea. She pulled and tugged until the setting was reversed. Physical activity made her feel good, the best she'd felt in days. She tried out the desk, her back now against the inner wall. Perfect. Not paranoid, just careful.

In response to a chat with the custodian, two strapping weretigers delivered a pair of file cabinets. Ari began to feel like a business professional with her own desk and file drawers. The fact they were empty didn't bother her. She had stacks of reports and folders in her apartment that would take care of that.

Satisfied for the moment, she plopped into the swivel chair, put her feet on the desk, and dialed Steffan's number. Voice mail. She left a message. Undeterred, she tried reporter Eddie West with better luck.

"Ari, how you been?"

"Fine." He hadn't known Yana, so she didn't need to get into all that. "I've been out of touch a couple days. Heard anything new about the drug traffic?"

"Not much. The drug's still available, but I've heard

complaints it's being cut. Less potent. Seems to be a good thing for the Otherworld version. Less fights."

"Huh, that's interesting. Lt. Foster didn't mention that."

"Doubt if he's noticed. No one talks to the cops about drugs." He changed the subject. "Any news on Angela's killer?"

"Nothing we can prove. But a Canadian wolf pack is up to their bushy tails in it. And a whole lot of other bad stuff. I'm going to end this, Eddie. Trust me, it'll happen."

"When it does, you'll call me?"

"You betcha."

She hung up, slowly tapping a forefinger on the desktop.

So the drugs were still circulating. Would the wolves be able to continue their drug trade with the wizard dead? Had they changed the formula again or were they cutting the amount because their stock was low? With the drugs here, it was a good bet the wolves were still in town. That was a plus. She wouldn't have to chase them to Canada. On the other hand, their continued presence meant Louie's original scheme wasn't finished.

She tried Steffan again. This time he answered on the second ring.

"Ari, just got your message." She braced for what was coming next. "I'm really sorry about Yana. I know you were close."

"We were, and it's been awful. But if you don't mind, I'd rather not talk about it."

"Yeah, it's been a year since my brother died. It takes time. Are you calling about the fight last night?"

"What fight?"

"Tigers versus lions. No one seriously hurt, but the weretigers were using Fantasy. The stuff appears to affect lycanthropes too, but less than the vamps. More like an irritant."

"I heard the dosage or purity had been cut. Maybe they can't get new supplies."

"I hope you're right, because they'll eventually run out. And we can get past this, unless they find a new cook. I'm not taking any chances. We've renewed the warnings in the lycanthrope community. What's Andreas say about the vampires?"

"Haven't talked with him since…well, you know. Ryan says there's a vamp problem, but I don't know if it's related to the drugs or not. Maybe it's more fallout from the attack on Prince Daron. I'm going to drop by the club and find out." Ari sighed. "How long do we keep putting out fires?"

"As long as it takes," Steffan answered. "What's the alternative? If a major disturbance breaks out in the Otherworld community, all of us are in trouble. Humanity's fears hover just under the surface. And that's on a good day."

Chapter Twenty-Five

Steffan's sobering words stayed with Ari after the call ended. A war between the races wouldn't just destroy Riverdale. In a world of instant news, the panic would spread across the country. The mastermind behind this was taking a terrible risk.

With that thought in mind, she headed for the door. She'd used up the afternoon; dusk had fallen. It was time to find Andreas.

As she reached for the knob, vampiric energy sent her witch blood racing, and the door swung open. Lucien, the vampire council representative, filled the passageway. Ari didn't like him, knew he didn't like her, and had no interest in talking with him today.

She scowled. "What do you want?"

As usual Lucien was dressed in a suit that made him look like a banker. Ari had a sudden vision of him as a successful executive, climbing the corporate ladder, until someone changed his career choice and he joined the ranks of the undead. On second thought, Lucien had never been that mainstream. Maybe he'd been an accountant for the mob.

Today the suit was gray, perhaps to match the hair.

"May I come in?" he asked.

She raised a brow. Way too polite for Lucien. "What do you want?" she repeated.

"I have a message for you."

Lucien was being congenial. Ari wasn't buying it. Maybe he should have shown a little courtesy at the Council meeting. "Then deliver it."

"I would prefer more privacy for this conversation. Perhaps I can come in, and we can close the door?"

"I don't think so."

Lucien's eyes dilated. "Andreas said we could trust you."

"That's nice, but I don't trust you. If Andreas has something to say to me, why isn't he here?"

"The message is not from Andreas."

Ari frowned, fast losing patience. The only reason she was still listening was because he implied Andreas knew something about this. "We're not getting very far with this conversation, are we? Either give me the message or leave." He'd picked a bad day for a chat. She pointed her chin at him and clenched her fists. Lucien clearly didn't know what to do, faced with conducting his business in a doorway or leaving before he accomplished his task. Part of Ari was amused by his dilemma, but it was wasting time. Her time.

"Oh, fine," she said, grudgingly ending the stalemate. "You can come in, but the door stays open."

She backed toward her desk, slipping behind it without taking her eyes off the vampire. Lucien pulled a chair from the conference table. As he sat, he arranged his jacket, checked the creases on his trousers. It was all for show.

Finally he spoke. "I am here on behalf of Prince Daron. He wishes to speak with you this evening."

"About what?"

Lucien's pinched face told her he didn't want to answer that. "We have had an incident." The creases on his face grew deeper. "One of the prince's staff was staked in his sleep. Normally we—"

"Who was it?" she interrupted. A heavy pulse beat in her temple. Not again. Too soon. Why wasn't Andreas the one here talking to her?

Lucien's frown became a fierce scowl.

"Who was killed?" she repeated.

"Does it matter?" he snapped. He caught himself—he'd obviously been told to play nice. "Frederick."

Ari's muscles relaxed, her heart resumed its normal beat.

"As I was saying," Lucien continued, his voice still heavy with disapproval, "normally we handle our own affairs. In this matter, the prince has decided to consult with you."

Yeah, right. Ari waited for the punch line. "Go on," she said.

"That was it. That is the message. I am here to take you to him. The prince wants to speak with you immediately."

"Consult about what? What exactly does the prince want from me?"

"He will explain when you meet."

She shook her head. "Not good enough. I'm not putting a foot outside this office with you, Lucien. Especially not to meet with the biggest, baddest vampire in the city. If Prince Daron wants to talk to me, have him come here." She wasn't sure she'd be safe even then, but she could arrange for others to meet with them. She'd learned from Sebastian just what the old ones could do. She wouldn't make that mistake again.

Lucien stared at her. "I don't think you understand the situation."

"Maybe not, but I know how to remedy that little problem."

She grabbed her cell and dug out the scrap of paper from Ryan. It rang so long she'd almost given up when Andreas finally answered.

"What's going on?" she demanded. "Lucien is here in my office."

"What has he said?"

"That Prince Daron wants to see me. He won't say why, except it has something to do with a dead vampire. This isn't another accusation of Ari is a vampire hunter, is it?"

"Unfair, Arianna. I apologized for that. Frederick was murdered in his sleep. Do you understand what that implies?"

"I think so." Among other things, it meant the vampires had a problem they couldn't handle. A daylight killer.

Lucien watched Ari during the conversation with a blank expression, but she saw the angry flicker in his eyes. She was pretty sure this "consult" hadn't been his idea.

"So, what's this got to do with me?" she said into the phone. "Come on, Andreas, talk to me."

She heard a heavy sigh. "I suggest you meet with Prince Daron and find out for yourself. I honestly don't know what he decided. And I would rather not speculate." The line was silent for a moment. "What concerns you, Arianna?"

"I don't know these guys. And no one, including you, is giving me much information. All I know for sure is a really old vamp wants to meet on his own territory. After Sebastian, I have trust issues."

Andreas chuckled. "Always honest. An invitation from Daron's court is an honor not frequently offered to outsiders."

"Yeah, well, it just feels dangerous to me. Why didn't you deliver the message?"

"The situation has been…complicated, since Frederick's death. And I didn't know they intended to approach you so soon. Would it make a difference if I told you I would be there? And guaranteed your safety?"

Ari thought it over, chewed her lower lip. Something had changed between her and Andreas on the night of Yana's death. She felt safer with him than other vampires, but did she trust him this much? Would he deliberately put her in danger? Probably not, but how could he guarantee her safety? Daron was reputed to be more than 500 years old. As old or older than Sebastian. Could Andreas stand against his prince or would he even try? Ari didn't think so. She had to be crazy to consider this.

On the other hand, Daron's request was unprecedented, a rare chance to see the inner court. It was tempting. Lucien had quit harping about the Second Chance incident, and she couldn't think of anything else she'd done recently to piss off the vampires.

Besides, Andreas would owe her.

"All right. As long as you'll be there, I'll do it," she said. She'd survived the encounter with Sebastian. Maybe her luck would hold. "But I'm not going anywhere with Lucien," she added.

"You are the most obstinate witch." Andreas's voice was both exasperated and amused. "Club Dintero. Say, forty-five minutes. Now let me talk to Lucien."

The vampires didn't talk long. When it was over, Lucien rose to leave. "Don't be late. Your absurd demands have taken Andreas from more important duties."

Since she'd won that round, Ari let him have the last word. She didn't even smirk at Lucien's back.

Chapter Twenty-Six

Andreas was waiting outside when she approached Club Dintero five minutes ahead of the agreed time. From a block away, she saw him leaning against a lamppost, casual, relaxed, as if he could wait forever. Then he saw her and straightened, his figure suddenly purposeful, a sleeping predator awakening.

"Arianna," he said as she drew near.

She smiled in return, rather uncertain. His dark eyes studied her face, and she finally looked away.

Ari hadn't seen him or talked with him since the day Yana died. They had forged an unexpected intimacy that evening, and she wasn't sure what it meant or what she thought about it. This first meeting felt awkward.

Andreas took the lead with a matter-of-fact tone. "We must hurry. I don't like leaving the prince, even in the capable hands of Lucien and Carmella."

Ari hurried to keep up with his long strides. "So you do protect the Prince?" She could do business talk. No problem.

"Yes. I am one of Daron's lieutenants. Lucien is another, and Carmella. Frederick was the fourth." He gave her a quick look. "I am telling you this because it will be helpful for your meeting with the prince."

"Can't you tell me what he wants?"

"We shall all know soon." He lengthened his stride again.

Resigned to waiting for her audience with the prince, Ari kept further questions to herself. They turned down a dark alley into the warehouse district. The big loaders and trucks had been put away, but their presence lingered in the smell of oil and gasoline. It was quiet without the roaring engines. Their steps were the only discernible sounds, except for the occasional call of a night bird and the distant hum of city traffic. They passed four long rows of buildings before Andreas stopped at the side door of a shabby warehouse.

"Once we enter, be careful what you say. Not all vampires will appreciate your candor and…unique sense of humor." He pulled a small cloth bag from his pocket. "Your bracelet. It would be an insult to wear it. Weapons?"

"None." After a long debate with herself, she'd left them at the office rather than cause a fuss. Ari dropped her bracelet in without protest. It wasn't likely her small protection charms would make a difference where she was going. She was placing a lot of trust in Andreas.

He knocked twice. A vampiress opened the door and beckoned them inside. Her fiery-red hair was cut in a short, manly style; she was dressed in what looked like black fatigues. Her stance said 'don't mess with me.'

"Andreas," she said, her voice low and sexy, belying the no-nonsense attire.

"Carmella," he acknowledged.

The female lieutenant.

"This is the Guardian?" The faint smirk said she wasn't impressed.

"Get on with it, Carmella," Andreas said.

"Very well. This way. The prince is waiting in The Blue Room."

The Blue Room? Was that kind of like The White House?

Carmella opened a door off the hallway, stepping aside so the others could enter first. It was a blue room all right. Dark blue wainscoting and a multi-shade blue carpet contrasted with white walls. There were five large oak chairs upholstered in midnight-blue tapestry. A table at the end was covered with a blue, white-edged cloth, four bottles of wine, and a grouping of glasses. The only occupants were two vampires, one was Lucien. Ari studied the other.

Prince Daron had never been a handsome man; his bone structure was too heavy, his jaw too square. His cropped, black hair was straight and coarse. But the news photos she had seen failed to convey his incredible presence. Ari felt his magical power the moment they entered the room. He made little attempt to lighten its effect. She knew he could have blocked it; Andreas did it all the time—was doing it now.

The vampires's supreme leader turned to look at Ari. She braced, remembering Sebastian's invasion. An invisible force flowed over her, probing, as a wild creature might sniff you out. It was impersonal. Not the evil she recognized in Sebastian, yet it was still a predator, looking for an opening, a weak spot. Goosebumps rose on her arms from the energy dancing along her skin. She stayed immobile, kept her eyes averted, and used every witch trick in her arsenal to strengthen her defenses. The magical assault never came. The power level abruptly dropped, and the prince moved toward them.

His movement wasn't the beautiful glide that Andreas could do but more like the flowing of an unstoppable wave. He came to a halt four or five steps in front of her. "You are part human," he said.

"Yes."

"I have not always found humans to be trustworthy."

And so the head games begin.

"And I don't trust vampires. We should get along fine."

Daron gave her a bland look. "Andreas warned me you would speak your mind."

Nothing she could say to that.

"You are the descendant of the witch Talaitha. But young to have many skills. What abilities do you possess?"

Not a good start as far as Ari was concerned. She resented the implications. Hadn't she been through this with Andreas?

And what was it with the age thing? Not everybody lived forever. This sounded like a freaking job interview. And Ari hadn't put in an application.

"Sorry, I didn't bring my resume. Why don't you just tell me what you want?"

"Arianna," Andreas cautioned.

Oh, yeah, Ari thought, he warned me vampires don't dig candor and humor. Guess that includes sarcasm.

"No, let her speak her mind. Are you not afraid of me, Ms. Calin? Most humans are." His voice held a note of perplexity and possibly warning. He closed to within an arm's length, and her witch blood reacted with a tingling in her fingers. She felt Andreas stiffen beside her. Prince Daron noticed the tension and stopped. "Andreas?" He stared at his lieutenant.

"I gave my word she would not be harmed."

The prince's head swung back to her. "Are you afraid, Guardian?"

"I would be a fool if I didn't respect your power. But I suffer from few human fears, your highness. And, I think I'm safe enough for now because you want something from me."

"No one is irreplaceable." The vampire studied her face as if trying to decide what to make of her. Then he smiled. It wasn't a bad smile. "But you are correct, I do want something. In fact, I am interested in your services. So let us relax with some fine wine while we talk. Lucien, would you do the honors?"

Within minutes, Ari found herself doing the unthinkable — sitting in a pretty blue room, deep in the heart of the vampires' court, sipping wine with the four most powerful vampires in the city. It was surreal, but apparently the games were over. Once they were settled, the prince got down to business.

"What have you been told of Frederick's death?"

"Only that he was staked in his sleep."

"That is true. His killer was not a vampire."

Ari nodded. "Not directly, but someone betrayed him. An insider, probably another vampire."

"Yes, I am afraid that may also be true," Prince Daron

conceded. "And there have been other disturbing incidents."

"Besides the attempt on your life? What incidents?"

"My prince, I must protest." Lucien's mouth had puckered, as if he'd been sucking on something nasty, the moment Ari entered the room. He couldn't contain his displeasure any longer. "The woman has no right to question you." He directed his anger at Ari. "You'll be told only what you need to know. Nothing more."

Prince Daron raised a hand to stop the angry flow. "I understand your concerns, Lucien. We may be getting ahead of ourselves, but if we come to an agreement tonight, she will need to know these details. For now," the prince turned to Ari, "it is enough to know I believe there will be another attempt on my life. And this unknown enemy has the ability to attack during the day. I trust you see the problem."

"But don't you have daylight guards? Someone to protect you while you can't defend yourself?"

Daron's look passed the question to Andreas.

"Of course we do," Andreas said. "But since we cannot identify the enemy, we can trust no one on the current staff. As you correctly pointed out, an insider was involved. Someone revealed Frederick's sleeping quarters to an enemy. Most of our day guards have been with us for years, but they are not vampires. I would trust them with my life. Not with the life of my prince."

"So you suspect everyone. No prime suspect?" She continued to look at Andreas.

"That is correct. We have a traitor, but unfortunately, I do not know who."

"So what's all this got to do with me?" Ari asked, turning her head to address Prince Daron. She wasn't sure where the conversation was headed.

"We will find those who betrayed us. Until we do, I need someone who can provide for my protection during the day. Take charge of the daylight guards and prevent the next attack. If the traitor is among the guards, I expect you to identify him."

"I can't take on a job like that," Ari said. "The Guardianship is 24/7. And the vampires aren't the only ones with problems." Too restless to sit still, she got abruptly to her feet. The vampires, except the prince, reacted by springing between her and the prince. Lucien crouched, fangs showing; Carmella held a wicked-looking knife. Andreas had his arms out, blocking both sides.

Ari straightened from her own defensive reaction to them. Her witch blood raced. "Sorry about that. Really." She showed them her hands, palms up. "I didn't mean to alarm anyone. I think better on my feet. But look at us. If you needed proof your proposal wouldn't work, here it is. How can I help you when we don't trust each other?" Her explanation didn't appear to make Lucien and Carmella much happier, but Carmella put the knife away.

Daron sighed heavily.

Andreas stepped into the breach. "We wouldn't ask you to do this, except there is no one as qualified. You're the Guardian, a neutral party with exceptional skills. Our court is requesting assistance from you and the Magic Council. That shows a certain level of trust. Can you afford not to listen?"

"Why didn't you apply directly to the Council? Why come to me?"

"We chose to limit our public exposure in this matter. If we reach an agreement, Prince Daron will inform the Council President."

She studied Andreas's face, but his lean features and hooded eyes told so little. The vampires were still hiding something. She wanted to refuse—she had her own mission to find the wolves—but Andreas had played their ace in the hole. He'd asked for the Council's help. What choice did he leave her? Hell, she could be such a sucker.

She looked at the city's vampire leader. "You have my attention, your highness. Give it your best shot."

Daron frowned, appealed to his lieutenant.

"I believe she wants you to make your proposal."

"Ahh." The prince's mouth spread in a broad smile, revealing a flash of fangs. "Andreas tells me that money would not be sufficient, so I propose an exchange of services. You provide protection for the vampire compound from dawn to dusk. In return, the resources of this court and my first lieutenant will be at your disposal to assist with this problem of the wolves. I understand you already discussed some kind of joint working relationship." Daron smiled again, and Ari wondered exactly what Andreas had said to him.

"I can relieve him of other responsibilities, when necessary," Daron continued. "Increase his availability." He waved a careless hand. "Of course, these arrangements will end as soon as the traitors are exposed." He unfolded his large frame and stood. "Are those terms satisfactory, Ms. Calin?"

Unprecedented entry to the vampire court. Access to their resources. And the vampires would be indebted to the Council. More than satisfactory terms. But most important to Ari, Andreas would have to help her track the wolves.

She darted a glance at Andreas. She thought she'd seen a smile when Daron asked if the terms were satisfactory, but she asked anyway. "You comfortable with this?"

"My duties are whatever the prince says they are."

That answer didn't help much, but it raised another question. She turned to Daron. "How can you offer me one of your lieutenants right now? Don't you need him here, protecting the court?"

Daron scowled and exchanged a look with Andreas.

"Fine," she said in exasperation. "You're still holding out, hiding something. It's your call. But in that case, I'm out of here."

Andreas grabbed her arm before she got more than two steps. "I suggest we tell her the rest of it," he said over his shoulder.

"Then do so." The vampire prince dropped back into his chair.

Ari brushed Andreas's hand away. "Well?"

"Solving one problem may solve both," Andreas admitted.

"The attacks on the court, the drug activities around town, all of it may be at Sebastian's orders. The moment he met with you in Toronto, I feared his ambitions had caused him to look in our direction."

"The drugs I get. But why attack your court? What does he gain?"

"I told you Daron and Sebastian were enemies."

"You said they weren't friendly," she muttered. "That was the understatement of the day. If he'd go to this much trouble, this must be a feud of ginormous proportions."

"I'm not sure what that means, but this is not a simple matter of bad blood between vampires." Daron raised his voice in irritation. "Sebastian is after my court."

Ari stared at him. "But he has Toronto. No offense, but why would he give up that for Riverdale?"

"Not instead of Toronto. He wants to add Riverdale to his control. Spread his influence and power," Andreas said. "We suspect Sebastian is waging war, a challenge for the throne, without coming here or declaring himself. If he can set up a puppet leader, he would gain immense status, especially with those in Europe. And I think we can safely assume he has already selected the successor prince. Someone who will do as he dictates."

"You've known this several days," Ari said, her eyes filled with accusation. "When were you going to tell me?"

It was Daron who answered. "I asked him to wait."

"Why? For how long? Until somebody else got killed?"

"Can the recriminations wait?" Andreas was getting angry. "You and I can discuss this later. Right now, we need to make decisions about moving forward."

"Fine. I can hardly wait for our little talk."

Daron looked at his lieutenant. The corners of the old vampire's mouth quirked. "I am not sure I pay you enough." He wiped the amusement from his face before he turned to Ari. "Does this mean you accept?"

Did it? In typical vampire fashion, both parts of this

agreement benefited the vampires the most. But if they were right, someone in Riverdale had done terrible things in support of a madman's ambitions. The deaths and violence needed a settling of scores. Ari wanted to be part of that. She'd felt the evil in Sebastian. If she had anything to say about it, that little toad would never control her town.

Ari lifted her chin and looked the vampire prince straight in the eye.

"Yeah, you have a deal."

Chapter Twenty-Seven

Leaving the warehouse district, Ari and Andreas walked in the general direction of her apartment. She'd gotten over most of her snit, for the moment anyway.

"Are you really fine with being part of this deal?" she asked.

"I already promised to help you."

"Yes, but offering and being ordered are different. What about the club?"

Andreas dismissed her concerns. "The club has an excellent staff. And Daron did not order this without my agreement. He isn't the dictator you think, but we don't have time to talk about the prince. Too many other things to explain before dawn arrives."

Ari listened with rapt attention as Andreas revealed detail after detail about the secretive vampire court. He started with an overview of the current daylight guards: three werelions, a werewolf and a halfling demon. All five had worked with the vampires for years with no smudges on their loyalty. Ari perked up her ears when he said the halfling's abilities included demon fire. She'd never met another being with fire ability, except Great-Gran. The demon part gave her a moment of hesitation— even a halfling could be evil—until she remembered she'd just agreed to protect a nest of vampires.

Without telling more than necessary, Andreas described the

general layout of the compound. The security station inside the side door held a secret entrance to Prince Daron's sleeping quarters. Beyond that hidden door was a complicated labyrinth of passageways.

"Without a map or detailed instructions, no one could locate the prince's chambers. Not before they were discovered."

"Then why do you need me?"

"We have a traitor. Someone may have revealed the path, drawn a map."

Ari blinked. "But I thought the passage was secret. Who would know the way…other than you, Carmella and Lucien?"

Andreas shrugged. "Nest leaders, court personnel, guards, maybe a few tradesmen. Most of the chambers are only secret to the outside world. Not to vampires. Daron's actual sleeping quarters are private, but a simple process of elimination could get you there if you already knew the layout. The entire complex is like a community center in some respects."

"How many entrances? Rooms? Corridors?" Ari flung out her arms. "This must cover an entire city block. A rabbit warren."

His lips twitched. "It is not as bad as that. There is only one way into the inner chambers. It is true," he said in response to her sudden scowl. "Daron believes that one entrance is easier to defend. The court is heavily fortified at night. And if we are asleep," he gave a rueful shrug, "what good is an escape route?"

"But that's such a stupid idea!" She put up her hands at his sharp look. "Never mind. We'll deal with it. But if one of the daylight guards is on the enemy payroll or someone else has talked, your only entrance and exit has been compromised." She sighed. "Fine, I've got the basic set up. Tell me about the other incidents the prince mentioned."

As Andreas talked, it didn't take long for Ari to see some possible links between the court problems and the wolves. Daron's attacker had been a deliveryman, a werewolf employed by the blood bank for less than three months. His background check turned out to be falsified, and they had no idea who he was. Six weeks before that Carmella had been ambushed by a vampire, another stranger to the Riverdale area. Three weeks later a wolf offered to pay, and pay well, for information on the vampire compound. The young vampire he attempted to bribe reported the incident, but by the time the wolf was located, he'd been shot to death. Again, he wasn't a local. In typical vampire fashion, the body was hidden.

"If you had reported it, we might have run DNA or something," she said as they crossed 10th Street and turned left onto a shaded boulevard.

"At the time, it seemed unimportant."

Ari suddenly looked at him. "That's what you were doing in Goshen Park when we first met. Following a suspicious wolf. As it turns out, you were right. I wonder if the kids interrupted a drug deal or a meeting with a local contact. Guess I should have killed Molyneux that night. You might have mentioned your earlier suspicions. You've kept a lot of secrets."

"Private vampire business. Up to the moment Sebastian questioned you, we had no proof our affairs affected the larger community."

Vampire business. As if that explained everything, she thought. To him it might. Vampire society had been closed to outsiders for centuries. But, dammit, if she had known from the beginning, it might have helped. She released a weary sigh. If their current arrangement was going to work, they'd have to get beyond the past.

"I'm curious, Andreas. You work with werecreatures, even a halfling demon. Why no witches or other conjurers before now?"

Andreas's eyebrows shot up. "I am surprised you have to ask. Have you no knowledge of the long-standing conflicts between the O-Seven and the Witches League? Their struggle for domination in the Old Country?"

"I've never even heard of the O-Seven. But what's some fight in Europe got to do with your court or what you do over here?"

"It was not just 'some fight.' The council of the seven original vampires—who are thousands of years old, by the

way—and the witches' covens nearly destroyed one another in
1329. In my country, no witch would consider aligning with a
vampire. With your abilities, she would be more likely to try to
burn us out."

"That seems harsh." Ari shrugged. She couldn't remember
Great-Gran mentioning a special problem with the vampires.
Except for them being violent predators, of course. For the
witches, the feud must have stopped at the ocean. For the
vampires, not so much. "So these old vamps are still holding a
grudge, huh? Somehow that doesn't surprise me."

She fell silent, losing interest in the O-Seven and focusing on
the other things she'd heard tonight. Headlights from a passing
car swept over them and highlighted the familiar surroundings.
Another two blocks and they'd be on her street.

"Out of questions?" he asked.

"Just figuring out what I haven't asked. It's a lot to take in.
The vamp who was killed, Frederick. How'd the killers get to
him but not the rest of you?"

Andreas swung his head to look at Ari. "I don't understand
the question."

"You live together, don't you?"

"Lord, no. Occasionally we might stay at the compound, but
that is unusual. We have our own homes. Frederick lived with a
human consort who guarded his sleeping hours. She was killed
during the attack. Shot three times. She hadn't been tortured, so
the killers knew exactly where to find his hidden chamber when
they arrived."

"And who would know that?"

Andreas shook his head. "It is not information freely
shared."

"Well, someone shared. The consort must have betrayed
him. Unless...could another vampire bespell her? Force her to
tell without using visible torture?"

"No, not possible." His answer was decisive. "Frederick
would have known immediately. Consorts are closely bound to
their vampire mates. It would take someone very powerful

indeed—someone as old as Sebastian himself—to overcome such resistance. The attempt would have destroyed her mind. And her willing betrayal is improbable," he continued. "Consorts often die from the breaking of a bond. Such action would invite her own death. No, Arianna, they were well mated. Their friends, including Victor, report she would have protected Frederick with her life. As apparently she tried to do."

"Then how'd this happen?"

"I have no logical explanation."

They had nearly reached Ari's front door. She still hated these steps, enough to look for a new apartment when she found the time. She made an automatic scan of the bushes. If Andreas noticed, he didn't mention it.

"I will be back at five o'clock," he said. "To introduce you to the guards." The vampire started down the steps.

"Andreas?"

He looked back.

"What about you? Who keeps you safe at home?"

A slow smile spread across his face, making his eyes glitter. "I have to wonder why you ask. Is this concern for my safety? Or that I might have a consort?"

Good question. She dropped her eyes and hedged. "Just curiosity."

He chuckled softly. As he disappeared into the shadows, his voice floated back. "Have no fears, little witch."

Which, of course, told her nothing.

Chapter Twenty-Eight

Five faces stared at Ari with a mixture of reactions: hostility, curiosity, indifference. The guards would be a tough crowd to win over.

Promptly at 5:00 a.m. Andreas had escorted her to the vampire compound. He'd already told the guards of her pending arrival, and she could imagine how the news went over. A stranger was coming to take charge.

When she had walked into the security office at Andreas's side, the guards were seated around a table with a deck of cards and poker chips in the middle. A TV ran in the background. No one, except Ari, appeared to see anything wrong with this set up. Andreas made introductions to a silent audience, then left to get home before dawn.

Now Ari was on her own.

When the determined silence continued, she finally asked, "Interested in knowing why I'm here?" Not the most original beginning, but she had to start somewhere.

"Not particularly. Already figured it out. The vampires don't trust us." The speaker was Lilith, a werelion with short black hair, a pair of size D breasts, and deep angry lines creasing her face. She wore two semi-automatic handguns, one at the waist and the other in a shoulder holster.

"Any reason for them to lose trust in you?"

"No, not really." Uncertainty flickered across Lilith's face.

"Well, maybe the attack on the prince. Which wasn't our fault," she muttered.

"Just let her tell us, Lil," the werelion next to her said.

"Why else would she be here, Russell?" Lilith spat. "We aren't so overworked we need another team member. And they put her in charge." Lilith snorted in disgust.

"I only want to talk about this once, so pay attention," Ari said, crossing the room and switching off the television. "Vamps don't trust anyone. Except maybe other vamps. And never completely even then. Not you, not me. They're suspicious and paranoid by nature. But if they thought you were a serious threat to the prince, do you really think you'd still be alive?"

She hoped a little plain talking would stop the bitching over their grievances and get them refocused on the job. Quickly.

"Frederick's death is what brought me here. The vampires are facing an enemy that kills during daylight, and the next target could be the compound itself." She let that sink in. "I'm here, on a temporary basis, because I'm the Guardian for this district and a practicing fire witch. I bring new skills to the group. Now you can get all bent out of shape if you want to, but somebody has to be in charge. For now, it's me. If you have an issue with that, deal with it. I'll be gone when this is over. In the meantime, our job is to make sure the bad guys don't win. And to do that, we have to work together."

Seconds ticked by, then Russell asked, "Do you play poker?" The cards made a soft slapping sound as he shuffled the deck.

Ari gave him a faint smile. "I know the difference between a straight and a flush."

So her first day on the job started with poker. It broke the ice. Not that they became instant buddies, but the tension eased. Ari tried not to disgrace herself by stupid card play while sizing up her companions. They talked freely, except for the wolf, and by the time the game ended, Ari had a pretty good idea of the team's individual strengths.

Russell was on the small side for a werelion but all muscle, even in human form. His movements were quick and smooth, very catlike. Not bad looking. Blondish-brown hair and somber, chestnut eyes. He was married to Lilith and her big guns. He admitted he knew some jujitsu, which drew laughter from his wife, who explained he held top status in four styles of martial arts.

The third werelion was Benny, a fair-haired, doe-eyed pretty boy with delicate features and a deadly stiletto. He was an outrageous flirt who Ari suspected didn't discriminate between sexes or species. He had been friends with the werelion couple for twelve years.

Ari didn't know what to make of Mike, a big, burly man, six foot three or a little more. Probably played college football. He was a werewolf, and his soft accent hinted of prior years in the Lone Star State. He didn't have much to say, and after the second poker hand he wandered off into the other room and signed on the computer. Ari couldn't ask about him while he was in hearing distance, so she filed a mental memo to ask Andreas.

The last guard intrigued her the most. She had never met a halfling demon before, but Maleban would never be mistaken for human. He was skeleton thin with a body always in motion. Brittle laugh, reddish complexion, spiky orange hair. Despite his exotic appearance, he was polite and painfully shy. Ari thought they'd get along. His bashful manner was oddly appealing. And he could breathe demon fire — a nice ace in the hole during a fight.

None of them struck her as candidates for the role of traitor. But she hadn't expected anyone to stand out. If it had been that easy, the vampires wouldn't need her.

When the poker game ended, Ari declined an invitation to join Benny and Russell in a game of gin rummy. She intended to check out the rest of the security area. In the adjoining room, she found Lilith refilling her coffee mug in a small kitchenette. At the other end of the room, Mike and Maleban huddled over an impressive array of computer equipment.

If there was an entrance to Daron's chambers somewhere, it

was well hidden. Another thing she'd ask Andreas.

Despite calls to update Ryan, Claris, and the president of the Magic Council on her current activities, by noon Ari was thoroughly bored. Protection detail wasn't exciting unless something went wrong, but this amount of inactivity was bound to lead to dulled perceptions, slow reaction times. She finally brought it up over lunch.

"How do you do this every day?" she asked when the plate of sandwiches Mike had made was almost empty. He'd had kitchen duty for today. As far as Ari could tell, duties like that took up most of the guards' time.

"Depends on what you mean?" Benny gave her a wink, which she ignored.

"It's so damned boring."

In the sudden silence, Benny laughed. "Yeah, it's a cushy job without much action. But usually we're not here every day. Not all of us. Until the attack on Daron, we came in two at a time."

"But what are your duties? Besides fixing coffee and lunch and waiting for the bad guys to attack you?" She looked at five blank faces.

"That's about it," Russell admitted, his manner a little cooler than before, a little defensive. He shoved his chair back and rested one foot on his knee. "A daily report. We keep a log of visitors." He looked at the others and shrugged.

"Did you know the vampires have had four recent breaches of security? Not all here, but each one involved the inner court members." She ticked them off on her fingers. "The assassination attempt, an attack on Carmella, Frederick's death, and a bribery attempt to get a map of this compound." Their eyes were focused on her now. Mike's heavy brows shot up when she mentioned the map. "The vampire leaders have become targets, and the enemy's growing bolder. How do we stop him? What's the next attack look like?" Ari's gaze lingered on each face, pressing for an answer.

Benny chugged his soda. "Is that a serious question? The vamps figure that stuff out then tell us what to do. We don't plan strategy."

"Why not?" Ari gave him a sharp look. "Aren't you the prince's security experts? His personal secret service?"

"Never thought of it like that," Benny mumbled.

"Well, that's a kicker," Lilith said, getting to her feet to dump her paper and plastic into the trash. "But, damn, I think she's right." She sat down again. "If we aren't anticipating the next threat, what kind of security are we?"

"I never liked all this sitting around," Mike growled. "We've kinda been rent-a-cops, but it's not what we trained for. If we're gonna keep the prince alive, we gotta be smarter than waiting for something to happen." It was a long speech for Mike.

"But the vamps protect the prince," Maleban argued. "We warn off nosey strangers. No one expects us to stop a serious assault."

"Well, things have changed," Ari said. "Frederick's killer wasn't another vamp. It was someone who struck during the day, when the vampires can't protect themselves. It's up to us to fill that hole. Are you telling me you can't or won't do that?"

Lilith put an end to the chorus of angry protests by asking the obvious question. "What do you expect us to do?"

"Be ready for everything."

* * *

It didn't take long to go over the current set up or for Ari to realize the vampires had depended on their reputations to protect them. The only security was the complexity of the tunnels and a simple screening process.

"We have a lot to do," she said. "For starters, a warning system and additional weaponry. What else? Mike, how would you go about killing the prince?"

The werewolf blinked his eyes. Finally he said in that soft Texas drawl, "I'd blow up the building and torch what was left."

A snort of laughter. Even Ari was surprised. This guy didn't mess around, but he had a valid point. A bomb or sudden fire would be a real threat. The warehouse would go up like a tinder box.

"So who does the building checks, inside and out?"

Russell's mouth dropped open. "Shit, Ari. No one."

"Then that's our priority. Starting now, we patrol the exterior. We'll secure the interior with a room-by-room check. Every box, every bag, check all the original doors into the warehouse and make sure they're secured. Check everything. I want to know this building hasn't already been compromised."

They dispersed, and within an hour they'd swept the building for unfortified entrances or dangerous objects, including explosives. Several items were removed, including two battered gas cans, and two doors required additional bracing. Nothing looked deliberate or suspicious and the building was cleared, except for the locked storage next to the security office. Ari was tempted to break down the door but decided it would be prudent to wait for Andreas and the key.

Russell volunteered for the perimeter checks. He slipped out for a circuit of the building every hour the rest of the day. They kept planning, tossing around possible scenarios and solutions, so caught up in their work that Andreas's arrival surprised everyone. In fact, they'd just been discussing how the vampires might react to the changes when he strolled in the door. Ari figured they all looked guilty as hell.

Chapter Twenty-Nine

A slight smile played at the corners of Andreas's mouth as he watched the team scatter. Whatever had put him in such a good mood, Ari hoped it would make him open-minded to the changes she wanted.

No one on the team said a word about their plans as they passed him on the way out. They trusted her to deal with Andreas, and she hoped she could pass this first hurdle. If she couldn't, they'd never respect her as team leader.

"They cleared out in a hurry," Andreas said when the door closed behind the last of them.

"Guess they had plans." She knew exactly what those plans were. They were scaring up more firearms. She'd asked them to bring whatever they were comfortable using, and extra ammo. Natural abilities were great; weapons added another dimension.

"Any problems I should know about?"

"No, everything went smoothly. Got some ideas for improvements."

"Would those have anything to do with Russell being outside the building so often?"

"Who told you?" Ari demanded. "You've got someone spying on us?"

He gave her a smug look. "No one told me. I saw him."

"You couldn't have. You were asleep."

"I still saw him." Andreas's eyes crinkled with humor.

"Come, I'll show you." He led her into the hallway and stopped in front of the locked storage room, producing a key.

When he swung the door inward, her mouth dropped open. "Wow, what is all this?"

The center of the room was filled with shiny equipment. A set of large screens covering all four walls displayed multiple views inside and outside the building. Andreas pushed a button and a picture of Russell walking up the alley appeared on one of the screens. The time and date displayed at the bottom. A different screen picked up Russell's image each time he turned a corner.

Andreas grinned at Ari's reaction and pushed more buttons. Hallway scenes began playing of the earlier building search.

"There are cameras all over the place."

"They automatically record hallway and exterior activity each day. I often review the recordings by remote, like today."

"And your security team knows nothing about this?" She frowned at him. Ari was incredulous—and indignant.

His mouth quirked. "They are now called the security team?" Not waiting for a response, he went on. "The camera system is new. Installed after the attack on the prince. By that time, we did not trust anyone. Only Daron, Lucien, Carmella, and I know about it."

"So you were spying on the guards."

Andreas shrugged. "I was being careful," he said. "Of everyone who came near or into the building."

"Can't believe we didn't notice the cameras." As a matter of fact, Ari was more than a little embarrassed. True, they'd been looking for explosives hidden inside the rooms, not surveillance equipment in the hallways, but it was a bad start.

"You seem upset," Andreas said. "I would be disappointed if you had found them. The cameras were designed and installed by surveillance experts with the latest equipment. The system was intended to be invisible."

"Still…" Ari shook it off. "We can put this stuff to better use. The team should take over running it. And there's other technology to consider, some that works for you, some that we need to guard against."

She talked about cell phones, motion sensors — he'd already arranged to have them installed that night — and the need to secure landlines and the computer network, which she discovered had also been done. When she described the team's brainstorming on new procedures and additional weaponry, Andreas appeared satisfied with their progress.

"Show me how the cameras work," Ari said. "I'll put Mike and Maleban on the system tomorrow. They seem to like tech toys. Mike's pretty quiet. A hard man to know. What's his background?"

Andreas's answer was brief. "Ex-military, special forces. The rest is Mike's story to tell or not. I should warn you that he hates werewolves."

"But he is a werewolf. Oh, not natural-born, I guess."

"Indeed." Andreas busied himself with more dials, clearly closing the topic.

Before Ari finished learning the cameras' operations, the crew arrived to install the motion sensors, and she got to play with those controls too. By eight o'clock everything was done and ready for tomorrow. She only needed one last piece of information before they left.

"So where's the entrance to the prince's tunnel?"

Andreas stilled, and for a moment, he said nothing. "I should have anticipated that question." He slowly nodded. "Of course, you need to know."

He led her into the main security room, where the poker game had been, and stopped before the west wall, one of two paneled in a dark knotty pine. Ari followed his pointing finger and saw what looked like a small nail head. It turned out to be a tiny latch hidden inside a dark knot. Andreas pulled it up with his fingernail. Ari heard a definite click, and a section of the paneling silently opened inward to a dark tunnel. He pushed the latch back in place and it closed. Simple but effective.

"Clever camouflage." Ari wanted a peek inside, but the

quick closing of the entrance reminded her the secret chambers were off limits to non-vampires, including witches.

* * *

Satisfied with her first day on the job, Ari was eager to get on with her hunt for the wolves. Maybe they could find and kill the enemy before they had a chance to attack the compound. She and Andreas stepped out of the warehouse, moving quickly down the street. A brief stop at Club Dintero, then they'd cruise through the bar district.

Victor appeared the moment they walked into the club and pulled Andreas aside to confer on some management crisis. Ari slipped into an empty booth, ordering a sandwich while she waited. Andreas returned with a bottle of wine just as her sandwich was served.

"We have plenty of time. It is early yet for the bar crowd," he explained. "Do you recognize our waiter?"

Ari studied the silent young man. "Lorenzo?"

He gave her a boyish grin. "Hello, Ms. Calin. I hope you enjoy your dinner." He blushed and left.

Ari laughed at his formal speech. "Such a change. So that's what caused the big grins when we left the caves. I suppose Reno works here too."

Andreas smiled and poured two glasses of wine. "He does. I wanted to ensure they suffered no harm from our visit. Have you decided where we should start our search?"

"The strip, for sure." She listed several vampire hangouts, including the Second Chance and the Bloody Stake, and threw in a couple of wolf clubs. "And Goshen Park. The wolves are bound to run sometime."

"There are other woods."

"Yeah, but we can't hit them all. At least not tonight."

Victor reappeared with another question for Andreas, and the two men left with their heads together. This time it was something about missing receipts.

Ari leaned back in the booth, rested her head against the

AWAKENING THE FIRE 233

cushioned surface, trying to relax. It had been a tense day. The club's dim lighting, the soft music, began to have an effect. The events of the last days floated in her head like remembered scraps of a dream. And for a moment she almost grabbed onto something important to the case. Something Andreas had said. But she couldn't hang onto the thread. They had discussed so much.

"Sleeping or day dreaming?" Andreas said without warning.

Ari sat up with a jerk. "Do you have to do that?"

"Do what?" He slid into the booth, retrieving his wineglass.

"Creep up on me like that."

"I am a vampire, Arianna. What would you have me do? Wear a bell?"

"Might not be a bad idea. Do I detect sarcasm?" she teased. "I thought you said vampires had no humor."

"I said *some* vampires would not understand your brand of humor." His smile was contagious, and Ari found herself grinning back. The moment was broken by the ring of her phone. Ryan. Considering the ongoing interruptions, Ari figured they'd never finish the wine.

Ryan had the report on Dubrey's flash drive. The data was damaged beyond full recovery. Only a few e-mail headings and spotty words or phrases had been recaptured.

"But they counted more than forty e-mails between Dubrey and Molyneux."

Another link confirmed, Ari thought.

"The word 'doses' appears twice in the text," Ryan said. "And references to 'the deliveries' and 'the vampire.' Sorry, it's not much."

"Except for the confirmed contact between the two men," she amended. "That's a biggie." Ari repeated the conversation to Andreas and then returned to the phone. "It's more than we had. Thanks, I know you put a rush on it. Um, Ryan," she said, watching Andreas, "there's something else. The vampires have had more trouble than we knew. Other attacks. And they seem pretty sure Sebastian's behind it. The drugs, the violence. All part of a scheme for him to take control of the Riverdale vampires."

"Where'd you hear this?"

"From the vampires. They're expecting another attack. Not Sebastian directly, but from the wolves working for him."

"And knowing this, Andreas let you go to Canada alone?" Ryan's voice was loud enough that Andreas heard him.

The vampire held out his hand for the phone. Ari shook her head. She wasn't about to let them start another argument.

"He didn't know for sure until I got back," she told the indignant cop. "Sebastian's contact with me was what raised their suspicions."

Ryan didn't speak for several heartbeats. "It would have been nice if Andreas had shared this earlier."

"Yeah, well, we know now. Our job doesn't change. We find the wolves, stop the drugs. And leave Sebastian to Prince Daron."

When she disconnected Andreas sat with his arms crossed, staring at the table. His face was unreadable except for the tight jaw line.

"You're not mad about what Ryan said, are you?"

"No." He unfolded his arms. "I was thinking about Sebastian. How he and the wolves have used my people, his people. Tortured them." Andreas finished his wine and stood. "Shall we be on our way?"

His calm exterior didn't fool her. Ari felt his energy vibrate with anger. Andreas wanted someone to pay. She and the vampire agreed on that. She hoped she got to Sheila before he did. Otherwise, there might not be much left for Ari to kill.

* * *

Later that night, after unsuccessful hours of searching, Ari slipped out to the woods where Yana was buried. She felt more peaceful there, more in control of the pain. She wanted Yana to know she was hunting her killers. That she wouldn't give up until they were found. It would be a week tomorrow, and Ari missed her.

It was a long time before she made her way home.

Chapter Thirty

"**A**nd no one told us." Lilith stared at the tracking screens and voiced what the group was thinking. "They've watched us every day." The accusation was plain in her voice.

"Since the assassination attempt. Before you get too bent out of shape, think about it," Ari said. "Someone had just attacked the prince. They were seeing the enemy everywhere. So they took precautions. Haven't we talked about the need for more surveillance? Well, here it is. I don't like the secrecy either, but at least they told us now."

"Hey, Mike, look at this." Maleban grinned as he turned dials and poked buttons; Mike's eyes lit up. Techies and their obsessions. In this case, it was a good thing. Drawn in by their companions' excitement, the rest of the team crowded around, and resentment was set aside.

The next two days flew by. During daylight, Ari worked with the security team, established the new procedures, trained on the use of equipment, sharpened defensive skills with sparring and mock attacks. In the evenings, Andreas and Ari continued to comb the Otherworld bars and clubs, patrolling the streets and Goshen Park, watching and listening for some word that would lead them to the Canadian wolves.

Ari was surprised how well they got along. Andreas was a charming companion with a dry sense of humor. As he chatted with many of the bar owners, Ari gained an appreciation of his business skills. No wonder Club Dintero was so successful. Andreas's keen eye noted every dirty counter as well as the friendly service or the sparkling set of glasses. Ari almost forgot they were looking for killers.

Late on the first night, they approached an establishment new to the strip. Ari had never been inside. Neon lights flashed in pink and orange and black. A rhythmic beat spilled into the street. The tall, brawny vampire at the door sported leather and multiple arm tattoos. He reminded Ari of the vamp in Toronto, except this guy was even bigger.

Ari started for the door, still thinking about the tattoos and the feeling of déjà vu she'd had with the tattooed vamp in Toronto.

Andreas nudged her arm. "Are you certain you want to go inside?

"Why not?" Ari gave the place a once over. The sign read Sin & Skin. Knowing vampires, that could mean anything. "Is it illegal?"

"Not exactly," he said dryly. "It is a vampire strip club."

"Male or female strippers?"

"Female usually. Both upon occasion."

"Oh. Well…" Women were definitely not her cup of tea. Nor were strip clubs for that matter, but no big deal either. "Nothing I haven't seen before. Might be the kind of place our wolves would go."

Ari strode toward the door. The bouncer checked them out, quirked a look at Andreas, and motioned them through the entrance.

The club was dark and smoky; it smelled of beer and cigarettes. Prior to the no smoking bans, this had been typical bar atmosphere throughout Riverdale. Now only the vampire strip remained immune to the bans. Since vampires, and most Otherworlders for that matter, didn't have to worry about lung cancer, smoking was allowed. Ari thought they should show a little more consideration for the human tourists. The music was loud and sensual, with a tropical beat. Three female vamps, in various stages of dress or undress, were pole dancing to the sultry music. After a quick glance that made her wonder if the undead could still get implants, Ari concentrated on the crowd.

She saw a mixture of tourists and locals, but no one who resembled the police photos of the wolves. She began to push her way toward the bar, ready to show the mug shots to the bartender.

Andreas spoke in her ear. "I don't see any indication of our pack. Shall we call it quits for tonight?"

Ari frowned at him. "Without talking to the barkeep? Do you have somewhere else to be?" A late date?

"Don't say I did not try," he murmured in her ear.

Sudden drums began a heavy beat, drowning out anything else Andreas might have said. The overhead lights went out. A spotlight appeared. Strobe lights flashed, and a female vamp with large breasts and long legs glided onto the stage. A red scarf draped around her neck, and three tiny triangles of red silk covered the most critical spots. She held a knife in her teeth. The predominately male crowd shouted as she gyrated her hips and swirled the scarf to the beat of the drums.

A male werelion climbed out of the audience onto the stage. He mirrored her movements and reached out one hand, capturing the top two triangles. As he bent his head and bit into a bare breast, the audience stomped and howled. Ari had been wrong; she hadn't seen this before.

Her feet seemed rooted by the spectacle, the violent, sexual display. When the dancer transferred the knife to her hand, Andreas took Ari's arm and steered her toward the door. As they reached the exit, Ari saw Sheila.

"There she is! The she-wolf." Ari dove back into the unruly mob, shoving toward the place she had spotted the wolf. Andreas stayed with her, searching from his greater height. Fights began to break out as the crowd stormed the stage. Bar staff waded in with clubs and Tasers. When Andreas and Ari failed to find any trace of the she-wolf, he finally dragged her outside.

"Are you positive it was Sheila?" he asked.

Was she? It was a brief glance, and all she had to go on was a mug shot. "Pretty sure."

They circled the building, hanging around until the show was over and the bar began to empty. They scanned every patron. When only stragglers remained, Ari was forced to accept she'd been wrong or Sheila had gotten away.

"I guess we're done for tonight." As they started up the street, Ari's curiosity made her ask, "Back there, were they really going to do it? Right on stage?"

"Yes. And much more," he said with a straight face. He struggled to suppress a laugh.

She didn't ask what he meant by 'much more.' Knowing vamps and werewolves, and with a knife involved, she figured blood was a prime ingredient. She wasn't sorry she missed the rest of the performance. There might be less desirable activities than having kinky, bloodletting sex on a public stage, but right now she couldn't think of one.

Ari grimaced.

And then he did laugh.

"That's why you wanted to leave. You knew what was coming. Have you been there before?"

"Yes." His eyes still twinkled.

"More than once?"

"That sounds like a loaded question." He looked at her with a grin. "And I have better sense than to answer."

* * *

By the second evening, they were running out of places to look. With no verified sightings, despite her "possible" from the night before, Ari began to think the pack had returned to Canada. She and Andreas had worked the side streets this evening. The next stop was Tillie's, a small bar and grill patronized mostly by weretigers. It was definitely off the tourist beat.

The owner's immediate response to the photos sent Ari's blood rushing.

"Yeah, I seen them. Recognize the woman." The owner pointed to Sheila's photo. "Heavy accent. Came in here two or three nights in a row. Ordered from the tap. But I suspected they were selling drugs. Told 'em to leave. Don't need the police shutting me down."

"Have they been back?" she asked.

The barkeep shook his head. "No, ma'am. Not since."

"Did you get the impression they live nearby?" Andreas asked.

The owner scratched his head. "Can't say about that. But the first night they asked about pizza. Told 'em about the carryout joint two blocks over. That's where they headed from here. Maybe the pizza folks can help you."

Ari was out the door almost before the barkeep finished. She sprinted the two blocks, Andreas easily matching her stride. But their luck ran out again. The pizza guy had no trouble remembering the wolves, but they'd used pick-up—not delivery. And paid cash. Another dead end. It proved the wolves were still in town, but that was all.

Tired and let down over the fizzled lead, Ari said good night and trudged home. So far they'd used good, old-fashioned police work, tromping around Olde Town, interviewing potential witnesses, and they had next to nothing to show for their efforts. Maybe it was time to try a little witchcraft. Scrying wasn't exactly one of her best talents, but it couldn't hurt to try.

Arriving at her apartment, she opened the cedar chest that doubled as her coffee table, pulled out the scrying bowl, and selected a small crystal pedant. While she'd never located people by this method, she'd found inanimate objects a few times. Well, once or twice. She knew people were harder. The searching spell worked best when the practitioner had personal items from the target—which Ari didn't have. She'd heard that sometimes images worked, and she had the police photos.

She uncapped a bottle of blessed water and poured two

inches in the bowl. Her biggest obstacle was the absence of a foolproof spell. For Ari, that meant she needed the missing family journal, the Book of Shadows. Lacking that, she could only borrow what had worked for her witch mentor in St. Louis.

Ari darkened the room and lit the candles of the four elements. Holding the police photos in one hand and slowly swinging the pendant with the other, she concentrated on the water and summoned the Goddess. Forming the image of Sheila inside her head, she repeated the she-wolf's name three times, asking the Goddess to grant her wish. The water swirled and clouded, but despite Ari's repeated efforts, it remained opaque, unreadable.

After an hour, she gave up the effort and went to bed. As she lay there still awake, she was glad she hadn't mentioned the attempt to Andreas. It was bad enough she had to live with her failures. It would be worse if others knew. Good thing she didn't have to depend on the witchcraft.

* * *

Since they had confirmed the enemy pack was still in town, Ari arrived early at the compound on Saturday morning. It was no longer a question of whether the wolves would attack again, but where and when. She wanted to share the news with her team and make sure they were ready.

When Maleban hadn't arrived by six, Ari called his home and cell without getting a response. Tension spread through the security room as everyone began to realize something was wrong. Concerned about splitting her team or leaving the compound a man short, Ari refused to send one of them to check his residence. She finally called police dispatch for an assist. Within minutes, they reported no one was home. The patrol officers agreed to cruise the neighborhood for anything unusual.

When Ari disconnected, she shook her head.

"This is bad," Lilith said.

The stillness at her words proved they were all having that sinkhole in the gut feeling. When the phone rang again, Ari flinched at the sound of Ryan's voice. Dispatch wouldn't have alerted the lieutenant on a welfare check, not unless it had gone sour.

"Your guy's dead, Ari. Looks like a sniper with a high-powered rifle. Two shots. Head, heart. A marksman. Patrol found the body around the corner, not more than a block from his apartment. You want to tell me what's going on? Is this connected to Sebastian?"

"Probably. Maleban was a member of the security team that protects Prince Daron."

Ryan sighed audibly. "You better warn me before this explodes all over the community. I don't want to get caught with my pants down. You hear me?"

"Sure, but so far no humans are involved." That's what he really wanted to know. As long as the problems stayed in the Otherworld community, Ryan's bosses would let the Magic Council take the lead. In fact, they'd prefer it that way.

He grunted an acknowledgment. "You want a lab workup and autopsy?"

"He's half demon. The body will decay like a vampire's. Send the remains to the Magic Council."

"Can do. Anything else?"

"Ballistics. I want to know if the bullets were silver. And, who knows, maybe we'll get lucky and find a rifle for you to match."

"Oh, yeah, like that'll happen," he said, disconnecting.

As soon as Ari took the phone from her ear, Lilith demanded to know what happened. Ari repeated everything. The team took it in silence. When she asked about notification, no one knew of any family. Nobody to care except the people in that room. And Ari didn't know how to help them. She felt the loss, and she'd known him only a week. The others had worked with him for years. They needed time to grieve, to recover, but she couldn't give them that time. The enemy would know their need too, might even try to take advantage of it.

Why had they gone after Maleban? Was he some special

threat? He could use fire, but so could she. Or was he just the most accessible? He lived the farthest away, and he lived alone. That might make him an easier target. A first target? Ari's stomach clenched. With a sniper at their disposal, maybe they intended to pick them off, one by one.

Not on her watch.

"None of you can leave the compound tonight." Ari's abrupt words got everyone's immediate attention. "You're all targets now. With a sniper it's not safe to go home. If you need to notify family or friends, do it. Tell anyone who lives with you to lay low, maybe stay somewhere else for a day or two. "

"What about our clothes? Toothbrush?" Lilith asked.

"Make a list of what you need. We'll ask the vamps to pick them up after dark. Any other questions?" She looked around. "Then let's figure out where you're going to sleep."

When Andreas arrived, Ari broke the news. He didn't say much, but his jaw hardened. The wolves were collecting bad karma from a bottomless cesspool.

During the following hour, quarters were assigned and set up in nearby rooms. Lilith and Russell in one, Mike and Benny shared another. Once she was satisfied the team was settled for the night, Ari headed for the door.

"Where are you going?" Andreas asked.

"I have work to do. There's a pack of killers out there, and I've got a community to protect. I'm neglecting my other duties. Like patrol, for instance."

"Not alone. If you go, we go together." He cocked his head. "And after patrol? What are your plans?"

Ari knew where this was going. "I'll be fine."

"Are you serious? You can't return to your apartment. The wolves know where you live."

"And I've been safe there for days," she countered. "I don't need a bodyguard."

"That was before they had a sniper. Maleban thought he was safe too. Arianna, be reasonable. Take your own advice. You just grounded your team."

A quick glance around the room confirmed the team was listening to every word. Otherworld ears were too damn good. While they could use some diversion right now, she didn't think a heated argument with Andreas would help.

"Can we settle this later?" she asked with a significant tilt of her head toward the observers.

"Of course," he said, his voice amiable enough, "but we *will* settle it. We have an agreement for your services. I believe that gives me the final word."

Lilith snickered, and Ari gave her a half-hearted glare. The werelioness returned a knowing smirk.

"He's right," Russell offered.

Traitors, Ari thought. This was so not comfortable. She lifted a hand in an abrupt wave and exited the door, Andreas in close pursuit. The cool evening breeze felt good on her flushed cheeks. Andreas caught her with a restraining hand at the curb.

"What?" she grumbled.

He waved at a silver SUV pulling to the curb. A young vampire jumped out, handed the keys to Andreas, and disappeared inside the compound.

Andreas jangled the keys in one hand. "Drive or ride?"

"Drive."

She caught the toss. Once behind the wheel, she glanced at him before starting the engine. "Why the wheels?"

"I thought that was obvious. If there is a sniper out there, walking the streets is somewhat risky."

"OK, I buy that, but you had the car waiting. You just tried to get me to stay in the compound."

"Yes. That is what I wanted." Andreas stared out the front window. "But I had no illusion you would comply. I called for the car thirty minutes ago."

Ari jabbed the key in the ignition, and the engine roared to life. Andreas was beginning to know her a little too well. At least he realized she wouldn't blindly follow his orders.

"But you cannot go home tonight," he added. "I will not indulge you in something that risky."

"Indulge me?" Ari couldn't believe he'd said that. "I'll quit before I let you order me around."

"And abandon your team? I doubt that. And if you do something so rash, the Magic Council will no doubt respond to an appeal from Prince Daron." He eyed her calmly. "If you won't stay with the team, then Club Dintero will have to do. We can protect you there."

"I'll stay with Claris."

"And endanger her? The wolves targeted you once before. Now you are working with us, which makes you a bigger target. If you stay anywhere that is not secured, you place yourself and others around you at risk. For no good reason I can comprehend."

Ari subsided, realizing Andreas had a valid point about risking others, but still trying to come up with an alternative. She didn't need anyone to protect her. They rode in silence for the rest of the trip. Andreas spoke once, directing her to stop at Club Dintero. They left the SUV at the front door. This had become a regular nightly stop, Andreas checking on business while Ari sampled the free food.

Tonight, Andreas had something else in mind. He led her to his office, opened the closet, and pulled the handle on a trap door. "This secret passage leads to Daron's compound. With the sniper threat, we may need to use it."

Ari peered down the narrow wooden steps that turned sharply to the right into darkness. "Who knows about this?"

"Hard to say. It hasn't been much of a secret. On the other hand, it has rarely been used. Daron and I built it when we first bought the Club. The other end is in the hallway near the compound security rooms." He dropped the trap door in place and stepped back into the office. Glancing at his desk, he frowned at a tall stack of papers, picked up one, and began to read through it. "Can you give me a few minutes? I would like to check if there is anything urgent."

While he perused the paperwork, Ari wandered around his office. She'd only seen it for brief moments prior to tonight. Not very fancy, she thought, and not nearly the size she'd expect for the owner's private office. Adequate, although the furniture was definitely upscale. His desk was polished cherrywood, the matching chair upholstered in leather like dark chocolate. She imagined she could smell fudge. A large, pillowy sofa claimed the same lush material. Two leather chairs of similar style, but in an off-white, provided color contrast, and a carved cherrywood file cabinet stood in the corner.

Ari poured herself a cup of coffee from the wine and coffee tray brought in as soon as they arrived. Sinking onto the couch, she watched Andreas work as she waited for the hot liquid to cool.

Showing no awareness of her scrutiny, Andreas's athletic body relaxed into the desk chair, his long legs stretched out before him, fine features intent on his work. He occasionally gave brief attention to his glass of Chianti. Ari wondered if he knew what an appealing picture he made. But she wasn't just enjoying the view; she was forming and discarding arguments to convince him she didn't want or need his protection.

As if hearing this inner dialogue, he lifted his gaze. "You can sleep in this room, if you like. That sofa is quite comfortable. I will introduce you to the night staff, and of course, I will be on the premises until dawn. You won't be disturbed."

Ari parted her lips to protest, but he stopped her with a sharp look. "Staying alone is not an option."

"Is that an order?"

He looked at her in silence.

"And you expect that to work?"

Andreas let out a long breath and laid his papers aside. He swiveled the chair toward her. "I hoped you would see the necessity for this precaution. The wolves will eliminate anyone in their way." He leaned forward, forearms on thighs, his eyes serious. "You would be the logical next target, and your team can't afford to lose its leader."

She released a sigh of her own. Why she was arguing with him? She knew her apartment wasn't safe. The longer she stayed there, the more she invited an attack and the more she endangered the other tenants. But damn, she resented Andreas telling her what to do. Of course, giving in gracefully, especially when she was wrong, could be a good thing. Yeah, right. It wasn't likely to become a habit with her. Maybe just this once, but no way would she return to the compound, hauled home like some willful adolescent. She could imagine Lilith's peals of laughter.

* * *

Later that night, as she lay curled on the sofa, patrol completed, her own pillow retrieved from her apartment and fluffed under her head, Ari's thoughts returned to the unproductive search for the wolves. How did they continue to elude her search? Who was the insider helping them? And most important of all, what were they planning next?

She woke when something brushed her arm. Terrified the wolves had found her, she grabbed for the dagger under her pillow. Strong hands caught her wrists. Before she panicked, a familiar energy registered.

"Arianna."

She relaxed, willing her pounding pulse to slow. Good thing he had quick reflexes. Andreas released her.

"I apologize," he said, so close she breathed in the scent of his cologne. "I didn't intend to frighten you. It is almost dawn. The SUV is at the curb. We have searched outside and nothing seems amiss. It is safe, if you depart soon." He moved away, switching on the desk lamp.

"OK." She sat up, trying to shake the remaining fuzz out of her head, and blinked at the sudden light. This was not the ideal way to waken. Adrenaline and a sleep-drugged brain don't mix well.

"Here." He handed her a cup of coffee. "This should help."

Ari half curled under the warm blanket. She must have been sleeping hard. She sipped at the dark liquid. Hmm. His special blend. Yummy. She lifted her drowsy lashes to peek at Andreas.

He looked good in black slacks and, surprise, a silver shirt. She never doubted the brand. The shirt hugged his chest and shoulders in all the right places. He looked rather yummy himself.

Whoa, scratch that thought. Vampire, she reminded herself. She sat up straighter and took another sip. "I'm fine now," she said. Whether the reassurance was meant for him or her, Ari wasn't sure.

Andreas smiled, his eyes glinted as if he'd read her mind, and he slipped out the door.

Chapter Thirty-One

Despite the abrupt beginning, the rest of the day on Sunday was quiet. Even the warehouse district shut down for the Sabbath, and the surveillance cameras only showed an occasional dog sniffing around, watering the dried weeds near the building. A couple of squirrels scampered across the roof and set off the sensors mid-afternoon. That caused a momentary stir until Mike pinpointed the culprits on camera seven.

Shortly after five o'clock, Carmella strolled into the room with two well-armed male vamps. Normally Ari might have been surprised to see the vamps this early, but Riverdale had switched to standard time, the regular 'fall back.' It got dark earlier. What did surprise her was Carmella's presence instead of Andreas's.

"You can all go do whatever you do now," Carmella said. "They," she indicated the two male vamps, "will take over for the night, and you have to clear this room. I understand you're staying in the compound, but keep out of their way."

Carmella had such a charming way about her. For a moment Ari thought Lilith was going to say something, then she shrugged. Good decision. Irritating old vamps was not a wise idea. Carmella didn't hang around for long, and the other two vampire guards kept to themselves in the surveillance room.

That left the team in possession of the TV and the kitchen.

Mike poked around in the refrigerator, and Russell recruited players for a poker game. Prince Daron and his court came through the hidden door about 6:15. As usual, they had little to say and headed straight toward The Blue Room, where the prince often conducted court business. Andreas still didn't appear.

Another hour passed. Ari rubbed the back of her neck, her tension growing with Andreas's continued absence. He finally strode through the door, his stride brisk, all business. He nodded to Ari before disappearing into The Blue Room. He wasn't gone long. When he returned, he stopped in the doorway. "Ready?"

He hustled her down the hall and opened the tunnel that led to Club Dintero.

"Has something happened? First you're late, now the tunnel?" When he didn't answer, she peered inside. "Are there spiders?"

That brought a faint smile to his face. "I will go first."

Ari followed, keeping away from the walls. "Why so late?"

"Business," was his terse reply.

"Ours or yours?"

He ignored that, turned on a large Maglite, and started down the tunnel. Ari hurried to catch him. For the first two or three minutes, the passage was a simple wood-framed hallway, wide enough to accommodate two people walking abreast. As they angled downward, the floor turned to dirt, and rock replaced the wood walls. On occasion Andreas ducked to avoid overhead rocky protrusions. The air was stale, stuffy, and the number of spider webs Andreas swept down with the Maglite spoke of the tunnel's long disuse. Ari watched for the web spinners, hoping to avoid any close encounters. The floor tilted upward again, the air freshened, and they arrived at the trap door in Andreas's office. The entire trip had taken no more than ten minutes.

"Now that's over, will you tell me what's going on?" Ari said as she brushed dust from her clothes. "It's obvious something's wrong."

"As soon as I return," he promised. "Just a few minutes."

Ari protested, but it was too late. Andreas had already disappeared.

With time on her hands, she cleaned up in the nearby bathroom, chose a fresh blouse from the bag she'd brought from her apartment, and even ran a comb through her hair. She checked her watch. Six minutes had passed. Now what?

Too restless to sit and wait, Ari wandered the room, absently letting her fingers trail over the surprisingly modern paintings composed in an array of jewel-tone colours. Her mind tossed around possible reasons for Andreas's mood. Some club problem? No. He would have said so. Some vampire issue unrelated to recent events? Maybe. But no, that couldn't be it. He said he'd tell her. And in spite of how much he'd recently shared, Andreas wasn't about to divulge vampire business unless he had to. So it must be connected to Sebastian or the wolves. Had he found the spy? Had someone else been killed? Why all the mystery?

* * *

She'd about run out of speculations when Andreas returned. He'd changed into a black sports jacket, and he was smiling. She didn't know how to interpret that.

"I would wager you are starved," he said. "A table awaits us."

"Us? You're joining me?" He didn't do that often. In fact, the only time they'd spent more than a few minutes together in the dining room was the night of Victor's interview. How long ago that seemed.

"If you do not object to my company." He held out an arm.

Ari flashed him a smile and walked by, ignoring the arm. She wasn't particularly fashion conscious, but she drew the line at a man in Armani escorting her in stonewashed jeans. He chuckled and followed her into the dining room. They were given a cozy corner table. As soon as they were seated, drinks appeared. Cabernet for her, Chianti for him. She sipped her drink and watched him. Andreas was pensive tonight.

Ari wondered if it was the mysterious business that was bothering him. Hopefully he would tell her in time. She glanced around the room. Business was good; the club was packed. There was a new maitre'd at the door. "Where's Victor?"

An emotion flickered across Andreas's face that she couldn't identify.

"An overnight buying trip to Chicago."

"So who's the host?"

Now Andreas smiled. "I am not surprised you failed to recognize him. The last time you saw Marcus was the night of his rescue."

"Marcus!" She turned to look again. "He's recovered completely. It's amazing! What a difference. You must be a fabulous doctor."

Andreas's smile broadened. "He has little memory of what happened to him. Probably a blessing. It has made his recovery easier than Gordon's. Marcus will make a fine head maitre d' when the time comes."

Ari look at the younger vampire again. With his dark good looks, Marcus would be quite a hit with the ladies. He greeted guests with a quiet formality that would someday match the elegance of the man seated across from her. Ari's lips curved in a smile. It was easy to identify Marcus's chosen role model.

She brought her thoughts back to the table. Andreas had returned to brooding, his shadowed gaze focused on the flame of their table candle.

"Are you ever going to clue me in?"

Andreas's eyes popped up to hers, and the corners of his mouth curved. "Run out of patience, madam witch?" He steepled his long fingers. "I am sorry to be so inattentive tonight. This latest development has been particularly hard for me to comprehend. We intercepted a courier last night. A vampire running information back and forth between Riverdale and Sebastian in Toronto. Unfortunately he did not reveal his local contact." Andreas's jaw tightened. "But the courier was here, in my club. And I fear I know who the contact may be."

"Who?" Ari leaned forward, lowering her voice. "Somebody on your staff? A member of the inner court?" Most of the vampire community hung out here from time to time, so she wasn't surprised the contact had been in the club.

Andreas's face clouded. "Forgive me, Arianna. But I hesitate to make such a serious accusation, even to you, until I am certain. Be patient for one more day. By tomorrow night my suspicions will be confirmed or refuted."

Ari frowned at him, tempted to push for a better answer. But how could she fault him? The community was teeming with suspicion and a mob mentality. A false allegation overheard in the club could be lethal. If waiting a few hours made Andreas feel better, she'd go along—unless she got an opportunity to quiz him in private.

She shrugged in tacit acceptance. "And the courier, are you going to tell me what happened to him?"

"No, probably not."

Better leave it alone, she thought. Vampires had their own idea of justice…and matching interrogation techniques. Someday she might try to change his mind. But to be honest, she didn't have much interest in the fate of some traitorous thug. She was more curious about the suspect, who could be Sebastian's candidate for the next Riverdale prince.

She studied her dinner companion. Now there was her candidate for prince. But he wouldn't make Sebastian's list. She almost smiled imagining Andreas as anyone's puppet.

No, Sebastian's choice would be someone weak, who only looked strong. She didn't know a single vampire who fit that description. She'd like to suspect Lucien, simply because he was a prick, but he was too arrogant to let Sebastian take control.

"I can't figure Sebastian out," she said, thinking aloud. "If he has the wolves and some hand-picked prince on the scene, why the drugs and the mind-control experiments?"

"A tough question. One I have thought about for days." He signaled the waiter to refill their wineglasses. When the young man was finished, Andreas continued. "Perhaps Sebastian hoped to keep us from seeing the bigger danger. Keeping the community in an uproar while he worked quietly behind the scenes. You have to admit it was effective."

"Well, maybe." She looked unconvinced.

"Or perhaps he fantasized about his own army of robot vampires. Whatever he envisioned, it is hard to believe even Sebastian would be foolhardy enough to want a drug perfected that controls vampires. A drug that could be turned against him."

"A good reason for him to have the wizard killed. Maybe Dubrey was close to success, and Sebastian finally realized how dangerous it was. I wonder what Sebastian's thinking now. Knowing we suspect him, what will he do?"

"Unpredictable. I am not even sure who is running the show. Master or puppet. Sebastian's pet may have struck out on his own." Andreas leaned back, picking up his wineglass. "Vampire ambitions have few boundaries."

And what were Andreas's ambitions? Ari wondered. When this was over, assuming they all survived, would he be content as a lieutenant forever? Somehow she doubted it.

* * *

Ari settled down to sleep early that evening. The short nights had taken a toll. She had a dull headache, and the wine had made her sleepy. As she waited to doze off, she tried to recapture those small things that kept nagging at her. The tattooed guy, something about Frederick's friends… She drifted into a restless sleep.

She woke with her witch senses shrieking. A vampire was in the room. Not Andreas. Not his magic. Her hand closed over the dagger under the pillow. Heart racing, she forced herself to lie still until she could identify the enemy's location. From the corner of one eye, she saw a dark shadow. A citrusy scent drifted toward her, one she'd smelled before. Ari forced her breathing to remain even. As the figure bent over her, she lunged against his legs, tumbling them both to the floor. The vampire let out a sharp hiss near her ear, and she slammed him with her fist, connecting on hard bone. Sharp fangs slashed open her arm, and Ari screamed. Striking blindly with the knife, she tried to roll away.

Pain seared her scalp as the vampire yanked her head back by her hair. She slashed upward with the knife, and the vamp reared back to avoid the blade. Ari wrenched free and scrambled away on all fours, knocking chairs out of her way. Surely the racket would bring someone soon. She heard her cell phone ring. An iron grip clamped onto her left ankle, pulling her toward her attacker.

In desperation, Ari snagged the wooden foot of the couch with her good arm and held on. The maneuver left her on her stomach, and when she tried to kick herself loose, she lacked leverage. She released the couch and flipped over to make another strike with the knife. Her elbow struck the floor, sending the blade flying to drop with a clatter.

The vampire laughed, low and mocking. Ari saw the flash of white fangs lowering toward her throat, and she head-butted him. A hard fist retaliated, making her ears pop. She finally heard voices in the distance. She groped along the floor, searching for a weapon, finding only her unzipped bag of clothes. As the fangs reared again, set to strike, Ari did the only thing she could. She dumped the bag over his head.

The door crashed and the lights came on. Victor's body was ripped away and slammed against the wall. Andreas pinned the assailant by the collar of his shirt. Victor's feet dangled in air, his face brought nose to nose with his furious boss. Victor's eyes bulged, his throat close to being crushed.

"Wait," Ari whispered. She cleared her throat and tried again. "Ask him about the wolves, where they're hiding."

Andreas hesitated, as if reluctant to allow Victor even a small reprieve. Finally, he said, "She has given you another few minutes of life. The longer you talk, the longer you survive." He loosened his hold enough for the tips of Victor's feet to touch the floor. "Begin talking now."

"I'm not telling the bitch anything," Victor gasped.

"Fine with me," Andreas growled, tightening his hold again.

"Are you willing to die to protect them?" Ari demanded. Her head throbbed, and she was slow getting to her feet. Blood dripped from the gash on her forearm. "Or maybe you think you're protecting Sebastian?"

"You don't know what you're talking about," was the sullen response.

Andreas shook him like a terrier with a rat.

"Don't delude yourself," Ari said. "Sebastian's sitting safe in Toronto while you take all the risks." She was on her feet now, next to Andreas's shoulder. "He doesn't care what happens to you. But you can help yourself. Tell us where Sheila is. Tell us their plan. And we'll talk about sparing your life."

"It is your only chance." Andreas's voice was harsh.

Victor hesitated. His eyes rolled toward Ari. He wanted to believe it. He focused on his former boss. "You'll kill me anyway."

"Perhaps," Andreas admitted. "But I can make it less painful. What more do you have to lose?" Contempt crept into his voice. "You have betrayed your prince. Betrayed me. And for what? Sebastian used you."

Victor struggled against the choking grip, his voice a ragged whisper. "You don't know anything. Riverdale was supposed to be mine."

Andreas's laugh was ugly. "You would have nothing. Sebastian would always hold your chain."

"Last chance," Ari said. "Where's Sheila? Tell me where I can find her."

"Go to hell."

"Oh, not me, buddy. But you have a nice trip. You're not only a traitor, you're a moron." Ari backed away. Unless Andreas had some mind thingy up his sleeve, they weren't getting anything from Victor. The would-be prince was at least smart enough to know he didn't have a remote chance of surviving the night.

Andreas leaned forward and whispered in his ear. Victor's body went rigid. Andreas released his grip, turning Victor over to the other staff now crowding into the room.

"Get rid of him," Andreas ordered. "Make this his last sunrise."

Victor didn't resist as they hustled him out. The fight was gone; his face was blank once again.

"What's that mean, his last sunrise?" Ari asked.

"Have you seen a vampire execution?"

She nodded. Andreas didn't need to tell her any more. The condemned vampire had burst into flames as soon as sunlight touched his body. It was a quick but painful way to go.

"You are hurt," he suddenly said.

Ari looked at her arm. She hadn't noticed the blood dripping on the floor. "Yeah, sorry about the mess." She grabbed a shirt from the clothes strewn on the floor and dabbed at the wounds. "Guess I could use a bandage."

Someone found a first aid kit. Andreas cleaned and wrapped her arm. The blood was starting to clot and the gashes smarted, sure signs of healing.

"Was Victor the one you suspected?" Ari asked as he put the extra supplies back in the box.

His hands paused. "Yes. I regret not telling you. If I had thought…" He closed the first aid box with a snap. "After the failed raid, I hired a private firm to investigate my staff, including the four men who were with me. The background reports arrived last Monday, and Victor's revealed he was born in Canada. That did not mean he had been a vampire in Canada or knew Sebastian, but it raised concerns. Since he came to us four years ago from South Carolina, we had no prior suspicion of any Canadian ties." Andreas's mouth formed a thin line. "He hid his ambitions well."

"Four years is a long time to plan a coup."

"Not in the life of a vampire."

Well, damn. Ari kept forgetting their unique point of view.

Vampires were bound to see time on a much bigger clock.

"So that's all you had on him? That he was born in Canada?" No wonder Andreas had hesitated to share his suspicions.

"That, and an uneasy feeling. Now I see other small hints that didn't mean much at the time. Like his failure to tell you Angela's companion was a werewolf."

"Yeah, I remember that one."

"And his antipathy toward you. His frequent reminders you were a witch, an enemy to vampires, and already involved in two vampire deaths. It was Victor who reported he saw you with Marcus. He said much to poison my opinion of you." Andreas's eyes held regret. "I should not have listened."

"You didn't know me then."

"A poor excuse." Andreas set the first aid kit on his desk. "Victor must have warned the wolves of the raid."

"Then he tried to talk Ryan out of searching the house. Afraid Gordon or Marcus would expose him." Ari suddenly put together one of the elusive pieces that had nagged her for days. The tattooed guy from Toronto—she'd seen him talking with Victor in a bar one night. "I think we all missed a lot."

Andreas grimaced. "Including his befriending of Frederick. I wonder if Victor intended from the beginning to have him murdered. Ironic, is it not? Betrayed by one of our own."

"Why'd he attack me? And why tonight? I thought he was on a buying trip."

"I thought so too. The trip was a way to keep him busy while we explored his Canadian activities. He must have figured that out, realized he was about to be exposed, and moved his plans forward." Andreas's gaze sought hers. "Removing you was his next step."

Ari shivered, not so much from his words as from the raw emotion in his eyes. She broke the contact and began gathering the clothes scattered around the room. He watched for a moment before gliding forward. Taking the items from her hands, he tossed them on the couch, and his hands settled on her shoulders. An instant spark of awareness brought her gaze to meet his.

Andreas slid a hand down to touch her injured arm. "I am sorry I was not here to prevent this. I received a message to meet Daron, and I went, thinking Victor was out of town."

Andreas's eyes darkened, and Ari's skin tingled where his hands touched her. Her witch magic hummed with pleasure. Magic or pure attraction, it was heady stuff.

"The minute Daron told me the message was a fake, I knew you were in danger. I called. When you didn't answer, I feared I was too late." He moved closer, both hands sliding to her elbows. "It was not a good moment."

Ari breathed in the masculine, musky scent of him, the allure of his cologne. She titled her head upward in invitation, and Andreas's mouth closed over hers. Gentle at first, the kiss became deeper and possessive as he pulled her into his arms, pressing their bodies together. Ari let the kiss take her under, full and sweet, a delicious moment. As she teetered on the brink of drowning in sensation, he drew back and gently, but firmly, set her away.

Ari stared at him, pulse pounding. Andreas had been like the forbidden apple, tempting but beyond possibility. Now he'd changed the rules of this game they'd been playing, and she wasn't sure how to react.

"It is late, and regretfully, this is not the time," he said. He retreated across the room, putting distance between them.

Why not? Ari wanted to demand. What better time? But something kept her from saying the words. Something that knew he was right.

She watched as he closed the open trap door. Victor's point of entry. He shoved the file cabinet against the closet door. "Secure locks will be added tomorrow," he muttered. Still not looking at her, he picked up the splintered door and examined the damage, as if the last five minutes had never happened. But a warm pulse lingered on her lips.

As Ari watched his dark head bend over the door, silent amusement bubbled in her throat. The ever-so-cool Mr. De Luca was acting as if he didn't trust himself. Probably a good thing, she thought. Deep inside, she was feeling very smug.

Chapter Thirty-Two

Ari threw off the covers. The clock on Andreas's desk read 6:30. Why hadn't someone woken her? Barefoot, she padded to the desk, switched on a lamp, and saw the note sticking under the door. It was written in a strong masculine hand. Andreas and the other members of the vampire court were holding an emergency meeting and would be staying at the compound. He suggested she sleep late and take the tunnel. It was signed with a simple A.

Ari's lips curved. A vampire sleepover. Lucien and Carmella and all the gang. Then it occurred to her what a bad idea that was. She grabbed her clothes, weapons, and pouch of spells and powders, searching under the sofa for a missing shoe. What were the vampires thinking? You don't put all your big guns under one roof. Not when you anticipated an attack. What kind of strategy was that?

She continued to mumble to herself while tying her sneakers, barely noticing her arm had healed to thin white stripes. Another Guardian ability she took for granted.

"They're arrogant," she grumbled, bouncing to her feet. "That's what it is." But Ari knew the real problem was the vampires were solitary hunters. Troop strategy was foreign to them. And the wolves would be watching for a mistake just like this. She raced out the door, her cell phone already dialing to warn the team. They might be called on to demonstrate all their skills today.

When Ari arrived at the compound, it was quiet. The kind of quiet referred to as the calm before the storm. The team worked in silence, scanning the cameras for trouble. Weapons were laid out on desks and tables. They'd already absorbed the news of Victor's treachery, understood his intimate knowledge of the compound, and that the dreaded map of the inner chambers was probably in the hands of the wolves. Determination hung thick in the room. The way to the vampires was through them.

"With Victor dead, is there a chance the wolves will give up and go home?" Benny asked her.

Ari shrugged, knowing Benny's question was just nerves talking. "Doubt if they know he's dead. They'll think he's sleeping like the other vamps. I'm more worried they already had a plan and were waiting for the right moment."

Benny plopped in a chair. "Yeah, that's what I thought you'd say."

* * *

Just before noon, the *whump, whump, whump* of a helicopter and an explosion on the roof announced the assault. Plaster and debris rained from the ceiling, and thick, black smoke filled the air. Ari dove for cover behind the TV. Mike upended the table and crouched behind it with an assault rifle. The smoke bomb continued to pour a heavy veil around them. Ari heard gunfire from the other room, returned from above. Then thumping and scrambling as feet hit the floor. The combatants were coming through the roof. Mike fired a couple rounds, but the smoke was too dense to identify the targets. A strong odor of werewolf confirmed the arrival of Sheila and her pack of assassins.

The smoke residue stung Ari eyes, temporarily blinding her. She released a powder from her magical pouch and the smoke thinned around her. Snarls and growls seemed to come from every direction. Ari glimpsed a furry hand, but wasn't sure whether it was friend or foe. A human form appeared in the haze carrying an Uzi, but combat was too close for him to use it effectively. Ari lunged forward, knocking his feet out from under him as she delivered two sharp jabs to his face and throat. He bucked her off, swinging the weapon around like a hammer and clipping her shoulder. He scrambled away. She threw a binding spell, but he vanished into the smoke.

A furry body crashed into her left side. Ari staggered and whirled to land a sidekick on the wolf's hindquarters. As the creature turned to swipe with its claws, Ari caught a good whiff of its scent. The same scent that had been all over Yana. Ari's blood pumped with the realization she'd finally come face-to-face with Sheila. The she-wolf's claws raked across Ari's waist, ripping her shirt and tearing away her belt. The dagger and bag of potions skidded across the floor. A gun exploded near Ari's ear and blood splattered her face, blinding her, as Sheila yelped and rolled away. Mike yanked Ari behind the table.

Ari took a deep breath. The sweet, metallic smell of blood saturated the air. She wiped her face, removing a layer of blood and bits of fur. Sheila would heal her injuries, but Mike's bullet had given the she-wolf something to think about.

A gray wolf face loomed over the table. Ari hit him between the eyes with witch fire. The face exploded in flames. Let him try to heal *that*.

The ventilation system kicked in, and the heavy smoke drifted toward the vents. Ari saw dark shadows to go with the various screams, growls, and loud blasts from the guns. She finally located the rest of her team. Lilith was in the surveillance room, firing from behind a computer desk that partially blocked the door. Russell, transformed into a small but muscular lion, was locked in a biting, clawing struggle with a large, dark-brown wolf. Ari figured Russell's greater agility would win that fight. Mike had traded the rifle for a handgun. All of her team members were armed with silver bullets. After that brief second of assessment, Ari went to Benny's aid. He had shifted into lion form but was outnumbered by three wolves who had trapped him in a corner. She blasted two of them with three stuns, at least temporarily evening the fight.

Two more smoke bombs exploded, obscuring the scene again, and she heard more wolves drop from the roof. Ari crept forward, stepping over two bodies on the floor. When she reached the wall, she spotted human forms directly ahead, one with an Uzi. They were running their hands over the knotty pine wall. Damn, damn, damn. Ari fired into the smoky haze with two more stunners, hoping to stop them before they found the latch. With her magic level now low and needing to regenerate, she was forced to retreat, leaping over the table to avoid the return fire from the Uzi. She nudged Mike. Although the smoke was still too thick to aim, he fired blindly in the direction of the secret passage. Ari heard an anguished yelp. She pulled the derringer from her ankle holster and started forward again.

Ari stumbled over the wolf Mike had shot. She had nearly reached the wall again, when she heard the distinctive click of the latch opening. Abandoning caution, she sprang forward, arriving in time to see three wolves escape inside. Sheila sprang out of the smoke to follow them, but her injuries made her one step too slow. Ari knocked her aside and fired the derringer into the she-wolf's gut. Sheila howled with pain and anger, falling back into the smoke. Ari yelled at Mike for someone to follow the she-wolf, then she plunged into the tunnel.

Like the passage to Club Dintero, there were no lamps, no electrical system. For the first ten feet, the light from the open panel revealed the way. As soon as Ari rounded the first turn, the light faded to total darkness. She squeezed her eyes closed, forcing them to make a quick adjustment. She heard the wolves ahead and moved in their direction. The derringer remained in her hand. Not killing power against werecreatures, but still damaging. And she had one bullet left.

She could smell the wolves' trail, but they had an advantage—they knew the way. Victor had committed the ultimate betrayal by revealing his prince's sleeping chambers. Ari could only follow, and she'd have to stick close. As the sound of their feet on the tunnel floor began to fade, she broke into a slow jog, trailing one hand along the wall to guide her in the dark. If she missed a turn, she might not find them again before they found the vampires. Somewhere ahead, the prince and his court were sleeping, defenseless. And Andreas was one of them.

She increased her pace again, concentrating all her senses on following the path. She was so attuned to the smell of the wolves, that she failed to register the sudden closeness. She collided with a furry mass. A rear guard. Ari stepped in close, pressed the derringer against his throat, and pulled the trigger. Blood spurted. The wolf grunted and slumped to the floor. Not dead, but down. She stopped long enough to mutter a binding spell to hold him an extra minute or two. She hoped it was enough. With the derringer now useless, she left it on the tunnel floor.

Ari hurried on, arriving at an intersection of four paths. The smell of wolf was all around her. She hesitated, listening, uncertain which route to take. Sounds came from the tunnel behind her. Had the injured wolf recovered so quickly? Was it her team? Or had Sheila returned? She didn't have time to find out.

Reaching out with her witch magic, Ari picked up nearby energy. Second tunnel on the right. Startled by how close they were, she slipped forward, more cautious now. Another misstep might not turn out as well. She kept her back against the wall, hands searching along the clammy walls.

Ari felt the familiar surge in her blood as her witch fire rejuvenated. Soon it would be strong enough to use. She crept through three more junctions. Only once did she make a false turn. Her senses alerted her quickly, and she corrected but lost precious seconds. She forged ahead, intent on her quarry, aware with every step that pursuers were also closing in from behind.

She began to pick up faint traces of Otherworld power. Not wolf. Vampire. Her witch magic reached out for the trace that led to Andreas.

"There!" The word rang out like a shot from the blackness ahead.

Ari sprinted forward. That single word meant one thing—the two assassins had found the entrance to the sleeping chambers. No! She couldn't let this happen. Not to Andreas. She put everything she had into a desperate sprint, her magic reaching out before her, witch senses screaming in her ears. *Danger. Danger.* Her mind formed terrible images of the wolves breaching the chamber door.

Rounding a sharp corner, she braked to a stop. She still had time to stop them. The guy with the Uzi held a flashlight in one hand and was running the other over a rock wall; the gun lay at his feet. A brown wolf guarded his back and immediately charged her. Ari backpedalled, firing a small burst of stuns into the lunging figure. He stumbled. She dodged aside as he crashed against the rocky wall. She sprang toward the man at the end. He grabbed for the Uzi, but her foot got there first, kicking it against the far wall. She body-slammed the assassin, forcing him away from the entrance. Ari whirled, back against the wall, making her body a barrier.

The brown wolf regained his feet and rushed toward her. The gunman crawled toward the Uzi. Pounding feet raced toward them from the tunnels. Ari summoned her magic for a last stand.

An enormous black wolf launched into the room, taking down her wolf attacker. The gunman reached the Uzi and swung it over his body one handed. Her crimson fire caught him as he pulled the trigger. Bullets riddled the wall. Ari saw the surprise on his face before he burst into flames and dropped the discharging weapon.

Ari didn't see him die. A ricocheting bullet caught her arm and sent her reeling against the wall. As she felt the rock impact on her forehead, the wall opened, and she fell into Andreas's arms. The vampire stared down at her, a strange look on his face. Ari slipped into darkness.

Chapter Thirty-Three

She opened one eye. Tan walls. Ari lay on a sofa in a room she had never seen before. Her arm was bandaged—again—and a damp cloth covered her forehead. She opened the other eye. Andreas sat on the arm of the sofa talking to someone she couldn't see without sitting up. She wasn't sure she was ready to do that.

Events and images flooded back. The deafening gunfire, the blood, the bodies. What had the vampires thought of the carnage throughout the compound? Jeez, Ari, she chided herself. They're vampires. Tame stuff to them.

She stretched her arm to see how bad it was. Andreas immediately crouched at her side.

"How do you feel?" he asked.

"Ready for another round," she said in a feeble stab at humor.

"Well, isn't she the bloodthirsty one," Carmella said from somewhere above her. "And they think we're bad."

There it was again, that vampire issue with humor. Before Ari thought of a suitable response, she heard Carmella walk away.

Andreas looked at Ari, his face unreadable. "Your magic woke me," he said. It almost sounded like an accusation. "An overwhelming sense of danger jolted me awake. Your magic filled the room, and I saw the wolves outside the chamber door.

Outside," he repeated, as if she might have missed it the first time. "What kind of a witch are you?"

Ari stared at his face, saw the tension, even the alarm in his eyes. But no one could wake a vampire. Could they? Or do the things he was suggesting. "What are you talking about?"

He raised an incredulous brow. "You woke me from the sleep cycle, Arianna. And now you say you don't know how?"

Ari frowned. "I don't, uh, I mean, I didn't...do anything. Whatever happened, whatever got you up, it wasn't me."

"And the image of the wolves? How do you explain that?"

Wide-eyed, she just shook her head. "I can't. How do *you* explain it? This is your deal, not mine."

He started to say something but seemed to change his mind when voices reached them from the hallway. "This is not a good time, but we shall discuss this later."

Yeah. Like never. She had a hard enough time coping with the tangible things, like killer wolves with Uzis.

She struggled to sit up and winced when she bumped the arm. Painful, but not too bad. With her constitution she should be fine by the end of the week.

Andreas soon dashed that hope. "The bone was splintered. It may need special treatment to heal properly. Should we find something for the pain?"

"No, I'm good for now," she said. "Tell me about my team. I want to see them."

"Everyone survived, and their injuries will heal. Lilith and Russell are down the hall licking their wounds. Mike morphed into his human persona and—"

"Is he a black wolf?" Ari interrupted, remembering the wolf who helped her in the tunnels.

"Yes, and very large. He left to look for Benny." At her frown he added, "We think Benny is still trailing Sheila."

"She got away?"

"Mike saw her and a gray wolf leave by the front door, right after you entered the tunnel. Benny went after them."

Ari snorted. "She left before the fight was over? Some leader.

And the rest of her pack?"

"Seven dead, one captured. We believe ten or twelve were inside the compound. The chopper pilot took off when Lilith and Russell climbed onto the roof."

"So Sheila and two or three others are still out there."

"At least," he said. "We do not have a good count. Sheila may have new recruits who were waiting outside. I hope Benny will return with a more accurate count—and a current location."

"They'll be long gone. Probably in that chopper," Ari said in disgust. "And trying to get out of the country with Victor dead."

"But they cannot know that yet," Andreas argued. "It is too early. We should have another hour or two before he is late enough they become alarmed."

Ari couldn't stand the thought of Yana's killer escaping. But in Sheila's place, Ari would head for the hills, or in this case, home to Canada. Hell, the she-wolf had already run out on her pack. Why would she hang around? Unless she needed time to heal.

Ari heard voices at the door. Andreas straightened his tall frame and left to see what was causing the commotion. She felt strangely disoriented, touched the large lump on her forehead, and wondered if her brains had been scrambled. What had Andreas been talking about? What really happened those last moments deep in the tunnels? She didn't have long to think about it, as Andreas returned, reporting Mike had checked in, without Benny. He'd been unable to find the missing werelion.

Now Ari had something worth worrying about. Benny had sense enough not to take on the werewolves alone, but what if they discovered he was tracking them? He could have been ambushed, outnumbered three to one.

She pushed off the couch. So far so good. She waved off Andreas's offer to help. Enough coddling. She brushed past him and was headed out the door when he reached out a hand to stop her. He drew back at the last moment, as if he was reluctant to touch her.

"Arianna, I meant to thank you. Would have earlier, except I was…ah, distracted. You saved the prince. We owe you."

Ari turned around, shaking her head. "I was just doing my job. But we're not done yet. First, we find Benny, then the remaining wolves. You want to thank me? Just keep your promise. It's not over until the last wolf is dead or in custody." She turned on her heel and left the room.

After checking on the lions, she walked into the security offices. Mike was in the kitchen frying bacon and eggs. Someone had done a good job of cleaning the mess; the table and three chairs were back in place, the broken furniture was gone, and the floor had been scrubbed. Of course the walls were still riddled with bullet holes. Her derringer, knife, and bag of potions lay on the kitchen table. Once Ari reloaded her pistol and pocketed the rest, she felt better with her arsenal back in place. She poked her head in the surveillance room. It was going to take a lot more work in there. The monitors and screens were gone, presumably shattered.

Ari checked the time on her cell phone. She'd give the missing lion another half hour. Then she intended to lead a search party.

Benny hobbled in twenty minutes later, his arms and legs covered with bites, claw marks, and blood. Mike and Andreas tended to his wounds while Ari and Lilith huddled over him, firing questions.

"This all happened before I left here," he muttered. "I'm all right. But if Ari and Lilith want to check me out, go for it. You dudes, get your hands off. They have first dibs."

That's when Ari knew he'd be fine. If Benny could flirt, he wasn't hurt too badly.

Basking in the attention, he spun out every detail of his lengthy absence. It boiled down to the wolves splitting up, doubling back and taking every precaution to shake off pursuers before vanishing into their latest hidey-hole.

"So where are they?" Ari demanded.

"Under the city. They're in the caverns."

The caverns. The officially unexplored labyrinth of tunnels

and caves under Riverdale were extensive. Carved by Mother Nature and enhanced by native Indians and possibly smugglers, the cave system eventually become the sole territory of the Otherworlders. Under the most recent treaties, it belonged to the vampires. The choice of hideout must have been Victor's. A good idea under most circumstances. No one knew their way through the secret passages. Well, no one except the vampires. When vampires were hunting you, it wasn't a smart place to be.

* * *

Within minutes of Benny providing the directions, Ari and seven companions — Mike, Andreas, Carmella and four other vampires — were on their way. Lucien and the werecats had stayed to guard the prince. At the last minute Andreas tried to convince Ari to stay behind, citing her wounded arm. He dropped the attempt when she grabbed her leather jacket and headed for the door. Injured or not, Ari was determined to go, with or without him. This was her fight too.

The trip to the cavern opening was mostly in silence. The only discussion was about the enemy numbers. Benny had followed three. Adding the pilot, there were at least four, and an unknown number of reinforcements. Ari wasn't worried about handling the wolves, no matter how many they found. She wanted to be sure no one slipped away this time.

The caverns on the Mississippi River cliffs were high above the river. No stairs on this side. No paths. One by one the hunting party slipped over the edge and inched down the rocks. Ari's fingers and feet searched for holds on the slick, cold surface. The splashing of the water on jagged banks below was a reminder how bad a slip would be.

The vamps led the way, dropping from one crumbly ledge to the next. With her weakened arm, Ari's drops were often clumsy, blindly hoping she'd find a solid landing below her feet and not a long plunge into an icy grave. To the vamps this cliff climbing was old stuff, and Mike's special ops skills were almost their equal. Ari found the trip more challenging. Once Andreas, and a second time Mike, gave her a hand. Ari hated it, but she'd do whatever it took to be there.

They stopped on a ledge barely a foot wide. The surface was slimy. When her feet slipped, Ari clung to a crack in the surface. The edge dropped straight down. The river was louder now, angrily smacking against the rocks.

Andreas whispered in her ear. "Are you able to continue?"

"Yes, fine. How soon?"

"Not much farther. I'll take the lead. Stay close."

He eased past her. They began to move again, stopping only minutes later in front of a large, dark opening. The entrance to the caverns.

They crowded inside. Carmella and the four vamps disappeared. When they returned, she nodded to Andreas.

"We can go in now," he said in a low voice. "The first two sentries have been eliminated."

They filed in, two or three at a time. Carmella and Andreas led the way, followed by Ari, Benny, and Mike, with the four vamps guarding the rear.

At first progress was painfully slow, as each side passage was checked. Once the wolves' path was certain, the hunting party moved quickly. The deeper they went, the cooler it became. Ari shivered, even in her leather jacket. No one else noticed the temperature change.

As the passage became narrow, they used their hands to feel the way. Ari's fingers grew icy, and she rubbed them for warmth. She peered ahead, hoping to see or hear something soon. The sound of dripping water was the only accompaniment to the quiet passage of their feet. The darkness was impenetrable. Even with Ari's night vision and the rare flicker of a penlight in tricky places, the absence of light was challenging. And creepy.

A dim glow appeared ahead, and they came to a halt. Ari saw two distant figures moving beyond the light. The only approach was through a series of two passages lit by flaming torches on both sides, a defense against vampire attacks. The passages were narrow. Even sliding sideways, the chances of being burned or singed were high. While the flames were uncomfortable for Mike and Ari, they were a major problem for the vampires. There was no such thing as a minor burn for a vamp.

Ari felt the unease ripple through the vampires. One mistake and the hapless vamp would be cinders. Even Carmella and Andreas were not immune, although they showed no outward discomfort. They were better at hiding it.

Ari nudged Mike, pointed ahead, and they crept toward the passage.

Andreas came up on her right. "Do you have a plan?"

"Yes," she breathed. "Let us take care of this."

Andreas pulled back, and Ari unsheathed her dagger. Catching on, Mike produced his military issue. "You know how to throw that thing?" she asked.

Mike grinned.

Their backs flat against the cave wall, they inched forward and through the first passage without serious burns or being noticed by the sentries ahead. Ari thought they were now close enough for reasonable accuracy. She checked for the wolves' current locations but saw only one. The male wolf looked bored, standing with one foot on a rock, so he could lean on his knee. Finally she located the second wolf, squatting near a small fire, a coffee cup in one hand, a cigar in the other. Easy marks for gunfire, but that would alert the others who must be somewhere nearby.

"We'll only have one chance."

Mike lifted his blade. It winked in the torchlight. "I'll take the cigar."

"OK," Ari whispered. "Now."

Two slivers of metal flashed through the second passage and across the intervening space. Each found its mark. Mike sped forward, knocking down torches as he went. Ari doused all but one torch in the passage behind her. By the time Mike had checked the sentries to make certain they were dead, the vampires had come safely through the passes. Mike returned Ari's dagger with a conspiratorial grin.

Four down. And still they hadn't seen Sheila. Wolf energy permeated the air. Excited by the blood, the younger vampires were edgy, pupils dilated. When a voice called from the farther caves, the hunting party froze. Knowing they were about to be discovered, they took the offensive and rushed forward. They rounded a sharp corner and abruptly entered a large, open chamber.

A male werewolf walked toward them, barely fifteen feet away. Sheila and another male crouched beside a second campfire. A third was stirring what smelled like beef stew in a cooking pot. Three figures wrapped in blankets appeared to be asleep. Seven, Ari thought. More than expected.

The male in their path gave a startled cry, rousing his companions, and unleashing an uproar. The vampires poured into the room. One of the werewolves grabbed an Uzi and fired at them. He was still firing when they swarmed over him. Some of the wolves tried to escape into side tunnels. The vamps gave chase, and the wolves didn't get far.

Sheila and two companions fled deeper into the cavern. Blood singing with magical rage, Ari hurled witch fire toward the retreating figures. Red and gold tentacles of flame arced across the room, just missing the she-wolf as she dodged around a corner. The wolf next to her wasn't as lucky. He burst into flames. His screams bounced around the walls until Mike shot him. The second wolf retreated from the fire, running straight into Carmella. She sent him flying across the room with one flick of her hand.

When the witch fire hit the wall, the explosion took out a large section of rock. Chunks crashed to the floor, shattering into small projectiles. The damp walls sizzled with steam. Ari stood in the middle of the cavern, staring at the fire, which hadn't died on impact. Glowing fingers spread over the rocky surfaces as if it had a will of its own.

The vampires hung back, staying clear of the deadly

reaching flames. Ari shrugged off her fascination and sprinted after Sheila. The flames followed, slithering across the walls and the top of the cavern.

"What the hell is that?" Mike said.

Ari's sentiments exactly. But she'd worry about it later. Her priority was Sheila and making sure she didn't escape.

But Sheila wasn't going anywhere. She'd boxed herself in. The side chamber, though large, went nowhere. Ari stepped into the entrance, blocking the way. Sheila fired a handgun from her sheltered position behind a large rocky protrusion, and Ari dropped to the floor, returning fire with her derringer.

The fire swept into the room, raced across the ceiling, fingers dipping down the wall and forming a circle on the floor, surrounding Sheila. Tails of flame flickered around the encircled wolf like dozens of tiny, malevolent lizards. A hundred eyes within the flames turned to watch Ari. Waiting. For what she wasn't sure. Orders? Recognition?

Suddenly, she *did* recognize them. Mythical creatures come to life. The ancient salamanders. She felt a surge of pure power. The fire spirits were awaiting her order to devour the wolf. It was exhilarating and terrifying. Her heart pounded like a thousand drums. The magic filled Ari, threatening to burst through her skin.

When Sheila moved, drawing her attention, Ari laughed, a strangely hollow sound. She was nearly drunk on power. And just because she could do it, she summoned a lesser magic, a child's magic, and took Sheila's gun away.

Thought to deed, heart's desire; with this thought, I shall acquire.

Bewilderment spread across the she-wolf's face as she looked at her empty hand and watched the weapon reappear in Ari's hand.

Sheila stood helpless before her. Ari smelled the sweaty stench of the she-wolf's dawning fear—and liked it. "You should have left my friend alone." Ari's voice was soft, almost conversational.

"It is our way," Sheila said. "An eye for an eye. It's the

code."

"Yana was an innocent."

"She was a casualty of war."

Ari laughed. "What war? Sebastian's? You were only a pawn in a vampire game."

Small, furry tufts appeared on the backs of Sheila's hands.

"You really think I'm going to let you shift?" Ari nodded toward the wolf's hands and tossed the gun aside. She stared into the eyes of the fire, focused her magic, and ordered the spirits to leave.

There was an instant puff of steam and smoke. The cave darkened as the flames went out, leaving a fallen penlight as the only illumination. Sheila tried to run. Ari leaped forward, the dagger in her hand and tackled the wolf. Sheila fell with a hard thud on the rock floor, Ari on her back. Sheila reached back, snagged Ari's hair, tearing at it until they rolled. But Ari came up on top, straddling the wolf's chest. Breathing hard, she stared into the face of Yana's killer, relishing the moment of triumphant, and raised the dagger.

And then she hesitated.

The world slowed, flipping frame by frame, as Ari struggled with her inner demons. She wanted this. A voice said no. The she-wolf smiled.

Then Ari was roughly yanked away. Andreas reached down and snapped the she-wolf's neck with a powerful twist.

Reality bent. And snapped. Ari's blood boiled with primitive rage. He'd stolen her kill. She sprang toward him. He turned, his lips drawn back, exposing white fangs.

Ari jolted to a halt and backed away, nearly falling over her own feet. Anguish clawed at her chest as the impact of the situation hit her. Her throat tightened, a scream stuck there. She and the vampire were ready to kill each other over the rights to take an enemy life. An unarmed woman. Ari raised a hand as if to ward off the truth and noticed the dagger still clutched in her fist. Shocked, she opened her fingers, and the blade clattered to the cave floor.

She looked at him. His dark eyes were hooded, a black curl had fallen across his forehead. The fangs were gone.

"Arianna."

"Stay away from me," she hissed. She whirled and ran as if all the demons of hell were at her heels. And maybe they were.

Chapter Thirty-Four

"Ari, wait. I'll go with you." Mike caught up with her near the cavern entrance and held out a flashlight. "They don't need me back there."

Ari had stopped her sprint through the dark. The finger fire she'd been using to light the way was almost depleted. Breathing hard, she rested her good hand on her thigh. "Thanks for the light. Give me a minute, will you?"

Mike nodded, his eyes saying nothing.

Ari's brain whirled with images and thoughts she couldn't reconcile right now. The dagger in her hand. The salamanders, their eyes flickering with fire. Andreas standing over Sheila's body. She willed her brain to shut them out and concentrated on slowing her pulse. She needed to quit feeling.

"Go help them with the wolves," Ari said when she was sure her voice was steady. "I can get back on my own."

"No. You can't. Not with that arm." Mike was matter-of-fact.

She had forgotten. Glancing down, she saw the bindings were tight; it was swelling. "I guess you're right. Let's go."

She started off in the lead, Mike followed. He didn't attempt conversation, and the return trip up the cliffs was completed in silence. It was harder than she had anticipated. Without Mike, she wouldn't have made it.

When they reached the top, Ryan was sitting in his off-duty car. The door opened when he spotted her, and he stepped out.

"I heard there's been some trouble."

"Yeah, you might say that. Who called you?" As if she couldn't figure that one out. She wondered how much Andreas had told him.

Ryan ignored her question, looking at her arm. "You're injured."

He was being careful, cautious. Andreas must have said quite a bit.

"It'll keep," she said. "Prisoners and bodies come first."

A brief frown crossed his face before he shrugged, accepting her answer. No barrage of questions. His restraint made it easier to stick to business.

Mike left, refusing a ride, and headed back to the vampire compound.

Ari filled Ryan in on most of the night's events. She didn't mention the fire salamanders. Not now, maybe never. And she didn't talk about how Sheila died. Surprisingly, Ryan took it all in stride. Of course, he'd already been primed.

"No human bodies," she said. "In fact, no one local. They thought they could walk into Riverdale and take over."

"Overconfident, huh?"

"Yeah, I guess. Too bad most of them aren't alive to learn by their mistakes."

Ryan gave a short, mirthless cop laugh.

He drove her to the compound. Mike was already there, and no one asked her what happened. The next hour was a flurry of activity. Carmella and the four vampires arrived from the caverns with the wolves, both living and dead. Carmella took no time in letting Ryan know the caves were off limits. He was fine with that, said the delivery saved him and the police department a lot of trouble. He called in officers to take custody of the prisoners and the coroner to handle the bodies. Ari started to follow the last officer out the door.

"So this is the vampire court, huh?" Ryan stood in the middle of the security area and looked around.

Ari stopped and turned back. "This is security. The audience chambers are down the hall. Sleeping quarters are far from here."

"Not very fancy. Somehow, I expected plush quarters."

"They were better before the fight." She started to shrug, grimaced at the discomfort in her arm.

"You need to see a doctor. We're done here. Unless you're waiting for someone." He paused and waited for an answer.

"No, no one. Let's go." Now the work was done, she was anxious to get away. Afraid Andreas might appear. She couldn't see him right now.

"Hey, Ari." It was Mike. He walked toward them, pulling something out of his belt. He held out her silver dagger. "You dropped this."

Ari shook her head. "You keep it. I don't want it anymore." As she turned away, Mike and Ryan exchanged a look, but she kept moving toward the door. "Are you coming?" she said over her shoulder.

"Right behind you." Ryan caught up with her outside. "You're not going to talk about it, are you?"

Ari didn't break stride. "No, there's nothing to talk about. The bad guys are mostly dead. The rest are in custody. Case closed. What more do you want?"

"Me? I'm satisfied, but I get the feeling you're not."

How could she be? Her personal life was a wreck. People she counted on had died or betrayed her. She had developed magical powers she didn't understand. But she'd cope. She always did.

She turned to Ryan and mustered a smile. "Quit worrying about me, partner. I'll be fine. A visit to the ER, a good night's sleep, I'll be a new woman."

"I kind of liked the old one," he said.

"Tough. You'll get used to the new me. Now come on before your pager or mine goes off. I couldn't face another crime scene tonight."

As she climbed into his car, she congratulated herself for not asking why Andreas hadn't returned to the compound. It was a start.

Epilogue

Six weeks later, Ari returned to Riverdale on a gray, gloomy afternoon. The feel of early snow was in the air, no more than a few weeks away. She was glad to be coming home. Her arm had healed, she'd undergone rigorous retraining with her childhood Sensei, and she was ready, even anxious, to get back to work. Martin was exhausted from covering both territories, but at least there'd been no vampire wars or drug outbreaks during her absence.

She hadn't heard from Andreas, but that was a good thing. At least she thought so most of the time. The manner of Sheila's death had stunned her, but she'd had many hours to go over the details of that night. In the honest light of day, she realized she'd reacted mostly from anger at herself, the irrevocable choice she almost made. And she'd been afraid, still was, not for what happened in the caverns, but at the compound. The magical link. The idea of such a powerful connection with a vampire, one that could break all magical barriers and wake him from his sleep…well, that was something she still couldn't wrap her head around. What if their magics consumed each other? Or the stronger one took control? And, Goddess forbid, what if it was all her fault? Or at least the fault of her family legend?

In her brooding, Ari almost missed the turn. She drove down the lane to the woods where Yana was buried and parked the Mini Cooper. She'd come to chat. She couldn't remember a time when she hadn't brought her problems to Yana. This time, she also needed to tell Yana why she'd died.

And how the story ended.

Ari got out of the car and entered the woods. The ground was hard, the brown grass brittle and crackly. It crunched under her feet. Finally, standing in the middle of a small clearing, Ari explained it all. The drugs, the deaths, Sebastian's ambitions, the compound attack, the caverns, and how Sheila died.

"I wanted to kill her," Ari admitted. "And I don't know why Andreas did it instead. His own reasons? Or maybe to protect me from stepping over the line. I'm still not sure I wanted to be saved."

With most of the story behind her, Ari began to walk. She turned onto a trail made by summer hikers and plucked a tall slender blade of grass from the edge of the path. She chewed on the end. It was dry, flavorless.

"I wish I could turn back the clock," she finally said. "Have you back. Do things better. But that isn't how things work. So I guess I just have to do the best I can." She paused to watch two squirrels chasing through the trees. "But I wish you could tell me what to do about Andreas. Until I figure it out, I'm going to stay away. There's so much about him…us…that I don't understand."

She fell silent, listening to the wind in the trees. The weather grew colder every day, the winds stronger, more biting. She turned to retrace her steps. It was time to go.

Ari chuckled as she rounded the last curve in the trail. "You'll be happy to hear Sebastian is having his own problems these days. Revolts among his vampires. Zoe heard Prince Daron had a hand in it. Payback can be hell."

Ari spotted her Mini Cooper through the trees. She'd reached the end of the path—and the end of her story. A gust of wind whipped the hair across her face. She shivered, pulled her jacket tighter, and said her good-byes. Pulling a pouch from her pocket, she tossed a handful of sweet grass into the air. It spun and twirled, scattering its seeds, ready to renew life when the ground warmed again. Spring was only a winter away. A smile tugged at her lips as she took a last look around. Yana would rest now.

Ari wouldn't be back.

~ About the Author ~

Ally Shields is the pseudonym of Janet L Buck, a former attorney and juvenile officer, residing in the Midwest.

Find out more about Ally Shields here:

http://allyshields.com
http://facebook.com/AllyShieldsAuthor
http://twitter.com/ShieldsAlly

~ Coming Soon ~

The Guardian Witch Series

Fire Within (Book Two)
Burning Both Ends (Book Three)

~ Available Now from Etopia Press ~

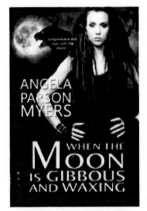

When the Moon is Gibbous and Waxing
Angela Parson Myers

Unspeakable evil rises with the moon...

Graduate student Natalie Beres can't remember who attacked her that autumn night under the full moon. She can't remember anything between leaving her lab in a secluded building at the south end of campus and arriving at her apartment in the wee hours of the morning. Covered in blood. Not her own. Other than the loss of memory, she's completely unharmed.

She can't say the same for the men who attacked her. The grisly campus murders force Natalie to dig deeper into what happened that night, to force herself to remember. But what she learns about herself is horrifying. When the police officer investigating the murders tries to get close, Natalie is caught between her attraction to him and her fear of discovery. But worse, can she avoid being found by the young man with a similar problem who's on his way from the West coast to find her...leaving a trail of shredded corpses along the way...?

Available now in digital format.

~ Available Now from Etopia Press ~

9mm Blues
Keith Melton

Christopher Hill is a brash young knight in the Order of the Thorn—a hard charger packing a submachine gun and a sword. His mission is simple: destroy the ancient, profane evils that prey upon humanity.

But Hill's mission becomes much more complicated when a young boy is kidnapped by flesh-eating ghouls. Barricaded inside a run-down house, the ghouls slowly gain the upper hand, while outside, mounting casualties and internal power struggles threaten both the mission and the boy Hill's vowed to see home safe, no matter what...

Available now in digital format.

~ Available Now from Etopia Press ~

Trust and Betrayal
Dani-Lyn Alexander

Trust is the ultimate weapon in the battle against evil.

Single mother Shay McKeon is no dummy—she's intelligent as well as street-smart. But when she receives a phone call threatening her children, she rushes headlong into the hands of evil.

Saved from certain death by Mason Constanza, who calls himself a Guardian, Shay is taken to the Realm of Light, where she learns her husband never abandoned her as she'd thought, and that good and evil are nothing like she'd imagined. Learning to deal with her own existence as a Guardian, Shay's attraction to Mason grows. But she has her own demons to battle, and when her daughter is abducted, she'll have to trust Mason and his team. But Mason has his own ancient battles to fight…

Available now in digital format.

Lightning Source UK Ltd.
Milton Keynes UK
UKOW050851010213

205702UK00001B/53/P